The Guardian of Arcadin

The Guardian of Arcadin

Dear Leila,
Warm wishes and
to your authentic self!
Sherdley S

Sherdley S

Dedication

To my cousin Diana, who is 70 percent patience and 90 percent leave me alone. Every day you let me talk, read the story through with you, demanding feedback. Without you, this book may have never been possible. And my love for you shall forever live.

Acknowledgments

A special thanks to those who encouraged me, believed in me, and cheered me on about my writing, giving me advice, and helping me to become a better writer. You know who you are, and I hope you know how much I appreciate you. Alyssa Williams, for being my most prominent advocate and my nonofficial public relations person eager to drag me out of my comfort zone. But most importantly, my mother, for supporting me through everything. You are my hero.

Prologue

Callum stood inside of the bar, DEVIL'S PLAY-GROUND, spelled out in big red letters. The words embedded in his mind, he wondered what Zachariah could want in this place. A mass of people was clamoring to get inside. An even bigger size was indoor. Unsure of exactly what he was looking for, he moved through the crowd eyeing the flock of heads dancing around him. "What were you doing here, Zach?" He whispered.

Suddenly a gray off-putting feel pulsated through the ambiance, and his ears shattered violently. With a slow, deliberate motion, he turned around. An Arcadien rebel was in the secluded area of the bar; a group of coerced mortal women surrounded him. Making his presence felt, Callum released the women from the rebel's mind influence, propelling them to leave the bar.

Immediately he was fenced in; the rebel telepathically communicated to the others in the room. Recalling Raphael's command about discretion and putting any mortal in danger, Callum molded a quick visual barrier blurring all three of his opponents in the left corner of the pub, manipulating reality, which was one of his many gifts. A quick second later, someone screamed high, followed by a second earsplitting one. A shot rang out, followed by another one. The pub shook with force. Feet pounded across the floor. Every mortal in the room raced to get out of the exit.

"You're trespassing, warrior," the taller Arcadien rebel voiced in their native language. "He's not just a warrior, he's a guardian. I recognized him the second he walked in," the other on the left snarled. "Fleeing the mountain is our only way to survive you, and our curse. Now you had to cross the other side of the world to your death."

Quiet, Callum stood rooted in place, anticipating their move, not the least surprised when an effective channeling of energy hit him. The strength and vitality beating at him strong, much stronger than he expected. It pounded his mind with thoughts of defeat. It was an attempt Arcadien warriors used to tear down their opponent's self-confidence in battle.

He didn't want to kill them, he had questions and needed answers, though he felt irritated that they thought of him as such a rank amateur. With ease, Callum reversed the fear, sending it winging back through them, strengthened by his influence and power.

A complete silence fell in the room.

Quickly he moved in a blur when the three rebels moved as equally fast toward him. An attack came to his right—a blur of motion impossible to see—but his heightened senses saved him from the hacking of a knife.

Spinning to the left, Callum leaped forward at once, whirled to his right, and thrust his blade to his first attacker's heart. The rebel roared with pain, blood coming out of his nose and ears. He fell on the ground. He was dead.

The air grew thicker, and danger swirled around them. Callum looked at his remaining opponents, challenging and daring them to make the first move. "What do you want?" one rebel stepped forward.

"Take another step, and it will be your last," Callum casually answered, his tone forthright with a hint of arrogance, indicating that he was not one to play with.

The rebel stepped back. Only one man he knew of, possessed these characteristics of furtiveness and superiority. Even the other Arcadien who visited the bar a couple of times didn't have that enigmatic and callous vibe to him. "Tell me about the man who came to the bar."

The man glared at him astounded, mindful that whoever was standing opposite of him wasn't just another guardian or warrior. There was more to him. "He was here seven nights ago."

"What happened to him?"

"Why should I tell you when you have every intention of killing me?" The rebel accused.

"I can easily compel you to tell me anything, and then I would have no reason to keep you or your pet friend alive. But I'm feeling rather merciful right now. Tell me about the man who visited a couple of times, and you have my word that I will walk out of that door the same way I came in," Callum said, pointing to the door.

The rebel sighed; Callum's tone was reassuring but menacing and intimidating.

"He mostly kept to himself. He tried to blend in, but it was obvious that he was looking for something or someone. Not long after that, Luke and his men came for him. They spoke in our native language, but it was more like a coded dialect. No one could make out what they were saying. They left together."

They were kids when they made up that coded dialect. It was their way of communicating with each other when they were in trouble and if something went wrong, not wanting their parents or the council to find out about it. Though Zachariah didn't like to fight, he was as much of a fighter as any of them. Callum thought it strange that he didn't put up a fight and followed Luke willingly. "Where is Luke?"

"No one knows the whereabouts of Luke unless he wants you to find him. Some of us escaped to the mortal world because we had no choice; not all of us want to fight Luke's battle," the rebel spat out.

"You had a choice; you always have a choice." Callum snapped.

"You called restraining my powers and treating me like a second-class citizen a choice. You're a guardian. You know what the council and the elders think of us once our soul is marked."

"With good reason. Our powers are our curse if restraining your power can save the lives of thousands, especially our women and our children. Indeed, it is a choice."

"Not all of us turn into murderers. I haven't killed anyone in my entire existence if I didn't have to. And I would never hurt women or children, no matter how dark I get," the rebel rebuffed.

"A tainted soul with a conscience?" Callum sneered, distrustful of the man's crossness.

"You should know. I can sense your darkness as much as you can sense mine, guardian. That's the thing about our curse and the predators that we are. The more we suppress it, the more it fights us to be free," Callum growled, warning the rebel off. The man lifted his hands in surrender and continued. "Whatever it is you're here for, I want no part. I happened to love the mortal realm. It's my home. So, I don't care what Luke is up to, especially now that the humans know of our existence. They are smarter and better equipped compared to decades ago, their technology is well advanced, and they are alert now more than ever. They know of our world."

"Explain."

"They apprehended one of our own not too long ago and have been on the lookout for our kind ever since. We must be careful now more than before. I don't know where Luke is, but I know someone who might."

Callum was in the rebel's mind. He was telling the truth. But still, that didn't explain why Zachariah crossed the portal or willingly followed Luke without a fight. Callum redirected his attention to the man, "Tell me of him."

"His name is Petrius; he works not far away from here. It's a little restaurant called Cuisine Douce. He runs in Luke's circle, but he's been pretending to be a cook at the restaurant for quite some time."

"Why?"

"I don't know why, and I don't care to know. As I said, I lost my battle with my darkness, but it doesn't define who I am."

"And what about your friend? Does he feel the same way?" Callum glared at the other rebel standing a few feet away from them.

"Please, we all have a past, but we're trying to be better, marked soul or not," the rebel pleaded, sensing the menacing aura glaring past him. "He's my little brother. He's still learning how to cope."

In the rebel, Callum recognized the ferocity he had when it came to defending his brothers, and he respected it. "Rest assured, I won't kill your brother today. but the next time we cross path, I hope you still feel the same way, and he does, too; otherwise, I won't hesitate to end both of you."

Chapter 1

*O*ut from behind the clouds, the waxing moon glowed. The forest was quiet except for the occasional hoot of an owl and the distinctive humming clicking sounds of an insect. A strong wind rustled; an overwhelming scent of decaying flesh and moldy corpses mingled in his nose.

"Ancenzia," Callum inhaled. The pungent scent led him deeper into the thick woods, steering him north until he found the dead creatures magically chained to a mapou tree. A cold shiver ran through his spine. He sank to his knees, a sharp pain shot across his chest. "Mierdei murio," he whispered, his senses heightened. The creatures' lamenting cries echoed from the ground and amplified his mind with grief.

"Freio."

"It's nothing I can't handle." Blood of his blood, their telepathy connection was deep, and their bond even stronger.

"Let me help you, brother. You're hurting." Raphael's voice rang in his head.

Callum took a deep breath. A throbbing thirst for killing took over him. The magic lingering in the air hit him at once. He recognized it. It was dark, tormenting, and precise. *"Two latnias are dead, and a dark spell is cast."* He curled his fingers into a fist—the killer inside of him fighting for control. Raphael couldn't know. Not yet.

"Can you trace the spell?"

"No, whoever killed them was smart enough not to leave any trace. It was a ritual, and they used Ancenzia."

"I can hear their cries in your mind."

"The latnias were tortured. Their souls aren't at peace, so they are bound to this realm."

"Can you free them or at least heal their essence?"

"I'm trying, Raphael. It is dark magic." Callum said. The dead creatures' agonies ran through him. His desire to slaughter everyone involved in the executing of the peaceful creatures became greater. Whoever cast the enchanting spell was no amateur. The magic was strong enough to constrain his power, seducing his darkness.

"There is a force field that separates our world. Can you feel the cloak?"

"Yes, barely," Callum whispered, struggling to free the creatures.

Losing his strength, he conveyed his healing energy to the earth, throwing a handful of dirt around the creatures' forms and spoke of their freedom in the old language. If they couldn't be free from this realm, they at least deserved to be at peace.

"I'll consult with the elders and see what they know. Allessio and Davide will join you. I'll put in the order at nightfall."

"I work alone—that hasn't changed, Raphael. I'm able to find our brother myself and bring him home safe and sound." Irritation was riding high within him, and he couldn't help it.

"I don't doubt that you will do whatever it takes to get our brother safely home. It's your shoot-first-and-ask-questions-later temperament that concerns me. That is why I want the two warriors to join you."

"My kill-first-and-ask-questions-later methods keep our people safe." The happenings of that night rose behind his eyes. Ire soared over him; he was convinced that Raphael felt it too.

"We can't reveal our identity to humans, and we certainly don't want to have any doubts about what it is that we're doing in their realm. Most importantly, I don't want you to lose yourself. If Luke is trying to get rid of the cloak or Zachariah is in grave danger, I need you to be clear-headed."

"Clear-headed? Are you too blaming me for what happened that night? Everyone else does." Callum snarled his irritation and ire transduced intensely in Raphael's mind. The spell was overriding his senses, the killer inside of him begged to be free.

"You're letting yourself get seduced by the spell."

"I'm trying to fight it." Callum bit exasperatedly, fighting for control.

"Let go of the past, or you will drown yourself, brother. Your demons are your weaknesses, and our enemies won't shy away from using them against you," Raphael coaxed, raiding his mind with force.

"I'd appreciate it if you didn't try your calming trick on me. I hated it when we were kids. I hate it now even more."

"You were an angry kid then, but a madder man now, and as always, you leave me no choice. The two warriors will join you; I'm not asking you for your consent."

A shrieking sound pierced the silence of the night. Callum's eyes widened; angst sneaked upon him. His pulse thumped in his ears, blocking out Raphael's voice in his head and all other sounds except his breath, unexpectedly and raggedly moving in and out of his mouth. He remained silent, puzzled at the increased pressure building in the pit of his stomach all of a sudden.

A faint sound brushed his ears. Fright consumed every cell in his brain, swelling them with terror. "Something isn't right," he whispered and stared east of the forest, unsure of the sudden intense feeling in his mind. *"Raphael, can you sense that?"*

"No, I don't sense anything, I'm in your mind right now," Raphael admitted.

"Someone else is in my mind; I feel them," Callum confessed, unsettled that someone was able to get past his shield.

"How? Is it Zachariah?"

"No, it's different," Callum whispered distantly. Fear of losing the connection to whoever else was in his mind, he

ignored Raphael's warnings. Nothing else mattered. Whoever or whatever was able to connect to him, he had to hold the link, lost without it if it broke.

A more profound scream echoed through the forest. Color drained from his face. Callum still stared east, wanting the connection to hold.

The painful sound ringing in his ears like a call, he raced toward the forest, led by the voice and the terror conveyed in his head.

Chapter 2

*R*ielle closed the small gate and sighed in relief. This part of the town always looked different at night, and everything had an unfamiliar slant to it as if the beautiful trees, flowers, and stones had gone away, but more ominous versions of them took their places. She glanced at her watch; it was a quarter to eight, ordinarily not a living soul would be on the street.

Strange things were happening in Kannan, but lately she couldn't shake the sentiment of being followed. The town was in an uproar since the governor's wife jumped to her death over the cliffs of the southern land, and the weird animal they found at the children's park didn't make things any better. "Be there in twenty," she typed in her phone before Syrah started berating her about being late to their usual Tuesday ritual at Omar's.

A high-pitched grating scream cut through the desolate street; a rushing wind roared. So strong, it nearly took Rielle off her feet. Rielle froze; she scanned her surroundings.

The trees dressed in shadows towered above her; their branches swayed in the coming and going of the wind. The air suddenly became cold; a shadowy figure moved from behind the opposite side of the road, drawing near her. Rielle went unnaturally still, quite convinced this was not one of her dreams. Shaken, a palpable sense of lingering fear wrapped around her. Her instinct screamed at her to run and she hurried to her old truck.

Faster than her, whatever lurked out of the shadow enfolded her in its captive embrace. Enclosed in a firm hold, she fought to breathe. Her eyes shut; a murkiness surrounded her.

Roughly, lightning flashed, sizzling the cloud. The leaves of the trees whistled with the wind, blowing harder than before. One instant, it enclosed Rielle in the creature embrace. The next, she was jerked away from it by unnoticeable hands. She fell hard on the floor, oxygen rushed back to her lungs; her eyes widened in utter shock, peeking at the man who had just helped her.

He was as quick as the creature. His speed was absurdly fast, blurring her images of him. It confused her. Thunder roared, and both man and creature disappeared in the sky. A loud thump followed; the man fell from the sky. The beast waved its eerie arms in the air in weird motions. The man struggled to get up. Scared, Rielle got up and ran toward her truck.

Sudden grief enveloped her, and an immediate melancholy swelled in her heart. The creature squealed. Rielle turned around. The man still struggled to get up, afraid that he might die. An unfamiliar commanding eagerness rose within her. Rielle closed the car door, walking back in their direction. Slowly, numbness moved up her body. A vibrant sensation went up to her form from beneath her feet. The motion of the earth flowed into her. Rielle didn't know what she was doing. The trees wavered back and forth. She had the sense to follow their motions, compliant to the mysterious liveliness coming into her. She closed her eyes, wanting and wishing the creature to halt its actions. It had to, otherwise the man would die, and she didn't want him to die.

The creature stopped and turned around to face her. Callum stared at her, dumbfounded.

Now, in her command, the shadow walker had wholly lost its purpose. Caught in her magical enchantment, it was unable to continue its ritual. She was in complete control of it. The earth, the trees, and the wind became part of her, guiding her. Her eyes shut; her free-spirited chestnut coiffed wild, loose, frizzy hair waved in the direction of the wind. Her umber skin was radiant under the moon. She was the most beautiful sight.

Intoning in a different language, "Rete sa vite m'komande," she repeated the four exact words. The shadow walker was entirely within her influence. The more she repeated the words, the more Callum felt the energy coming out of her and the shadow walker fading into the night. The words seemed familiar, but he was unsure where he'd heard them, before the depth of her emotions struck at him.

Rielle fell on the ground. The creature disappeared into the night; it vanished.

Callum had never seen anything like it. Hastily he went to her. "Who are you?"

His voice, alluring, was almost like a magic charm. Hazily, Rielle opened her eyes. He was tall, his shoulder-length hair tousled over his face. In the dark she couldn't see his face, but bright eyes were gazing at her. So dazzling and so inviting, Rielle became fretful all of a sudden.

"Are you a necromancer?" Callum helped her on her feet while holding her to his side.

His gaze pierced at her. Rielle felt a pushing throb in her head, and it made her dizzy. "I mean you no harm, you have my word." He stared her down.

Fear crept into her; Rielle's body quivered, sensing in the man next to her an animalistic wickedness and a fiery authority she had never detected in anyone before. His eyes were hard on her, unflinching. Quickly, she moved away from him, not sure where she found the strength after all. Pushing past him, she ran into the forest at a fast speed, stumbling as she fought to keep running, weak and scared. Thorny stem and brushwood tore at her legs.

Rielle clenched her teeth, pushing down the pain. She didn't know anyone who could fight whatever that thing was the way he did. He screamed danger. Swamped in the darkness, she slammed hard into the bark of a tree, stumbling backward. Two firm hands caught her before she landed on her butt. "Let me go!" she shrieked, kicking and frightened.

Callum sensed her fears and uncertainty, but he didn't expect her to run. Since he was faster than most, it didn't take him long to reach her before she went too far. Holding her close, he spun her around. Her shirt half ripped, her breast slightly brushed against his chest. His skin tingled in anticipation, every cell in his body heightened.

"I mean, you no harm. You have my word," he whispered, startled and confused by his body reaction. With his finger, Callum tipped up her chin. A sudden heat went up to his chest. He studied her face through the thick night. Arcadien had excellent eyesight, and the darkness didn't impede his vision in any way. In his ears, her heartbeat sounded like a hammer beating on cloth, a sweet scent of aroma imprinted into his brain. Impelled, Callum nuzzled his nose against her neck, the riveting scent drawing and pulling him closer to her.

"Please, don't hurt me," Rielle pleaded. Her frightful voice aggrieved his mind.

Granted, she was scared, but weirdly so. She was as awakened as he was, with the two of them inches away from each other. Callum stepped away from her. "I'm not going to hurt you, Rielle," her name seared into his brain like her cry for help earlier.

As an Arcadien, his senses were transcendentally acute, and as a guardian, it was common to feel human terror, but the unusual fretfulness that sneaked upon him was unfathomable. He didn't merely feel her fears. She had conveyed them to him. Her mind unconsciously had called out to him, and that was how he had found her.

"Who and what are you? How do you know my name? How are you so fast?" The alertness in Rielle's voice broke his thoughts, the impact of her gaze burning into him.

Fearfully, Rielle moistened the tip of her tongue. Every part of Callum's body clenched in hot hard impulses' demand, and his heart pounded with an intensity that was unfamiliar even to him. *What in the devil is happening?* He whispered inwardly. His senses strengthened, more acute than ever. He pushed into her mind. Vibrant energy rushed in his head, bringing his compulsion to a standstill.

"Entrei Sine," Callum cogently said, coaxing her mind.

Rielle looked confused, feeling the melodious spellbinding tone in every muscle of her brain. She collapsed on the ground; a pain as intense as a sledgehammer throbbed in her head. Groaning and panting with anguish, she writhed about on the ground, holding her head, tears blurred her vision as her breathing came out sharp with shallow rasps.

"What are you doing to me?" she croaked. Her desperate tone made her words almost inaudible. "Stop it!" Rielle screamed. Her mind pushed together; something was fighting to gain control of it. Dimness swallowed her vision; everything inside her mind went dark.

Callum closed his arms around her, drawing her into his chest. He'd used the ancient charm to merge his mind with hers. "Soivhe Nui," he whispered in her ears, using his full ability to get deeper into her head.

Two elementals sacrificed, she got through his protective shield and summoned him. Most importantly, she killed a shadow walker. It wasn't a coincidence.

Chapter 3

*R*ielle jolted awake. Her eyes shot open, sweat beaded down her face and her hands. She glanced around the room wide-eyed; she was home. What was happening to her, these dreams? This one was so vivid and felt so real. A gentle breeze rustled out of the windows. She removed a full amount of hair out of her face. She looked at the clock next to her bed.

The moonlight glimmered against the protective cover of the curtains and, inside of the room, shielding her eyes from the light cutting right through the room, she slowly got up and yanked the curtains shut.

Immediately, an unnerving feeling crept upon her. Her whole body went cold with a sudden numbness that felt spookily close to fear. A pair of eyes locked on her, Rielle's breath caught in her throat. Her shaking hands gave away her apprehension. From a distance afar, she heard her name, but she couldn't quite pull herself together. Confused, everything seemed fast-forwarded while she stood motionless in the middle of it all. "I must be still dreaming," she whispered, recalling her dream. The man from her nightmare was standing right in front of her.

Callum didn't want to scare her, but as soon as she woke up, he knew. He'd sent her into a deep sleep, but was surprised that even his sleeping charm didn't work on her.

As a guardian, his powers were more enhanced than most, but her mind was different. Her shield was more of a spell than a telepathy block, and it made her partly immune to his gifts. Even with the charm, he couldn't reach beyond the protection wall embedded in her mind. Wary and conscious, the thought of him dying had triggered something in her.

"It wasn't a dream." Callum eyed the window, and immediately the curtains opened. The brightness of the moon glimmered back inside the room. Stunned, Rielle stared at the windowpane, then back at him. Alarmed, her gaze remained on him. "My name is Callum Castallante. I am an Arcadien." He continued. If Raphael was ever to find out that he had divulged his identity to a human mortal, his head would be served on a platter. "I'm not going to hurt you, Rielle. You know that. Your level of awareness sets you apart from most humans I've encountered." Callum marched toward her.

"If you take another step, I will scream, and my neighbor won't hesitate to call the police," she warned. "Shadow walker attacked you, and you conveyed your fear to me. That's how I was able to find you." Callum ignored her threat. "You killed the creature of the night by just chanting words. How?"

Fast, Rielle ran toward the bedroom door. But in a flash, Callum was in front of her and gripped her arms. Without hesitation, she swung her tight fists into his jaw. Hard. "Damn it!" she cursed out loud, her right hand in pain.

"You hit me," Callum said, taken aback. Pleased, he watched her squirm around in pain, Callum was convinced that she would hit him again if he approached her as the thought weighed heavily on her mind. He stayed put. "Come to me," he pronounced. Her boldness intrigued him.

His voice was calm but firm; it felt like a magic trick. Rielle felt charmed by it. Forceful energy pushed in her mind; trepidation came crashing at her. She remembered how he fought the creature and how fast he was. The thought of him dying had made her anxious and melancholic. *It wasn't a dream. The words? How did I know what to say?* "No," she shook her head in denial.

"Come to me," Callum repeated. His eyes searched and locked with hers, and his voice was seductively low and raspy. Although he couldn't thoroughly read her or compel her, he would coerce her mind even if for a few moments. "Come to me," Callum whispered, his voice more compelling. Every Arcadien had mastered the art of coercion by the time they were a decade old.

His face was sharp and defined. His high cheekbones perfectly accentuated his face. Effervesced cerulean eyes beholding her, Rielle was positive that something flashed in them. Something feral and brave, warning her of his authority. Dark and dangerous.

Resisting, Rielle fought every cell in her body to stay rooted in place. Whatever and whoever he was, he was bewitching her. And she was wrapped around his magic charm; there was no question she would go to him.

"Come to me." His tone softer and more intimate, ocean waves brushed at Rielle's stomach; it was alluring.

Rooted in place, Callum realized she was fighting the urge to do as he asked. Her brown yet defiant eyes stared back at him, daring him. Not to be challenged, he boldly walked up to her.

"If you don't want another fist to your jaw, I suggest you stay where you are," Rielle uttered. Her trembling voice gave away her false threat. Callum kept walking. "I said, stop!" she yelled. The mirror on the wall cracked, and the sound of glass shards filled the room.

Stunned, Callum turned around.

Rielle clasped her hand over her mouth. Her heart raced, her chest pounded. She looked around the room; everything suddenly faded to grey. Slowly she tried to walk, but her knees went weak, and her vision became hazy. She couldn't see it correctly. Everything went pitch black as she fell backward; Callum caught her just in time. Her head against his hard chest, his arms enfolded her. "Shh . . . duermei," his voice sang in her ears. Rielle closed her eyes, feeling sleepy all of a sudden.

Chapter 4

*C*allum strode over the veranda of the old house, over-looking the forest. He drew in a breath and closed his eyes. This wooded area reminded him of the mountain. The smell of the earth slightly made him feel at home.

"Any leads?" Raphael slipped in his mind automatically.

"I'd appreciate it if you didn't pop in and out of my mind like that, but as you feared, Luke is in the mortal realm and might be behind all of this."

"Devil's playground?"

"Owned by rebels, Zachariah visited the place."

"So, Luke is holding him hostage?"

"I'm not sure. Zachariah walked out with Luke without putting up so much of a fight."

"Do you think he's working with Luke?" Raphael asked worriedly.

"I don't know what to think. Nothing makes sense. But there's a mortal restaurant. Luke has a watchdog in the café."

"Did you find him?"

"No, he hasn't shown up, but I've been keeping an eye on the place."

"The council agrees that you need back up. Alessio and Davide will be on your side of the realm shortly. You're going to need them now that we know Luke might be involved."

Callum stayed quiet; an unexpected heavy scent of gardenia filled his nose. The sweet smell of the earth and the rain mixed with the cool gentle breeze, His body stiffened at the thought of Rielle's scent. Someone had gone to a great length to hide her powers from her, and Luke had a watchdog in her restaurant. Callum wondered why.

Shielding his mind from Raphael, he didn't want to reveal anything about the mortal woman or his instincts to keep an eye on her. *"Fine, Raphael, if it would make you sleep better, I'll accept your overseers,"* he conceded.

"You want the warriors with you?" Raphael staggered.

"Don't act so surprised, you know I had no choice in the matter. It means that much to you." The relief in Raphael's mind brushed over him. *"How are Priscilla and my niece?"*

"We're keeping it a surprise so it could be your nephew. She's well, and I intend to keep it that way."

"Of course, you do, she's told me of the limitations you've set around the manor."

"I'm merely taking precautions for the sake of our baby. I knew you were the one that told her how to get rid of it," Raphael chided.

"It was either that or agree to come to her winter feast. So, I made a choice," Callum chuckled, mindful that when it came to his mate and their unborn child, Raphael was a different man.

Living in their family estate, he'd witnessed how attentive and fond his brother was of Priscilla and how obsessed the two were with each other. He was happy for his brother, though at times it pained him to know that he would never experience those feelings.

Silence fell between them for a moment.

"Elder Perouse's daughter is spending some time at the palace. She sent her well wishes. I believe she always took a liking to you, brother; she was disappointed to find out that you left the manor."

"Send her my regards," Callum replied callously.

As much as he tried to hide his feelings and sentiments, there was no escaping Raphael from finding out about his burdens and his pains. And he hated when his brother invaded his mind like that.

"You've become a loner living by yourself in the deep end of the mountain. Some companies might do you right. I worry about you."

"Do you worry about Zachariah?"

"No, Zachariah isn't a loner, and he's not a guardian. He's not a—"

"Monster? He's not a monster like me. Like Luke, like our father? Is that why you're not worried about our little brother?" Callum said sharply aware that he'd just let Raphael entirely in his mind.

"That night changed all of us. Our demons hunt you, freio, you don't have to carry this guilt with you." Raphael tried to appease his mind.

"I will let you know of my findings." Callum ended the conversation, not wanting to deal with Raphael's calming tricks.

He was aware of his demons, and whether he wanted to admit it or not, Raphael was right. They haunted him. That night did change him, guilt and resentment drove him.

He had become cold and detached, removed from everything a normal Arcadien man should relish. Like their father, the darkness inside of him was getting forceful, and it was harder to fight it. An Arcadien man turning dark was something Raphael and the council could deal with, but his turning dark was going to be everyone's problem. Only Zachariah had a small glimpse of what he indeed was. And if the council or the elders were to find out, they would not only strip him of all his powers, they would also chain him to rot. Fear of history repeating itself. For so long, he'd kept his secret from his brothers, knowing they would do anything and everything to save him instead of granting him his release as their law applied.

The cold one they named him; he heard the whispers. It was why he isolated himself in the woods on the mountain.

As a guardian, his oath was to defend and protect his people. Strike first and ask questions later was how he survived.

Although he wouldn't come out and say it, he knew exactly what Raphael was getting at. Callum sighed out loud. "I don't need and certainly don't deserve a companion brother, not after what happened with our parents and not when I'm every bit of a monster as our father."

※

It wasn't so much the loud sound that woke Rielle up. It was her nightmare about her dead aunt screaming about the broken spell. Rielle jumped off the bed, trying to figure out what was going on. *Spell? What kind of dream was this?*

With no warning, numerous screeching sounds echoed throughout the house. Terror snuck into her, and her bedroom door busted open as three shadow walkers breezed inside the room. Her eyes enlarged; she questioned how they found her home and why weird creatures were targeting her. A spit of black smoke. She ran to the corner of the room just in time. Another creature strolled in; black smoke spat from his mouth, just like the first one. Taken aback, it was too late before the creature sped toward her and enfolded her in its shadow. Rielle's watery eyes widened, the hairs on the nape of her neck bristled. Her lungs were slowly shutting down; darkness gradually enclosed her. Someone screamed out her name, and the creature flung away from her. Weak and tired, Rielle fought to open her eyes and stood up.

On her left, Callum was fighting with both creatures. A murky substance wrapped around them. One creature waved its hands. Callum became paralyzed on the floor, unable to get up. The murkiness cleared up a bit. Rielle saw him on the wooden floor. Both creatures looped around him, towing at his lungs.

Like before, the same feeling of fear for his life washed over her. Her nostrils flared, her eyes flashed, and closing slits, fury, and the fear of something happening to him flooded over her like a volcano releasing its pent-up emotions into the world. Her hands closed into a fist, the desire of wanting the creatures to cease to exist took over her. Concentrating on them, Rielle closed her eyes. Energy was pouring out of her. A chant came to her mind. Even to her ears, the language sounded foreign. "Rete kenbe kanpe edisparet." She felt elevated from the ground; her skin was burning hot. Hearing the creatures' screechy screams, an amplified liveliness that wasn't hers arose within her. Whoever was controlling the creatures had felt her powers and stopped battling with her, as they were astounded. "Rete kenbe kanpe edisparet." The creatures exploded into pieces. Dark smog covered the room.

Rielle fell on the ground, and her heart raced uncontrollably. She opened her eyes. Callum was on the floor, lifeless.

Feeling weak, slowly she crawled toward him and cradled his head on her lap. "Callum," she faintly called, remembering his name.

His eyes were shut. Rielle checked his pulse—nothing. Placing her head on his chest, she listened to his heart. Relief swept over her; he was alive. But the creatures had done something to him. Hours later, she placed a cold cloth on his forehead, wondering if she should call an ambulance or not. There was a man in her bed, but she wasn't sure if he was sleeping or unconscious. He wasn't breathing, yet his heart was pounding very loudly in his chest. "You're not dead. I can hear your heartbeat, but you might as well be. How could this be?" She questioned.

His copper thick brown hair fell in tousled locks around his face, Rielle took her time to look at him. Unable to stop herself, she gently touched his face. His warmth seeped into her, and it comforted her as if she had known him forever.

With a mind of their own, her hands started to explore. He had a scar in the middle of his chest, and it ran across his left side. Rielle continued her light touch. Her hand rested on his right bicep. There was a strange tattoo, and she could swear it moved. "What are you?" she whispered.

The heat from her fingers crept into his consciousness; his body was heating up. Callum wanted more of it. Touch. So long without it, he wasn't sure if he'd ever been comfortable being touched. It was an invasion, an unwanted intimacy, but his body was yearning for more of her touch. *Take what you deserved; it's been so long. You deserve this.* No, Callum said, fighting with himself. *Make her mine. I deserve her.* A growling sound escaped his mouth once her hands reached his abdomen.

Firmly, Callum grabbed her wrist, stopping her. He was wide awake. Promptly he sat up, watching her intently. She was flushed.

"I'm sorry. I didn't mean to," Rielle quickly said. "I just . . . you were . . . you were out for more than an hour," she stuttered.

"And touching me was your way of waking me up out of my unconsciousness?" Callum spat, not liking the way his body reacted to her. Especially now.

"I'm sorry," Rielle apologized. She held her face directly at him. "Well, you're awake, so I'd say it worked, didn't it?" Something glinted in her eyes.

Callum growled, getting out of the bed. He looked around; everything came rushing back to him. His mind went awestruck the minute he realized and took in what she had done. Standing still, he was in disbelief. She killed two shadow walkers at once. And it was beyond anything he had ever seen.

She didn't just have magical abilities; her magic seemed powerful. No one could kill the creature of the dark, not even necromancer. The only ones who were able to kill the animals of the shadows were pureblood enchantresses, and that was centuries ago—a period before his time, and all of them were dead. He studied her face. She wasn't a witch, as witches couldn't hide their true selves to Arcadien. It was easy to identify their souls marked by the evil they do. She couldn't be an enchantress either because he would have known the minute he tapped into her mind. Whatever she was, someone had gone to great lengths to hide it, as her soul was pure mortal. Whoever was after her, they knew what she was, they also knew she possessed these powers, and they weren't going to stop coming after her.

"What are you?" Callum questioned.

Rielle slightly moved away from him. "You're welcome."

Callum turned her around to face him. "What are you? Tell me the truth," he sternly said as he tried to glamour her.

Rielle could feel the erotic sound in her mind. She remembered he had done that to her before. "Stop that!" She rubbed her temples. "I should ask you the same question because, clearly, you're not like the average of us around here."

"Tell me how you can kill two creatures of the night at once?" Callum's hard gaze was on her, unflinching.

"You can't do your magic tricks with people's head; the buzzing is annoying," Rielle replied.

"Answer me, what are you?" Callum harshly glared at her, not liking the fact that he couldn't even glamour her.

"I don't know how I did what I did. But whatever I've done, it saved your ass, didn't it?" Rielle answered. She didn't like his tone. "As I recall, twice now."

Callum forcefully towered over her. Rielle backed up immediately. He stared down her brown yet scared eyes. Intuitively he acknowledged that this woman was going to challenge him in ways he couldn't even anticipate. His body responded to her when he was around her, and it surprised him. She might have some powers, but she was mortal first and foremost. He had no business having any relations with her. Why was he thinking about having a relationship with her—a mortal? But his magnetism to her was undeniable. Boldly he pulled her into him, slowly he wrapped his hands around her waist. The urge to kiss her was driving him mad.

Rielle wanted to pull out of his arms; she didn't want to feel this way about him. She didn't know him, and she didn't want to be affected by his touch, but she found herself shivering in anticipation. He leaned in close to her face, his lips barely touching hers, her lung shunt for half a second. She closed her eyes, holding her breath. He moved just a bit, inclined his soft, warm lips, and tasted hers.

Rielle's heart pounded in her chest, blood flowing rapidly in every part of her body. She felt so hot she feared she was about to erupt when he pressed her more into him, leaving no space between them. Her lips parted beneath his, giving him the opening. Callum took complete possession of her mouth. The feel of his body against hers made her dizzy, and she hung to him to keep steady and not faint.

His hands wrapped around her waist, he brusquely lifted her into his arms. He held her tight against his hard chest. Not a care in the world that the woman he was holding in his arms could be in danger or was the danger. All Callum's brain could register was the delicious feel of her slender body against his body, the press of her soft breasts against his chest, and the sweet taste of her mouth kissing her. Her scent filled his senses, his sex hardened pressing against her belly shamelessly, but he didn't care.

Consumed with a new sensation—a pleasurable pain he had never felt before, hot and fiery, centered on his heart, plunging to the lower part of his body. He felt passion ignited from both of their souls, flowing through both of their lips, causing an electrical surge. Straightaway the darkness inside of him became aware of her. Taking control over him, Callum wanted to claim her. With or without her permission. The feeling became so great he fought to keep control. Hastily he moved away from her. Rielle barely landed on her feet. In a blur, Callum moved to the other side of the room.

Raw emotions beat at Rielle. Dark rage, and ice cold. She realized they weren't hers. *How was this possible? Was he capable of making her feel like this?* She asked inwardly.

If she had any common sense, she would run for the hills. But she couldn't, not when the feelings manifesting over her were so raw and heart-rending.

He needed help.

"Stay away; you're not safe right now." A low growling sound came out of Callum's throat.

Rielle knew she should listen to him, this was her opportunity to escape or call the police, but she had a feeling that they would hurt him as things lately in Kannan were strange. People were on edge ever since the governor's wife died, and two other women were found dead near the cliff. *Why do I care? I just met him*, she inwardly thought. Ignoring his command and her inner voice to stay away, Rielle reached out her hands to touch him. Callum knocked her hands away hard, and she tumbled on the floor. He was so strong she felt the impact right through her body.

Their eyes met and held.

A muscle jumped in his jaw. Callum saw the terror on her face. He knew that look. It was the same look he got when he entered a room; it never bothered him until now. "I told you to stay away. Don't you listen to commands?" He chastised. Irritated at himself for forgetting he was stronger than her.

"Does everyone always do what you asked?" Rielle retorted. Blinking, fighting back the tears. She felt a slight pain in her hand.

"Yes, always." Callum watched her intensely. Amazed at how calm and collected she was. When the brute that he is, he physically caused her pain. "Come here. Let me see your hand," he voiced, agreeably this time.

"No, I don't think so," Rielle said defiantly. She didn't dare look at him.

"Come to me." Callum's tone was now more in-depth, thrilling. She was irritated, and he didn't like the rollercoaster of emotions coming out of him.

Rielle's body quivered at the sound, urging her to do as he said. "Whatever you are, you can't just do your magic trick and be rude to people, then expect them to do what you want." She was fighting internally with herself not to give in to his order.

"You are a stubborn woman," Callum growled, frustrated.

"And you are an uncouth man," Rielle fiercely rebuked, annoyed all of a sudden, not knowing why.

Callum was surprised at her resolve. Using his Arcadien speed, in a second he was in front of her, and gently he pulled her by her waist, closing the gap between them and lifting her chin. "Everyone, do as I said." Delicate lines formed around the corner of his lips.

His confession startled her a little, but looking into his eyes, Rielle wasn't afraid of him. Oddly, she felt safe with him as if they had known each other for a long time. But that didn't stop her from pulling away from him.

"What are you? What is an Arcadien?" She questioned.

Callum stared at her. "We have human traits, but we are physically and intellectually more advanced than mortals. We have certain abilities, talents, and gifts that allow us to do most things mortals can't. For thousands of years, others like me have been around and have lived approximately close to mortals. What separates us is a magical portal. Pure mortals can't see it, but others can. Some call us supernatural, and some call us paranormal." Yea, Raphael is going to have my head, Callum inwardly voiced.

"Not only are you not human, but you're telling me there are others like you? And there is a whole different world that exists, that humans don't know about?" Rielle asked, perplexed.

"Some humans do; some of our counterparts are mortals. Like a necromancer, mage, or a witch, they are part of your world but also part of our world."

"What are those creatures that are after me? And why?"

"You were attacked by shadow walkers. They are creatures controlled by someone, and whoever it is, they know about your gifts. They are either trying to scare you or trying to hurt you. And now that they know you're able to kill the creature, they won't stop coming after you," Callum confessed to her, relieved and satisfied she wasn't the enemy. *We don't know that yet. Maybe you don't want her to be the enemy*, his subconscious lectured him.

"Why? Why would someone want to hurt me or send some creature after me? I'm not part of your world. I don't know anything about your world," Rielle said agitatedly.

"You saw the creature, and you killed the creature. It confirmed to whomever it is whatever they suspected about you."

"This is senseless. How do I know you're not behind all of this? Things are weird around here, and you're a strange man yourself, yet here you are twice when I get attacked." She raised her eyes and met his. "How did you know my name? How did you found out where I live?" A nervous flutter in her stomach, Rielle's heart was thudding wildly. There was no denying she was attracted to him. But how? Why?

Callum held her eyes, stood, and approached her. The air between them sizzled. Rielle knew he felt it, too.

Why did she feel this way? That indescribable pull that defies logic—she barely knew him. Why did she feel safe with him when it was apparent he was a dangerous man? Everything Rielle was thinking flew out of her head. She stood immobile, barely breathing as Callum closed the distance between them. He looked threatening as if she had just insulted him. There was something else in his eyes: hunger and possession.

Callum pulled her along his arms. Her pupils dilated.

Rielle's entire body trembled in his arms. His mouth covered hers, the flame of desire that she wanted to ignore flared up to life. Like a wildfire, it consumed everything and flamed into her life in every part of her body. She had no understanding of anything outside of his lips and his hands touching her waist and her back, pulling her closer.

His legs slipped between hers, pressing against her while his hands pulled her hips against his. Hard. Rielle whimpered with an increased need. Her arms slid up to his neck, pulling herself closer to him. She felt his hands shift, covering her breast through the fabric of her cotton shirt. She gasped, ripping herself out of his embrace. Rielle stared up at him, not sure what just happened or even what was happening between her and this enigma of a man.

What had he done? She watched him with growing confusion as the fire in his eyes increased, and for the first time since they met, she saw a slow sexy smile grow on those lips that had just been kissing her.

Unlike most Arcadien men, he didn't need a companion and never looked forward to that fragmented part of his life. He was the cold one, the one everyone feared. The one who would walk into a room where people glared and didn't dare talk to him. He didn't mind the glares or the disquieting atmosphere. On the contrary, he liked the fact people didn't want to have anything to do with him. Rielle didn't understand the compelling force that passed between them when he kissed her, but he somehow was familiar with it and recognized it.

How? How could he have a bond with her? It should have been impossible. But there it was, growing stronger by the second every time he saw her, or they were in the same room. Arcadien only paired off and mated with their equals and it was said that it was impossible for them to mate with others. The latter reasoning in his mind, "Give me your hands," Callum said. It was more a command than a request.

"Why?" Rielle swallowed nervously when two strong hands held her small hands. Callum inclined himself a little closer, and she looked down, afraid her eyes would reveal how he was making her feel. She felt a thrust in her mind, and her eyes flew up to clash with his.

Her eyes locked on his perfect lips, thoughts of the two of them tangled in scented sheets plastered all over her brain. Rielle cringed at herself. Feeling rattled at her fantasies, she blushed.

"You're a defiant woman." Callum reached out and tipped up her chin with his finger so that he could stare directly into her eyes. His enhanced hearing attentive, he listened to her heart pounding in her chest with an intensity that couldn't have been an average heart rate for a mortal. Her skin felt hot against him; he wondered if mortal humans ran hotter than Arcadien. Focusing on her heartbeat, he realized that she was as aroused as he was, with the two of them being inches away from each other.

Her concern filled his brain, and her mind was going crazy with doubts and questions. The atmosphere suddenly was not only daring but was equally passionate. When the images she conjured up in her mind conveyed to him unconsciously, Callum found himself wanting to entice her desires—imprinting his hard frame on the softness of her body, claiming her as his so that every man knew that she belonged to him. Especially the officer from the other day.

He had made it a habit of keeping an eye on the restaurant since he found out who Petrius was and that she was the owner. Callum had watched her talk and smile at her customers, and most of them adored her.

She was everything he was not. Gentle, kind, and patient. He treasured watching her until the officer seemed a little too intimate with her. He had observed the officer hugging and laughing with her. Never in his life had he felt the need to end a mortal's life. He had to restrain himself and not compel the small man. Not only did he want to harm the man, but he also wanted to make Rielle know of the consequences of letting another man touch her in that manner. His mind conjured up the images of the small man caressing her face, and jealousy swelled over him. *She should be mine. She belongs to me, and the only way is to make her mine.* Jealousy was eating him alive, foreseeing the officer and her now in a tangled sheet—desires to claim her overrode his logic.

The urgency beat at him, the thought of her with anyone but him maddened him. No, this wasn't right; the bastard had cursed them, and he wasn't going to put anyone through that, especially not a mortal. Struggling with himself, he took two steps away from her. It was becoming unlike him.

"Callum," Rielle softly murmured, sensing the threat in him.

"I don't want to hurt you," he confessed.

"We both know you're not going to," Rielle confidently reassured him.

"You don't know that. I'm a dangerous man, Rielle." His voice was cold and detached.

Rielle didn't know why, but his confession pained her. He stood immobile as she marched toward him. "It doesn't control you—whatever it is inside of you, that you fear. It doesn't control you." She pleaded with him, unsure how or why she could feel his anguish.

How did she know? Callum pulled her hard against him, covering her lips with his.

The way he kissed her was nothing gentle like before. It was hot, coarse, and needy.

Harshly he pressed his body more into her. His hand slid down to her waist and up her breast. He couldn't help himself. A soft sound escaped Rielle's mouth, Callum wrapped his hands around her waist. Roughly he lifted her. She wrapped her legs around his waist, her hand tunneling in his long thick hair.

"Weirdly enough, you don't scare me," Rielle whispered against his lips, determined not to let him intimidate her.

On knowing about her resolve not to be intimidated by him, Callum felt an unusual sensation through his body. He closed his eyes, feeling passion and desire for her instead of anger and entitlement. A sense of relief moved over his body. Rielle had managed to calm him down, and it all made sense to him now.

How she conveyed her terror to him, how he triggered her magics simply because she assumed he was going to die, why his body reacted to her as it did, why the need to protect her consumed him, and his impulses to claim her, needing her.

Callum stood tense, silent for a long moment. The realization that he might have found his mate and she was a human lost him a little. But humans could not kill a shadow walker; humans could not even see a shadow walker.

Slowly, the tension left his muscles.

Callum sat her on the edge of the bed and looked at her. Much to her relief, the dark vibrations coming out of him moments ago retracted. "I don't feel it anymore," Rielle whispered. Callum nodded stiffly. "Why can I feel it? Why can I feel your anger as if it's mine? And how did you know."

Callum briefly debated telling her about their connection. It was unusual for him so he could only imagine what it would be like for her if he told her the truth. *I'm Arcadien, yes, we just met, but you might be more than a mortal, and you are mine. We have a bond until one of us dies, so it's only natural that I know when you're in danger.* "As a guardian of the supernatural, I can sense terror, but yours called out to me each time. Call it my superhuman senses," he answered instead.

"Even you have to admit this sounds crazy." Rielle sounded thoroughly lost.

Callum's face warmed. She was having a hard time accepting what he was and everything that happened, yet she wasn't afraid of him and wasn't looking at him like the monster that he was—his compulsion and desire to protect her, to mark her.

To brand her with his lips, to claim her as his own was painfully sharp. He stepped back from her. The small distance between them centered him a little. He managed a normal breath. "Not as irrational as killing the creature of the dark."

"I don't know how I did what I did. I was trying to help when I saw you on the floor. Am I a witch? Is that how I knew the chanting words?" Rielle softly asked.

"I don't think you are, you would have tried to kill me otherwise and your soul would be marked." Callum smiled, surprised at the simple reaction.

"Ever since they found these two weird looking half animals in the forest, things haven't been the same around here. Three women have jumped to their death near the cliff in broad daylight; most people around town believe they were possessed. And everyone has been on edge. Now I find out I can do things, and there are magical creatures after me because someone wants me dead. My friend Jao has been talking nonsense about how we need to prepare ourselves. That Kannan is cursed, I didn't believe him. But he was right, wasn't he?" she voiced more to herself.

At the mention of the officer's name, a cold shiver ran through Callum's body. He tried to pick her brain. She cared about the officer. It irritated him a little bit. He breathed in, and calmly answered, "They were latnias, spirits of nature. Whoever killed them did that for a reason and wanted the human to find them."

"Is that why you're here?"

"No, I came here to retrieve my younger brother, but things seem complicated."

"Are there more of you in Kannan?" Rielle asked, troubled. When Callum didn't answer, she continued, "Does your brother's disappearance have to do with the women dying and the animals? Or me, for that matter?"

"I intend to find out."

Rielle sensed the difference in him. There was no warmth to him all of a sudden. She found it interesting how his moods changed to cold, deadly, and heat in a space of seconds. "You should be careful. The special forces aren't child's play."

"Have no fear for me. I'm quite capable of keeping myself safe," he curtly said.

"Somehow, I don't doubt that." Rielle watched him intently.

Her eyes on him, Callum felt exposed all of a sudden as if she was reading everything that he was and wasn't. "I told you I'm a dangerous man," he rejoined.

"No, you wish people to see you as such, but deep down, I think you're really sweet," Rielle smirked at him.

Callum didn't like it one bit. There was nothing sweet about him. Not when he was contemplating killing her officer friend and certainly not when all he wanted to do was claim her. "Come to me," he said with a lingering threat.

Every part of Rielle's body shriveled, wanting to do as he said. "No. I told you, you can't do your magic tricks and expect people to obey." She fought her instincts.

Callum strolled toward her in anticipation, swarmed over her. She held her breath once he kneeled in front of her between her legs. "I'm a dangerous man, Rielle. The sooner you accept that I am, the better it will be."

"I don't," she defiantly said, aware she was playing with fire, and something told her he probably didn't like being instigated. His hand firmly cupped the back of her head for a moment; she feared what he was going to do until his lips crushed over her, hard.

Aroused, Callum feared his manhood exploding as a painful throb surged between his legs. She was as challenging as can be, and he exulted in her boldness.

His desire was to show her that he wasn't what she thought he was. That he wasn't gentle, but still she opened for him, and was kissing him back as ferociously as he was. She was mirroring him.

Rielle grabbed his face in her hands, pulling him closer into her. Abruptly he pinned her down on the bed, his hands roamed everywhere on her body. The smell of her arousal filled his head, and he wanted nothing more than to be inside of her. Forcefully, he ripped her shirt.

So close. Yes, mine. Callum ignored the voice in his head. "No, not like this," he whispered, ashamed of his actions.

No, he couldn't claim her, not like this, not when her eyes were so inviting and wanting. He merged his mind with hers and seductively coaxed her mind to sleep. Her mind fought him, but ultimately, she went to sleep.

Chapter 5

"Rielle," a too-familiar voice said across the room. It was enough to wake her up. Slowly and reluctantly, Rielle opened her eyes. The flash of the sunlight in the room blinded her. How long had she been asleep? She tried to sit up but felt too weak.

"Sy, what are you doing here?" She whispered faintly.

"Checking up on you. I've called you several times last night. And when I went to the restaurant this morning, the staff were waiting outside. They said they've called you several times. That's unlike you, and I got worried."

Rielle glanced around, hoping that she might have dreamt of being attacked in her home last night. "I'm sorry, I took a nap. I must have fallen into a deep sleep." She tried to rationalize what happened last night. Callum—Rielle remembered him kissing her, and then she fell asleep.

"What happened here? It looks like a tornado remnant in this room. What's going on with you? Are you still having those dreams?" Syrah asked, concerned.

"I'm fine, Sy. I'm sorry about dinner." She didn't want to freak out her friend as she was freaked out and didn't understand what was happening. Creatures were after her, and then there was this superhuman. He kissed her into oblivion, and each time they were in the same room, her attraction to him grew. Rielle sighed. "I just really need some good sleep Sy." She forced a smile. Syrah was the only family she had left; she didn't want her to get involved with whatever was going on, especially when people were after her. And women were dying in this town.

"They found another woman near the cliff this morning."

"What? When?"

"Early morning, probably before the sun came up. We have to be careful out here, Rie, especially when we don't know what's happening or why it's happening."

"I know," Rielle said, wondering if others like Callum were responsible for these deaths.

"People are frantic, and they think Kannan is cursed or that the supernatural is among us. It's crazy. I say close that side of the cliff and the problem will be solved."

"Maybe not that crazy, Sy."

"Now, you're starting to sound like Jao. People aren't possessed, Rie. These women committed suicide. That's all."

"Even the governor's wife?"

"He's a sexist misogynist—we all saw her black eye on the news. I wouldn't be surprised if he really did abuse her even though she came out and said otherwise," Syrah seethed.

"Sy, Jao said that there was no foul play in her death, and the governor is innocent."

"I know, I know, but I can't help but think about what I think. That man is evil." Syrah sighed. "Anyways, if you want to take the rest of the day to get some sleep, you can. And you need to clean around here. What happened?"

"I just need a bit of cleaning," Rielle lied.

"I have to go back to the restaurant. Petrius still hasn't shown up to work, and Celia called out earlier."

"No, the convention is in town, and we're short of two employees. I'll be there in a couple of hours."

"Are you sure? I can handle it, you know, and frankly, you deserve a day off. I know these dreams keep you up at night, and you haven't been sleeping lately."

"No, we're short-staffed, and it's going to be a packed house."

"Alright, see you in a bit! And please be careful."

"Yeah, I will, Sy."

Removing a full amount of hair out of her face, Rielle glanced at the clock next to her bed. It read 10 a.m. She got up and headed to the bathroom. Grabbing a towel, she made a quick work of showering then returned to the bedroom for fresh clothing. The lunch and brunch shift was their busiest one, and Syrah would be way over her head.

Sometime later, she was in the middle of inventory when loud knocks sounded at the door. Startled, she looked at her watch; it was 7 p.m. The restaurant was closed, but her car was still parked outside. She glanced through the crack of the window. Two men stood in front of the door. Judging by their vehicle parked on the curb with the guns in their hands, she knew they were a special force team. "I'm sorry, but we're closed," Rielle yelled out, pondering what they wanted.

"Open the door. It's a matter of security. We have an order from sergeant Jao," one of the men persisted.

"Sergeant Jao?" relieved, Rielle was unsure what kind of order Jao would possibly have his men execute concerning her. In the last weeks, he was acting stranger than usual, and he couldn't stop talking about something big coming or that they needed to prepare themselves. Was he talking about superhuman and Arcadien? "Open the door," the man shouted once more.

Reluctantly, Rielle opened the door. Both men came in. "Can I help you, gentlemen? As you can see, I'm in the middle of closing, and I'd like to make it home not too late and safely," she said serenely.

"That's why we're here, Miss; the sergeant has given specific orders to take you home," the shorter officer voiced.

"Why would he give that request?" Rielle doubtfully asked.

"With that sweet little tail of yours, I'd want to get you home safe too," the other one responded. He was tall, and he had a small scar on his left cheek. The way he looked at her, Rielle felt apprehension all over her. Although she had a bad vibe about both men, the contrast between him and his partner was as night and day.

Finding his attitude and comments uncouth, Rielle shook her head. No way she was going to let these men take her home. "Gentlemen, I appreciate this concern, but I still have a lot to do here. Besides, I'm sure you have better things to do than wait here for another hour for me to finish up." She politely smiled, trying to persuade them that she was okay.

"Look, sweetheart, you should have been home hours ago, and that's why your boyfriend has his panties in a bunch because he doesn't want anything happening to you. You've heard the stories. Things happened to people around here, particularly women. Besides, we are at war."

"At war with whom?" Rielle asked warily.

"Even if I told you, a woman like you wouldn't understand. Now we're all tired and want to go home. How about you stop whatever it is that you're doing, get your bag, and get your sweet little ass home," he rejoined in a clipped tone.

"You kiss your mother with that mouth?" Rielle asked sarcastically.

The officer pushed past his partner and stood in front of her. "You're a feisty little thing, aren't you?" A smirk cornered the left of his mouth. "You must taste as sweet as you look too for the sergeant to have people on the lookout for you." He smelled her from head to neck.

"I'd rather you keep your distance away from me, officer," Rielle said.

"And if I don't?" the man forcefully grabbed her by the neck and pulled her toward him.

"Anything happens to me, we both know how this is going to end," Rielle quietly bluffed. A painful sob came out of her mouth.

"You little wench, you are threatening me?" the man snapped. "I've wanted to take your bastard of boyfriend down for a long time now, and nothing ever works. I think I might finally find his weakness. Who does he think he is putting me on babysitting duties? Maybe I should have a little fun with you, put you in your place." He drew his gun and aimed it at her. "Take off your clothes."

"Excuse me?" Rielle's eyes widened, shocked at his request.

"I said take off your clothes—you need to learn your place, and I'm happy to teach you."

"Enough, Ben," his partner interjected.

"Can you imagine Jao's face when I tell him that I fucked his girl raw and dirty, and she liked it?" He continued looking at his partner then back at her. "I said, take off your clothes! Now take them off, or I will shoot your little brain out," he threatened.

Fear crept inside of Rielle, and it was all over her face. Seeing the man's eyes, she knew he meant every word coming out of his mouth.

"Ben, I said enough!" his partner shouted again. "She's right. If anything happens to her, Jao might kill us both with his bare hands."

"This is our chance to stand up to the bastard, and you're a coward right now."

"We have to choose our battles, and she's not it, as good as she looks."

"She's his girlfriend; we can use her as leverage, hurt him where it hurts." He licked the side of her face, his gun still aiming at her.

"I'm not his girlfriend," Rielle spoke.

"Shut up." The officer snapped and slapped her hard, knocking her backward. Rielle staggered but kept on her feet. She put her hand to her stinging face, fighting the tears coming out of her eyes. She wasn't going to let these men think they had the upper hand on her, guns or not.

The door of the restaurant was kicked down. What felt like a rushing wind blew into the room. A dreaded feel swept over Rielle, seeing Callum in front of them.

Callum stood in the middle of the room. Hot rage burned inside of him. A man had a gun over her head. He hit her, and the other one was standing by the window. They were both mortals. Without hesitation, something inside of him arose. Fury took control of his body. He wanted nothing more but to massacre both men. His senses were becoming less rational. How dare he treat a woman like that? How dare he touch her like that?

"Callum! You're losing sight of your task," Raphael voiced quietly in his head.

"This guy is a murderer, and I'll be doing the people of this town a favor by killing him."

"We don't get involved with the human dilemma, and whatever this man did, it is not worth killing him."

"I am their karma, Raphael, and their time has come."

"Does your anger have to do with the mortal woman?" Callum stopped in his track. He had forgotten to put up his shield. He didn't want Raphael to know about Rielle, not now, not until he figured out her powers and what she was or why Luke had a watchdog in her restaurant.

"I'm in your mind, and I can sense how you worry about this woman. Do not kill the men. Send them away, but do not kill them." Raphael's tone was commanding this time around.

"You don't get to tell me how to do my job, Raphael," Callum said, riled up.

"The human dilemma is not your job!" Raphael directed. "Please, brother, as a guardian, you can't kill human mortals. It's against our law."

"These men deserve to die," Callum sneered the darkness in his tone for Raphael to hear.

"I won't let you turn into the very thing we are fighting against; I won't let you lose your way like them. Don't kill them. Send them away," Raphael pleaded.

"I need to do this." Callum broke their mental path. In a rapid movement, he used his enhanced speed and threw himself at the officer, pointing his gun at Rielle. Callum grabbed him by his neck and dragged him to the wall, fast and hard.

"Let him go, or I shoot you." The one standing by the window pointed his gun at Callum.

"I wouldn't," Callum hissed, compelling him to put the gun in his mouth.

"You're not human. You're the filthy thing we've been searching for the past weeks, but instead, we have your partners," the man in his hold disgustingly intoned.

"What did you do to them?" Callum questioned in a threatening but enthralling voice.

"They are down at the lab. Rest assured, all of you will die. We aren't afraid of your kind."

"Give me one reason not to rip apart your wretched head from your body," Callum squeezed the man's neck.

Rielle had never been so terrified in her life. Her superhuman was a blink away from killing another man in her restaurant. And she couldn't get through to him. She called out his name several times, but he wasn't in control anymore.

Overpowered by rage and ire—it ran deep in his core. Rielle felt it, and it was calling out to her. She didn't want a man killed in her restaurant. She needed to get through to him.

I can't let you kill him, Rielle said inwardly.

Callum went still. Entranced by the mellow tone of her voice in his mind, not a muscle in his body moved. She had spoken to him telepathically, and it was not on the same path used by his brothers. Her voice, like a drowsy caress, was sexy and exotic. It was more intimate,

"Callum, let him go, please." He finally heard her ear-splitting voice. Reluctantly, but obediently he let go of his hold on the officer's neck. Her voice overrode his thoughts and senses. He took a deep breath; Callum compelled the other man to put the gun down as he erased their memory and compelled them away.

Immediately he walked right up to her. His hands gripped her arms hard. "What were you thinking? He wanted to hurt you. I felt it." The nefarious expression on his face startled her. He was fuming.

"He didn't," Rielle said, barely above a whisper. "He didn't touch me."

"He hit you," Callum rejoined furiously, his adrenaline kicked into overdrive. He stared at her with a dark gaze, not understanding these reactions coming out of him. His hand slid back to her face. He cupped her cheek and pressed his palm to her burning skin, the overwhelming sense to take her pain away heavy on his mind.

Urging to feel her close, Callum wanted to touch her. The need burnt him up. The thought of her being harmed did something to him, and he didn't like it. The things that man was contemplating doing to her maddened him all over again. Struggling internally to appease himself, he stepped away from her. He needed to regain control.

"Are you okay?" Rielle quietly asked, noticing his discomfort.

"Stay where you are," Callum growled under his breath.

Rielle cautiously treaded toward him. "I just want to help."

"Don't come any closer." His tone was intimidating.

Rielle swore, she felt her skin quivered. "We both know you won't hurt me, Callum, otherwise you wouldn't be here. Besides, you said it yourself." She took another step toward him and touched his arms lightly. Callum spun around and pushed her hard against the wall. He pinned her arms above her head. An aching sob came out of her mouth—the overwhelming need to kiss her shattered at him.

"You don't scare me," Rielle faintly whispered, wondering where this bravery came from or why she was feeling all hot and bothered by him all of a sudden.

Her voice, her scent, a strange sensation rocketed through his body. "Your face, does it hurt?" He asked.

Recalling how the officer had slapped her, rage started brewing inside of him again. Callum closed his eyes, his nose flaring. Gently he stroked her face and forced his way into her head, merging his mind with hers, fighting her shield. A rush of energy poured into her. In a nanosecond, Rielle didn't feel her face burning anymore. Freeing her arms, she took his face in her hands. Callum flinched, moving away from her. He growled, and in a blink of an eye, he disappeared.

Chapter 6

*C*allum moved back. Deeper into the shadow, his gaze steadied on the security man, forcing him into a deep sleep. Walking past him, he entered the room. The lab was underground with some sophisticated equipment systems. Blood samples were everywhere. He had never seen anything like it. Davide was unconscious, linked up to a machine monitoring his heart and another one regulating his blood. The young warrior was bleeding out. His left side cut open, a tube draining out his blood to a large flask. There was no sign of Allessio.

How was it possible for a human to be able to capture something as powerful as them? Callum questioned. He unhooked the young warrior from the machines. "Davide!"

"Callum, you shouldn't have come," he weakly answered.

"What have they done to you?"

"Allessio is dead. They injected him with something. Whatever it was, it killed him. I couldn't help'." Guilt filled his voice.

"You're not to blame, warrior," Callum reassured him, accustomed to the emotions of letting another fellow warrior down. "I'm getting you out of here, and we'll figure this out. Are you able to walk?"

"I'll need your help because I don't have the strength."

"Merge your mind with me. Can you do that? I'll teleport us both out of here."

An alarm went off. Callum was positive the humans had figured out that he was in the building. How were they so equipped? He helped Davide up. In seconds they were inside of the hidden house Zachariah had found in the forest and the place he'd called home the past few weeks. Placing Davide on a bed, Callum tried to heal him with his healing powers.

Merging their minds, Callum saw what the mortals had done. They used a magnetic force field to catch the two warriors, making them powerless. It was the same one the elders used to restrain their powers and what he had felt near the portal in the forest. How did humans know about the portal? How did they know the two warriors were coming? They waited for them in the woods and trapped them. Whatever they injected Davide with, it was hard to heal. It was poisonous and venomous and could infect him as well. What was this? And why?

"Raphael! Raphael, can you collect my memory? Alessio is dead, the humans have killed one of our own."

"*I saw it.*"

"*They know about us and can catch us. It is a declaration of war.*"

"*We can't be at war with them; it's going against the truce.*"

"*Did you not hear me? They've killed Allessio and injected Davide with something that even I can't heal. If not careful, it might infect me too,*" Callum barked.

"*I heard you, brother, but we can't go to war with the humans,*" Raphael voiced in Callum's head the neutrality for him to hear.

"*So what? We're just going to sit while they kill our kind. What's to say they're not going to kill every other supernatural being out there?*" He was frustrated.

"*No, our kinds were just in the wrong place at the wrong time, and we let the others fight their own battle.*"

"*Mierdei! Raphael, we protect our kind and others. Bad or evil, we protect them!*"

"*You said it, brother, our kind. We don't get involved in others' battles, otherworldly or not. And Callum, you're there to find our brother, that's it, so you find Zachariah, and you come home.*"

"*I'll find Zachariah, and he'll go home,*" Callum snapped. "*Guardian, I'm your leader, and I forbid you to get involved in any situation that's irrelevant to finding our brother and put-ting you and our people at risk,*" Raphael commanded

"*As a guardian, I took an oath to defend and protect all, from human to supernatural, and that's what I intend to do. The council can sanction me after I've done my job, which is to defend and to protect."* Silence fell over them. *"I'll see what I can do for Davide, and I'll make sure he goes back home. That way our people don't get involved. Not when our leader forbids it."*

Callum closed their mental path. His temper didn't like being told what to do. Using all his power, he sent healing energy throughout Davide's form, focusing on the poisonous fluid flowing through the body, making sure that it didn't affect him. It took him more time than needed and more energy than expected, but he succeeded in sending the warrior into a deep sleep until the healing process was complete.

Chapter 7

$\mathcal{C}$allum paced around Rielle's home, trying to find some clues or anything that could help him figure out what she was or how she was able to kill the shadow walkers. She was mortal, yes, but her abilities weren't like her counterparts—a witch or a necromancer, even a mage. This town was filled with magic; he felt it every day. And Luke was at the center of everything, he could feel it. Why? What was Luke's end game here? Why this town?

"Callum, are you alright? Your worries are strong enough to wake me up from the deep sleep you sent me in last night," Davide brushed his mind.

"Sorry, my friend, I didn't mean to, I forgot that you are connected to me as well now."

"The woman you're worried about, who is she?"

Callum growled, infuriated he didn't put his shield up. *"She may be in danger and needing my protection."* In a blink of an eye, the young warrior was next to him. "What are you doing here? You should be resting to gain your strength back."

"I feel much better. What happened here? Shadow walkers . . . they are after her?"

"Yeah, I wanted to see if I can trace whoever sent them after her while she was at work."

Davide looked around, summoning what happened. The gift of recollection was the young warrior's ability. His enhanced cognition and ability to recollect things that have happened just by being in a room or touching objects were what set him apart from other warriors like him. Staggered, Davide's eyes widened. "She killed both of them all by herself, how is that possible?"

Callum stayed quiet, not sure how to explain this to the young warrior either. "How is she able to kill a shadow walker, let alone two at once?" Davide walked up and down. "No one can, unless you're a pureblood enchantress; is she a pureblood enchantress?" he asked, concerned.

"I don't know, but I'm starting to believe that she is, and Zachariah was trying to protect her. That's why he crossed the portal."

The warrior kept quiet. "There must be another enchantress in town. Only an enchantress can control the creature."

"I thought so, but they were before our time and none survived, and why kill one of their own?"

"Maybe they are trying to capture her and not kill her. Maybe they are aware of her powers and want to use her."

"That makes sense."

"Does she have anything to do with what's going on around here? And the mortals, how are they able to kill Alessio with some injection? It isn't just about protecting themselves; they are studying us, Callum."

"Maybe so, but can we blame them? Rebels took over their towns, and things are happening. things they can't explain—like women are falling to their death and people doing things they don't remember afterward."

"We need to look into this so we know what's happening and deal with it. What do we do?"

"There's no we, you're going back to the mountain," Callum said, matter-of-factly.

"These people killed Alessio and nearly killed me. I want to help."

"I can't ask you to do that; it's treason against our people and our leader. Besides, Raphael forbids that we take action."

"Raphael doesn't see what's going on around here. If Luke is behind all of this, which I'm pretty sure he is, there is more reason I should help you out, you can't do this alone. Besides, we all know the consequences of crossing the portal without permission. Zachariah wouldn't have crossed if it wasn't important, and he wouldn't have called out to you if it wasn't serious."

"Davide, listen to me; you are going home, and as guardian of our people, I command it," Callum pronounced.

"I am a warrior, and as my superior, I have to abide and do as you command because it's the law, and I don't want to go against your ruling. But as a friend, I'm respectfully telling you that I am not going home. I'm staying here with you to fight because it is my choice."

Callum looked at the man in front of him, and man to man knew that he'd already made up his mind. "Do you have any idea what will await you back home?"

"Yes, sir, and I will deal with it then. We took an oath to defend and to protect evil or bad, human or supernatural, and that's what I intend to do by your side."

"You sure you want to go against the council, the elders, and Raphael?"

"I know Luke is your brother, but I want him dead. I want to find Zachariah, and I want to know what's going on. Magic and evil are rampant in this town, and people have seen things they shouldn't see. Whoever or whatever is happening, I want to put an end to it."

"There is no going back once you go rogue," Callum tried to scare him.

"I know. Now, what do we do?"

"Help me keep her safe," Callum looked into Davide's eyes. "Help me keep her safe. I have a feeling she's at the center of whatever is going on in this town, and she's not safe from our people, the humans, or others. Raphael can't know she's able to kill the dark creatures, not until I know how Rielle can do what she did or what she is."

"You have my word," Davide grinned. "Especially when it's not every day I see you taking a liking to someone, and a mortal on top of that."

"It's not too late to send you packing," Callum glared at the warrior, not the least amused by his remark, wondering if his sentiments for Rielle were that obvious.

─❈─

Rielle closed the front door. An eerie feeling ran down her spine. Aware that someone was after her or wanted her dead, she was becoming more and more paranoid, conscious that Jao was right, that things were happening in the city, and most people weren't aware of it. Things such as otherworldly beings living among them, and the fact that she was attracted to one.

At times, she swore she could feel Callum's presence next to her or that he was watching her. That's how much she was attracted to him. She'd been researching on his kind, and they were all supposed to be children's books. Children's book Callum wasn't, and myths weren't a creature called shadow walker. It was strange how her attraction to him was grow-ing by the day; most importantly, she didn't understand why she felt like she had known him for a long time.

The back of the restaurant door swung open. Rielle turned around and saw Petrius standing in front of the door. He stared at her with a sinister look, his face hardened into a malignant grin. A little spooked, Rielle wondered if he was okay. "Petrius, you scared me." She forced a chuckle. "Where have you been? We've been calling you. You can't just disappear. If you needed time off, you could have asked me." The cook didn't say anything but kept looking at her with terrifying eyes. "Petrius are you okay? You seem upset." Something was wrong with her cook; this wasn't the same jovial Petrius she had come to like.

"I have no choice. I have to do this," Petrius said, remorsefully.

"Do what?" Rielle didn't understand.

"You have to come with me."

"Where, Petrius, what are you talking about?"

"I know what you are, he knows it too, and if you don't come with me, if I don't bring you to him, he will kill me."

Fear crept up from the pit of Rielle's stomach; a cold wave embalmed her as she felt the hair rise on the back of her neck and her mouth dry. "Who, Petrius? Who will kill you if I don't come with you?"

"The commandant, he knows what you are, that's why he had me spying on you, keeping a close eye on you, but now we have to move fast. I'm sorry, Rielle. I've come to like you, but I must obey my commandant. I don't want to die. The commandant, he's not one to mess with." He wept.

"Petrius, you're not making any sense."

"Don't play stupid with me, I know what you are, we all do. I know about your powers."

"What powers?" Rielle pretended to be oblivious. Was Petrius behind her attacks? Who was this commandant?

"Stop playing dumb with me. You know what I'm talking about," he shouted.

"Let's just calm down," she softly said, not wanting to aggravate him. "You don't have to do this."

"I do, you don't understand. I have to do this, it's the only way," he confessed.

"What do you mean?" Rielle gently asked, trying to calm him down. But all of a sudden Petrius's voice resonated in her mind as if she could hear his thoughts on what was happening.

"You're in my mind. How dare you? Are you trying to get past my shield? Luke was right—you are a danger to us."

The menacing aura holding her in a tightening grip, Rielle knew she'd made him angry. "I'm sorry, I didn't do it on purpose. I don't know what's happening to me," Rielle said, feeling a hammer pounding her head.

"Now come with me, I don't want to hurt you, Rielle, because I like you, but I will if I have to," he threatened her.

Uncertain that Petrius wouldn't hurt her, Rielle wasn't sure what to do. She wished for her cook to walk away, but that didn't seem to be working.

A rushing wind came into the room, followed by another one. Callum was standing next to her, and another man by her side. *Who was this?*

"Petrius, it's finally nice to meet you. I've been looking for you," Callum scathingly said.

"You know my name?"

"Your friends told me all about you," Callum wickedly smiled.

Petrius took a glance at Callum contemplatively. "You're the warrior; I thought the human caught you."

"You thought wrong."

"You kill me now, there will be more to come for Rielle."

His threat upset Callum. He ran to the man using his speed, pinning him to the wall. "Where is he? Where is Luke hiding?"

"You will have to kill me because I won't tell you."

"I can just read your memory, but we both know Luke is not that stupid. So, tell me where Luke is hiding, and I won't cut out your eyes and feed them to you." Callum's words sent a chill down Rielle's spine as she looked at him and saw no warmth but rigidness and a cold expression on his face.

Taken aback, Petrius looked at Callum as if he saw a ghost. "You're the one he talks about, the one he told us to be wary about; you're Callum, our guardian."

"So, you know who I am. Tell me where Luke is." His tone was unassailable and powerful.

"I can sense the darkness in you, and every time you kill, it gets stronger." Petrius laughed almost maniacally. "So, you see, you can't kill me, because if you do, you are one step closer to turning into the very thing you hunt us down for."

Callum watched the man with an unnerving serene smile on his handsome face, and it disturbed Rielle. It wasn't so much the expression on his face but the glint in his eyes, cold, hard, and emotionless, filled with a dark glow as if he didn't have any ink of humanity in him. With one quick move-ment, she watched him pulling out a blade from his jacket and pressing it into the man's heart. A scream resounded; blood came out of Petrius's ears and nose.

Immediately Callum fell on the floor, his head between his knees, shaking. "Get her out of here." He growled a gut-tural sound that sounded more animalistic than human.

"Callum," Rielle impulsively took a step forward.

"Get out of here, Rielle." This time his voice was louder, and it shook the entire room.

Callum didn't need to look at her to know what she was thinking. "Go now!" he fiercely screamed at her. When she didn't do as he said, Callum growled, cursing himself.

"Do you need my help?" Davide asked worriedly.

"Mierdei! Fuei ire con Elle Davide." Callum spoke in his native language. His voice was louder, and it shook the entire room.

Davide stepped in front of Rielle as if he was trying to protect her from Callum.

Rielle blinked, worried about Callum.

"Come with me." The young warrior dragged her outside of the restaurant.

"He needs our help," she argued outside of the café when she heard another growling uproar coming from inside of the restaurant. She felt his agony, and the urge to go inside to comfort him was thrashing her.

"He will be fine," the warrior tried to reassure her, unsure himself.

"No, he's not, I can feel it. He can't control it; whatever that's inside of him, it's fighting with him. I have to go back in."

"You can feel it?" Davide questioned.

"Yes, and we need to get back in there, please," Rielle pleaded with him.

"He'll be fine." *"Callum, she feels your emotions, how is that possible?"*

"I don't know, but I have a feeling Luke wants something from her; otherwise, he wouldn't spy on her for all these months, and Zachariah's last word would not be the name of her restaurant."

"I can't read her mind; she has a shield, an unusual one."

"Yes, I know," Callum said telepathically to the young warrior.

"Are you even listening to me?" Rielle's voice snapped the young warrior from his thoughts.

"You can feel whatever it is that's happening to him right now?" a bewildered Davide asked.

"Yes."

"Can you hear his thoughts too? Has he tried to speak with you in your mind?"

What was this guy deal with twenty questions, when Callum needed their help? "I'm going back inside," Rielle snapped. Davide advanced on her, inhaling her scent. "Are you sniffing me? What the hell are you doing?" Rielle backed away from him. A smirk appeared around Davide's mouth, he chuckled. What a weirdo. "What is so funny?" Rielle asked, irritated.

"No wonder," he smiled at her.

"No wonder what?" Rielle repeated, confused.

"Now, more precisely, we can't go back in."

"Why not? We can't just leave him."

"He'll be fine, trust my words," *"Callum, I think it safer to take her to our place."*

"Ok."

"Everything alright?" The young warrior asked.

"Yes, I need some time."

"Raphael doesn't know, does he?"

"About her? No." Callum confessed.

"About you, Petrius was right, wasn't he?"

There was a silence, Callum said, *"Don't let her persuade you to go to her house. She's a little stubborn."*

"It seems to me it's a great pairing," Davide said.

Chapter 8

*R*ielle tipped her head back and assessed the elegant house that rose in front of her. They weren't in the city anymore and were deep into the mountains. Sunflowers were grown wildly in thick huddles by the gate. Flowers led the pavement to the house.

The crescent moonlight cast a glimmering glow on the house. The hoots were singing loud as if welcoming her. Vines formed on the side of the house; trees fenced them in. She was new to this part of the town. "What is this place? As I said, I'll wait to make sure Callum is okay, and then I'm driving home." She looked around.

In front of her, Davide walked and opened the door to one of the most ravishing houses in Kannan. Everything looked rich, from the gleaming wood floors covered in loving throw rugs to the sheer curtains flowing like mist on the wall and the floor to ceiling windows that faced a slope and then the moon—nothing else. The furnishing was old but had a story to tell, so they had to be antiques with what looked like hand-carved quality, each area of the room melting into the beauty of the next, with some delicate settees next to more heavy bookcases and fireplaces that paired off with the walls. "Wow," Rielle whispered.

"Zachariah has always been a charming one with an expensive and good taste," Davide smiled.

"Who is Zachariah?" Rielle asked.

He is the youngest of the Castallante nobility and Callum's brother. I'm sure Callum will tell you all about him when he's ready." Davide smiled at her.

"Like I said, just here to make sure he's alright." She rejoined a hand on her hip.

"I'm just following orders; Callum thought this would be the safest place for you, and I agree with him."

"Do all of you just take it upon yourself to decide for people without their consent?"

Davide laughed. "It's in our DNA to look after our women." Seeing her expression, he cleared his throat, "I mean those that are under our protection."

"I'm not his woman first and foremost. I just met your friend or whatever relationship you two have."

"He's our guardian," Davide corrected.

"So, he's your boss?" Rielle asked curiously.

"I guess you can say that my boss and boss of every warrior from our land."

"So why would you think I was his woman?" She was curious.

Davide smirked once more. "Your scent—though lightly, you bear his scent."

Rielle smelled herself but smelled her lotion on her. Davide laughed out loud this time. "It's not that kind of scent, the human sense of smell is different than ours. Yours is finite, but ours is enhanced and boundless."

"I don't understand. How come? I didn't touch him. And having someone's scent on you does not make you their woman."

"It's your fate. You've always borne Callum's scent. Now that you've both found each other, it's amplified. And indeed, if you bear someone's scent, you are his woman."

"There is no reasoning with you," Rielle sighed.

"I like you already." Davide continued to laugh. "It sure is going to be fun to watch him turn into a *mauvieitei* when it comes to you."

"Excuse me?" Rielle said, confused.

Davide continued laughing. "I think it's what your mortal calls a puppy dog."

Before he reached the house, her laughter echoed in his head, and a smile came on Callum's lips. "For god's sake, I am the most feared warrior on the mountain, and my reputation was the cold one," he said out loud. But being around her did not make him feel as cold. Contrarily, she brought warmth to his life. He stood behind the door, watching her. She was teasing Davide, and they seemed to get along fine in a short amount of time.

Callum knew the warrior was himself, charming and easy to get along, but watching her laugh so carefree and touching Davide's arms was enough to invoke suspicion in the pit of his stomach, and he was ready to pound the young warrior. *She is mine. He can't have her. He wants her. He is going to take her from me.* No! Callum shouted firmly to himself.

Rielle stopped laughing and turned her head around in the dark corner, looking straight at him. Callum knew she was aware of his presence and had spotted him. Staring at each other at that moment, Callum knew he wanted to make her his, and if he didn't, he would be a danger to both mortals and his kind. He walked to their direction, and already Davide could feel the threat from him as he immediately stood away from her.

"Callum, it's not what you think." The young man quickly blurted out, knowing how dangerous an Arcadien man can be when they have found their life mate and were in what they called the days of obscurity, especially with the Castallante brothers and considering what happened to their parents.

Callum stared at the young warrior fighting internally, not to launch at him.

"It's not what he's thinking?" Rielle asked, put off by at all the male testosterone that was going on in the room all of a sudden. She wasn't stupid, and she knew what was going on, as both men kept quiet but were ogling each other like it was a pissing contest. "Davide here thinks I bear your scent and also got it confused that I am your woman." She air quoted the word woman. "I am not, although I thank you for your sudden appearances with my troubles lately. Besides, I think it is archaic to think that being someone's woman gives you the right to be a narrow-minded person. And even if I were, I'd have the right to talk and laugh with anyone I want to." She shot daggers at him.

"Rielle, I wouldn't advise it." Davide tried not to laugh, loving how quickly she caught up on things.

"Stay out of it!" She retorted. "It seems like you're all the same; your society needs major reform."

"I was just trying to—"

"She said to stay out of it!" Callum roared at the warrior, his eyes still on Rielle.

"Okay . . . I'll . . . I'm not here," the young warrior smiled.

"I need to go home, Callum," Rielle said, turning on her heels and out of the room.

Both men looked puzzled. Callum looked at the young man.

"Don't look at me; go after her," Davide chided. "And just so you know, I know she's your life mate, so know that I would never cross you," Davide grinned.

"I know." Callum did not have to look in every room to find her. Just by thinking of her, he teleported to her. *"Rielle."* He used their telepathy path. It was more intimate, and it was how life mates communicated with one another often.

She turned around, shocked that she could hear his voice in her mind. "I heard your voice in my head; why can I hear your voice?" Rielle asked, baffled.

"It's telepathy, and you are telepathic." He watched her reaction.

"No, I'm not."

"Yes, you are, that's how you were able to stop me from hurting those men that attacked you in your café. Your voice, I heard your plea telepathically."

"This is insane!" Rielle paced around. "Everything that's been happening is insane. How do you keep finding me or know when I'm in danger?"

"You call out to me unconsciously, and our bond makes it so that I can find you," Callum explained calmly, trying his best not to scare her away. Now that he knew Luke was indeed after her, he had to tell her of their bond.

"This is crazy, what you're telling me is crazy, I didn't call out for you. I didn't even know who you were." She looked at him and squinted her eyes. "You too believe what Davide said, don't you?" When he didn't answer, she gasped. "I need to go home; I can't be here."

"I can't let you leave, not when you're in danger. You heard your cook; more will come for you."

"You have no say in this, Callum. I want to go home. I can't be here. I have a business to run and friends who will worry if I don't go home." She needed to escape him; this was too much too soon.

"I'm sorry, Rielle. I can't allow you to go home, not when you're under my protection." His voice was stern, warning her she had no say in the matter.

"Callum, you can't keep me here against my will. That's kidnapping. I have a friend who's a police officer. I'll tell him what's been happening, and he'll help me. I'm not staying here."

Callum approached her, staring hard at her. Rielle saw a flick of yellow-green glint in his eyes as she read fury on his face. He snarled more than he spoke. "Your officer friend, the one who visits you at the restaurant every two days?"

Rielle had enough of his anger manifesting over her. Whatever connection they had, it was insane how she felt his emotions as if they were hers. How did he know about Jao? At times, she'd felt his presence but thought she was exag-gerating, until now. "You've been keeping a tab on me?" She accused.

"Your restaurant name came up, so once I found out an Arcadien rebel was your cook, I had to find out why."

"Callum, you are under no obligation to protect me," she could only reason to say. When he didn't answer, she con-tinued. "There shouldn't be any attraction between us. You control people with your mind and . . . and you're not human. How do I know I'm not under your spell? That you're not controlling my mind?"

His eyes ogled her. They turned into an intense gaze. Suddenly, a dark blue rim and white rays flashed around his iris. Silence fell before them.

Rielle felt uncomfortable. She writhed under his gaze. For an infinite moment, she felt a rush across her chest. Slowly he moved closer to her and leaned into her. "What are you doing?" Rielle asked as she leaned back against the wall; her breathing caught in her throat once he wrapped one hand around her waist then slowly pressed his mouth to hers. Tenderly at first, then harder when a moan escaped her lips, and she kissed him back. She closed her eyes; the fervid sensation of his tongue filled her mouth. Within only a few seconds, a spark of sexy static electricity hit at her with an insatiable need for him. His breathing hardened.

"I don't need to control your mind to make you feel the way you're feeling right at this moment, mortal," he whispered against her lips. His deep voice was harsh and condescending.

Rielle opened her eyes and raised them to look at him. His brows furrowed, he stared her down with an intense gaze. She read fury in them, and a moment later, something else flashed in them.

"You want me, I can smell it, and I sense it," Callum challenged and pulled her more into him as he brought her lips once more to his. Their lips pressed together, ragged breathing and dancing tongues brought a fiery heat to his body.

Infuriated, she brought up the officer friend to protect her, thinking herself to be under a spell when it came to their attraction. Callum had wanted to prove a point to her. But nothing else mattered at this moment as desires ignited in him, and he was losing himself into her. He pushed himself more into her as he became engulfed in their lustful burning flames, and their kiss grew more urgent, vital, and more passionate.

Waves of passion fired through them; it was just the two of them in the world. One arm enfolded tightly around her waist, and briskly, he lifted her from her feet. A soft sound came out of her mouth. She wrapped her legs around his back.

A rush of wind between the two of them, in nanoseconds Rielle was lying on a bed as his hands raced over her body. Slowly he unbuttoned her shirt, his mouth closed over one nipple, and she lost all common sense. "Callum." This was insane. The way her body responded and connected to him. Her attraction and need for him were undeniable.

Callum felt his need for her exploding at the center of his legs when she whispered his name. He went back to her mouth, his heart pounding the moment their lips touched again. When their mouths began mating with an intensity that shook every nerve on his body, Callum fought the urge to break the connection, fear of losing control as the possessiveness in him was flipping, fighting to surface. But now he didn't want to be aware and didn't care about anything but the feel of his tongue stroking hers. A rush of sensations flooded and overpowered him. Fire stirred in his loins, and his body began to ache. He kissed her neck, his breath hot and moist against her skin. She was shaking with need and passion beneath him. "Ilia mie," he growled, the possessiveness in his voice for her to hear. She was his. *Yes, mine. I need to claim her, so I don't lose her. She belongs to me.* "Ilia, mie."

The urgency pounded at him; Callum couldn't help his actions even if he wanted to. The words filling his brain at a fast rate, he couldn't stop himself from saying them and sending her into a deep sleep. His lips curled back as he erotically nibbled on her neck.

"Tui aparatenie a mie Io lomeia aparatenie a tui."

"You belong to me as I belong to you."

"Tui sei la mie vitale, etui sei illo Mio mondole lomeia Io sonoto tuio."

"You are my life, and you are my world as I am yours."

"Io prometole loivia, feidelità, feiliciotà, eme ti protegarò seimprei."

"I promise you love, loyalty, happiness, and I will protect you always."

He spoke the words, his voice enthralling and glamorous, wild with magic. The magical words marked her, whether she liked it or not. They were one. "Mine," "yours"—the words echoed in his mind.

Chapter 9

Rielle woke up to strong masculine arms around her waist. What happened last night? Callum kissing her rushed her memory, but anything else she couldn't remember. She must have fallen asleep in the middle of their make out. Slightly she turned around, taking her time to look at him. He was probably one, if not the most handsome man she'd come across.

Around his face were his long copper hair tousled locks. Rielle gently removed a fringe. The connection between them was fearsome. He wasn't even human, for god's sake. "Did you hex me?" She whispered, not understanding the feelings overcoming her all of a sudden. She didn't know the guy, yet the way he made her feel just by looking at her or kissing her, she had to admit that her attraction for him was inescapable and grew by seconds.

Rielle let her finger run along his face as if she was memorizing everything about his look. Outlining the line of his lips, she remembered how they felt on her breast, how she felt. She blushed just thinking about last night. If, by only kissing her, he was able to ignite every cell on her body, what would happen when she acts out all her fantasies with him? And why was she thinking of acting out her fantasy with him? *No, no,* she inwardly said and glanced around the room, trying her best to move as little as possible.

A loud groan, and words in a language that she didn't understand, Rielle gulped. He was up. "I'm sorry, I didn't want to wake you up," she timidly said.

"You didn't, your thoughts did."

"You can read my mind too?" She asked, perplexed, wondering how much of her thoughts he had heard.

"I can't compel you or see deep into your mind, but I can read your mind," Callum confessed. "You're a telepath. You can read my mind if you want to. You have to concentrate."

"Callum, we have to talk." Rielle quickly got up. "I get it. We are sizzling hot for each other, and physically attracted to each other, but that doesn't make me your woman. These kinds of things take time; around here we get to know the person, we go on dates, we start dating, and the rest is just history." She nervously ran her hand through her hair. "Yes, I feel like I do know you, but this is strange. Unusual. A couple of weeks ago, I was just an average person, but now I find out that I can do certain things. And people are after me or might want to kill me. And then there's you."

"You were never an average person, and what about me?" his brows furrowed.

"You and your looks, and your charms. And whatever that you are, it's all too much," Rielle confessed.

"You think I'm charming?" An amused looked crossed Callum's face. No one would ever dare claim him to be.

"You know you are." She needed to sit down. She took a step back, and out of nowhere, a chair was suddenly next to her. Rielle looked at him with an overwhelming look. "Do you see what I'm saying? It isn't normal." Feeling defeated, she sat down, her face in her hands.

Callum felt her apprehension about all of this. She was scared and confused. He had marked her last night and joined them together; their mind did become one, so it was only natural to know her thoughts. He heaved a sigh. Now was not the time to tell her the truth.

She was legitimately and officially his life mate.

"I understand that all this could be too much for you to handle, but I swear to you with my life that I will not let harm come to you," he calmly said. Kneeling in front of her, Callum awkwardly removed an amount of wild curls away from her face and removed her hands from her face.

The way he looked at her, Rielle knew he meant every word. "I'm not scared of you, Callum; I'm troubled by everything that's going on. It's just too much too fast." A vibrating sound echoed in the room. It was her cell phone; Rielle pulled away from him and quickly ran to the other side of the room, searching through her bag. It was Syrah, and Morris was with her. "What's wrong, are you okay? Where are you, and what is all this commotion?" Rielle spoke on the phone. Minutes later, she hung up the phone. Something wasn't right. She glanced at Callum. "I have to go," she said, not waiting for his answer, and just walked out of the room.

Callum did focus on the conversation and even heard the woman's voice on the phone. He focused on the sound and the surroundings of her friend, using his enhanced hearing. Rielle's friend wasn't in trouble, but something had happened. It could be a trap, he thought. The woman was a mortal, and easily she could be compelled to lure her to the restaurant.

By the time she was out of the front door, he was already right behind her. "What are you doing?" Rielle asked him.

"I'm coming with you; this might be a trap."

"Trap or not, Syrah might be in danger, and it would be my fault," she stubbornly said.

"And falling into the trap is not a good way to help if she is in danger for real."

"We can debate about this, but she's at the café, and I have to see what's wrong with her," she said, not backing out.

"Davide, see what's wrong with the mortal while we drive down there," Callum instructed the warrior, using their minds.

"I'm on it."

Police cars were everywhere. A fire truck was in the middle of the street. Pulling over the curb of the road, Rielle felt antsy about what was going on. She looked to the passenger side to find it empty. Callum had already disappeared. *"Special team force is everywhere. Just don't use any of the superpower things that you do."* Rielle found herself slipping in his mind as if she was always a part of his mind. She was shocked that she was even able to do that.

"I'll be fine."

"These people are nuts, and if they feel like you're not human, which you're not, they will kill you," she pressured.

"If you are not in danger, I won't use any of the superpower things that I do."

Her worries warmed his heart, and for the first time in his existence, Callum wanted to be careful.

She walked to the opposite of the street to talk to the first officer she found. "I'm sorry, Miss, you can't go in there."

"What is going on?" Rielle queried, trying to glance behind the officer. She smelled fire, and there was smoke everywhere.

"Rielle!" It was Jao. He spotted her and was walking toward her. "Let her through. She's the owner of the place," he signaled to the man.

"Jao, what happened?" Rielle tried to hold back her tears. Half of the dinner was burnt to the ground while the firemen were trying to salvage the other half.

"Whoever did this, we will find them. I promise." Jao pulled her into his arms and hugged her.

Rielle couldn't hold back the tears anymore. Sobbing on Jao's chest, she hugged him back. Her whole body went rigid, her ears ringing, and her skin went from heat to coldness. Part of her mind throbbed with an excruciating, raw discomfort. Hastily she pulled away from Jao's embrace.

"Are you okay?" Jao asked, touching her face. "Your face is cold. And you're shaking. I think you're going into shock." He kissed her forehead, calling out the medics on the scene.

"I'm fine, I'm fine." Rielle sobbed, confused about her body reaction. *What was that?* She inwardly thought.

"No, you're not, Rie." An officer signaled to Jao, nodding his head. "I got to go, Rie. A case we're working on just fell in. I just wanted to be here when you get here so I can tell you that whoever did this will regret messing with you. Are you going to be ok?"

"Yes, go." She wiped a tear out of the corner of her eyes.

"I'll call you later to check on you." He touched her arm and walked away.

Rielle swallowed hard, suddenly irritation riding her, and it wasn't hers. Immediately Callum crossed her mind. It left her feeling unfilled. Like something wasn't right. Ignoring her emotions, she glanced around and spotted Syrah. "I found it on fire when I got here. Whoever did this, they did it this morning."

"You didn't do anything wrong. I'm just glad you're okay and that you weren't in there when this happened." Frozen, Rielle stood in front of the scorching café as she watched it burn. "This was my everything, Sy! Who could do such a thing?"

"I'm so sorry, Rie." The short-haired woman hugged her tightly.

Two hours later, Rielle sat in her car, dazed. Too much to hold in, she bent her head on the driving wheel, sobbing.

Wiping her eyes, she turned on the car ignition deciding to drive. Home. That's where she was heading. Her house. She needed to be alone and digest everything. Why were people trying to kill her?

"I think you're going the wrong way?"

Startled, Rielle pushed on the brakes. "Davide, where did you come from?"

"I teleported to your car." He smiled at her. "You're going the wrong way."

"I think it's best if I stay over my house, I need to process all of this."

"Rielle, I meant it when I told you that I agree with Callum and that you would be safer at our place." His tone, intimidating, sounded a lot like Callum.

"I have no personal items over there and—"

"No, ifs and buts, you are in danger. When the rebel said more would come after you, he was telling the truth. Whatever Luke wants from you he will not stop until he gets it."

"I have no other choice, do I?"

"Thank you." Davide smiled his goofy smile like he didn't just scold her.

Rielle scoffed out loud. One she could deal with, but not two. She turned around, making her way to the isolated house. An hour later, they arrived, and Rielle took a deep breath, wondering if he was inside.

"You have to understand you're his world, and if he loses you, we lose him too. When it comes to our women, we are overprotective, and our downfall is our jealousy. Whatever you're feeling, he feels it too, and having another man comforting you is as disturbing to us as it would be for you if another woman even comes close to him once he officially makes you his life mate. I understand this whole situation might be overwhelming for a mortal because, at first, it was a little hard on my brother's life mate, too, and she's from our world. But you're here, meaning that it was fate, and we can't fight fate. He's your world too, and soon you will accept the truth. Just give him time. It's hard on him, and he doesn't understand it, just like you."

"I'm not his woman," Rielle tried to argue, but deep down knew she was lying to herself. Their attraction was undeniable.

"You can't fight it, Rielle. It'll simply get worse." Davide smiled, instructing her to follow him out of the car.

The heavy scent of gardenia filled his nose. Callum immediately knew Davide had convinced her to come back to the house. He was inside the café looking for clues, and what had caused the fire, when her crying tears pierced his mind, followed with a dreariness that clogged his senses and his heart.

Watching her hugging the officer, sobbing on his chest, Callum pictured her on his knees, and it scared him, reminding him what he was. The officer was not only smitten with her; he was beyond infatuated with her.

Though he wished to make the officer disappear, Callum had tried his best to remain calm and was vastly surprised that he did. Granted, she didn't understand what happened.

He knew she felt whatever he felt, as she immediately pulled away from the man.

Much later, Rielle had unconsciously brushed his mind but, too furious, he had ignored her. When she decided to drive back to her house, that's when he told Davide to stop her. The warrior had found the word "witch" written on the kitchen wall. Using his powers of recollection, and his acute senses, he discovered that humans had started the fire. But Callum wasn't going to tell her yet. Not until they figured out what was going on.

After much thought and debate to leave her alone, he walked to the bedroom she occupied. The shower ran and then stopped. Quietly, Callum opened the door. Every part of his body ached the way she looked at him. Her hair was damp with water; wrapped around her was a white towel.

"I have no clothes here," Rielle quietly said, not surprised to find him in the room. Following his gaze, out of nowhere, a t-shirt was on the bed. It wasn't there seconds ago, but she was mentally too tired. She had seen enough of magical and supernatural things in the last few days to ask him how he did that. Grabbing the shirt from the bed, Rielle headed back to the bathroom and pulled it over her head. Running her hand through her wet hair, she walked back into the room. Callum was gone. Tears fell down her face, a comforting feel pushed in her head. Rielle knew it was him. She wiped her eyes, and in a matter of seconds, Callum stood in front of her.

Slowly he pulled her in his arms, holding her tight as he kissed her hair. Rielle wrapped her arms around his back, weeping like a baby. "I'm sorry, I'm not usually this emotional."

"Don't apologize to me." He held her face in his hands, kissing her tears away. "What can I do?" Her tears were affecting him.

She wanted him to kiss her. She didn't want to think about her burnt down café, or people who wanted her dead. She just wanted it to stop, wanting to forget for the moment. But she didn't dare tell him that.

Callum smiled inwardly. He had received her request loud and clear as their mind was now linked, tying them to one another. He lowered his face to hers, capturing her lips in what seemed to be a bone-melting kiss. It was aggressive, it was fervent, it was obsessive, then it was passionate, and it became tender, soothing. It was everything all at once. He pressed her body to his, leaving no space between them. His hands slid down her back as he gently grabbed her rounded rear brusquely. He lifted her, wrapping both of her legs around his back. With her, he marched to the bed as he laid her down carefully. Callum took a minute to look at her. He saw everything she was feeling right at this moment in her eyes.

Rielle pulled him down on her. He captured her lips once again as he slid his hand under the oversized shirt she was wearing. His heart nearly stopped; he stopped breathing. She had nothing but the t-shirt on her back. "I shouldn't—"

The gate exploded. He heard footsteps in the house. Quickly Callum pulled himself off her. *"We have company,"* he communicated to Davide.

"I'm already outback; they're not alone."

"Don't do anything stupid hold on until I find you," Callum commanded to Davide.

"I want you to stay here and don't come out until I say so." Rielle frowned. Callum was almost sure she wasn't going to listen. "No. I mean it, Rielle, stay here and don't come out of this room," he yelled.

"So, you expect me to hide under the bed or in the closet?" He detected sarcasm in her voice.

"Please, I'm begging you, stay here."

Chapter 10

*C*allum followed the men's footsteps and launched at them using his agility and heightened speed. He threw one against the wall while holding the other one by the neck. He pulled out his blade, thrusting it in the man's heart. "Let go of the warrior, Callum!" A commanding voice came from behind him.

"Raphael?" He'd recognize this voice even in his sleep. Holding on to the man, he turned around. "What are you doing here?"

"Let him go now!" Raphael ordered. Callum freed the man from his hold. "You're dismissed. We're taking over your task," Raphael uttered.

"If you honestly traveled to the other side of the realm to tell me this, then you wasted your time, brother."

"You don't get it. I'm trying to save you. We can't fight the humans; orders of the council we find Zachariah, and we go home."

"This is more than just finding Zachariah; the humans have teams and labs to dissect each one of us. They captured Allessio and Davide. Raphael, they can kill us without the blade."

"I read Davide's memory. We both know this is about your mortal woman more than it is about Zachariah or the humans being able to kill us." Callum heard the disapproving tone in his brother's voice. "Whatever you think you're doing with this mortal, it is against the law, and it needs to stop now." Raphael turned to the soldiers. "Get him to the portal effective immediately, and my brother isn't just another warrior, so he'll likely try to kill you all," he warned.

"You're making a big mistake, Raphael. I don't want to hurt anybody, and you need to hear me out."

"You've disobeyed my orders. You went against my decree. That's treason to our people, to your leader. You've put another warrior in danger. You've killed two mortals after I told you not to. Cuff him now, so he doesn't try anything." Raphael signaled.

"I'm warning you; I don't want to hurt these men," Callum said calmly but in a deadly manner.

The soldiers looked at both brothers, confused as to what to do. "Do it now," Raphael shouted angrily. Two soldiers used their speed. They were each on Callum's side, holding both of his hands while another one pulled out his gold shackle.

The cuff was designed to restrain their powers, and their strength. Callum wasn't about to let that happen. Using all his strength, Callum pushed the man on his left side and banged his head against the one with the cuff. "I said I didn't want to hurt anybody, but anyone of you come at me again, I will kill you." His gaze was on his brother all the while he talked.

"You've left me no choice," Raphael uttered. In a flash, he ran toward Callum, knocking him down forcefully. With one hand he tossed him against the wall. Callum went through two different walls before he landed on his back in the back of the house.

Angry, Callum got up. Using his speed, he ran toward the house only to find himself knocked down again. He felt his dark possession rise, but Raphael was his older brother and his leader; he didn't want to fight him.

"You are so stubborn, just like him. You're everything that he used to be. *Mierdei mie*, if I let you become him, or what he is!" Raphael roared angrily for the first time, letting himself get to that point.

"I am nothing like Luke," Callum snapped back.

"You're exactly like him. Not following rules, killing mortals. I lost one brother to his darkness, and I'm not losing another one." Raphael picked him off the floor and held him by his shirt. "You're going home. You're trying to hide from me, but I can feel it inside of you. This place is turning you into the very thing we fight against, and I'm not letting you get sucked into it." He turned to the men once again and roared. "Cuff him now!"

"Get your hands off of him." A soft but confident voice echoed behind them.

All heads turned. Raphael tightened his grip on Callum, and his eyes were on Rielle. There was something about her, it was unfamiliar, and he couldn't quite put his finger on it. "And who might you be?" He charmingly said, coaxing her mind.

"Who I am is of no importance, so I'm only going to ask this last time. Let go of him." Rielle didn't know where this confidence came from all of a sudden. Whoever this was, he was as handsome and as powerful as Callum, exuberating the same characteristics and mannerisms. Softer and gentler on the edges, in him, she didn't feel the danger she felt in Callum the first time they met. He had a graciousness and nobility about him that was different and seemed fair. But still, he wasn't a total saint. He was just as much of a fighter as Callum, and she knew that she should be afraid of this man.

"You should have stayed in the room as I asked you to," Callum reprimanded her.

"You're getting an ass-kicking right now, and I can't stand it. Why aren't you fighting back?" Rielle bit back. She wanted to stay in the room as he asked her to, but the minute this powerful man attacked him, she knew. It worried her.

"Raphael! Trust me. She has nothing to do with this." Callum pleaded to his brother telepathically.

"She has everything to do with this. She's the reason why you've shielded your mind from me. Even now. What are you hiding from me?" Raphael asked Callum distrustfully. *"Very well then, if you're not going to let me into your mind, I'll just do what I have to do with hers,"* he continued, as he tried to read Rielle's memory, wanting to erase everything she knew about Callum and whatever else she knew about their race. But instead, he found a white wall. *"I can't read her mind."* Using more power, Raphael tried again forcefully. He felt a compulsive throb in his head, and it hurt like hell.

Raphael let go of Callum. An incredible power surged into his whole body; it was electrifying. A weakness in his legs, he went down on his knees, fighting to take back control of his body and his mind.

"Rielle, stop it!" Callum looked at Raphael on the floor, then Rielle. He felt the energy coming out of her the minute Raphael tried to manipulate her mind. She was trying to protect herself as Raphael's intent was not only to read her mind.

"I don't know how," Rielle said, losing her nerve.

"Focus on me, look at me, Raphael meant you no harm."

"He tried to do something with my mind. I felt it."

Raphael's men took a step toward Rielle, and Callum knew they would not hesitate to kill her. "If one of you touch her, I will rip your hearts out with my bare hands," he growled, warning the men off. "I know, Rielle, but my brother meant you no harm, I promise you."

"Your brother?" Rielle looked at Callum. He was telling the truth. Immediately she felt mortified. The energy stopped pouring out of her.

Raphael stood up and was looking at her, baffled. Then he looked back to Callum.

"What are you?" Raphael demanded.

"She might be a pureblood enchantress," Callum acknowledged, using their mental path.

"What?" Raphael was staggered.

"Read my memory; this is the reason why I didn't want you in my mind."

Raphael did. Stunned and amazed at how she killed the shadow walker. Taken aback to find out she was the last pureblood enchantress in over a century if Callum was right. *"Impossible. She holds too much power to be an enchantress. How is she able to control my mind? Enchantresses can't control our mind even with spells. She could be a threat to us."*

"She's not."

"She tried to take control of my mind just now."

"You tried to wipe and manipulate her mind; she was protecting herself," Callum defended.

"And protecting you. I know you're taking a liking to her, but I'm sorry, Callum, we don't know what she's capable of. I must report her to the council. Any being that can control our mind like she just did is a danger to us," Raphael said, unsure. "Cease her," he yelled out to the men.

"No, Raphael! Don't do this." Callum stopped the men on their track.

Raphael disappeared in the room for a second, and the next, he was behind Rielle, his blade around her neck. "Callum, we have no other choice. Stop fighting my men, or she's dead."

"If anything happens to her, you're dead." Callum looked at his brother with the same intensity in his eyes. Raphael was unyielding, and so was he.

Rielle could see the fierce glow in Callum's eyes. She sensed something dark in him, ready to take control. She didn't know why she was confident that Raphael wasn't going to hurt her but would try anything to make his brother listen—also convinced that neither one of them would back out. She blamed their mothers and their society for raising them like that.

"Raphael, I will appreciate it if you get your knife away from me." The threat hung in the air between them for a long moment. She was irritated.

"What?" Raphael said, confused.

"Look, I don't know you, but it's obvious that you are just using me to tame your brother as you should. However, I don't like being in the middle of people's family issues, yet somehow it seems that I'm right at the center of your family issues. If you wanted to kill me, you would have done it already."

"Excuse me?"

She rolled her eyes. "I'm sorry I did whatever it is that I did to you, but you tried to use your magic thing with my mind in my defense. I will go wherever it is that you want me to go to show you that I'm not a danger to anyone. For god's sake, you are the dangers, not me. I was fine until your brother showed up and turned my world upside down. So, if someone is a danger, it's you, Arcadien men, with your testosterone and your backward views and prejudice against women."

Raphael let her go, amazed by her shrewdness. "Prejudice against women? We love our women; they are our number one priority." He didn't know why, but he felt the need to defend their view.

"Telling me what to do, being an angry idiot the minute a man whom I knew before you touches me innocently, or because I'm talking to your friend. Expecting me to hide like the little woman that you think I am while you are out there putting yourself in danger and getting your ass kicked does not show that women are your priority," Rielle snapped at the powerful warrior.

More confused than ever, Raphael glanced at Callum, the men around the room, and then back at her. "Why do I feel that this is more about my brother than it is about Arcadien men?"

"Because apparently, it's your society. You all are arrogant and cavemen."

"What did my brother do to you?" Raphael was now amused but trying his best to keep a straight face.

"Besides being an arrogant son of bitch—"

"I can assure you that our mother was pure noble." Raphael was offended. Still, her words amused him.

"I'm sure she's wondering where she went wrong," Rielle snapped. She had enough of these supernatural dramas. "Look, if you're not going to murder me and you're not going to take me to some dark place and torture me, I'll go back to my assigned room now. Simply because I can't go home."

"You can't go home?"

"Your brother won't let me go home."

Raphael ogled at Callum disapprovingly. "You've kidnapped her?"

"It's complicated," Callum quickly defended.

Rielle sighed out, frustrated. "I've been through enough with the likes of you. I'm not a threat to you or to your people or anyone else for that matter. Honestly, I want my life back." The room got quiet, and Raphael moved away from her. He'd never met a mortal like her before.

"Where is Davide?" Callum asked his brother, breaking the silence.

"Handcuffed outside."

"She's not a threat, Raphael. You have to trust me on this." *"Rielle, go back into the room. Let me talk to my brother."* He used their mental path.

"Are you going to be okay?"

"I'll be fine," Callum reassured her.

"How can you be so sure?" Raphael uttered, once Rielle left the room. "And what is it with this mortal woman that got you so worked up. And seven hells, Callum, you've kidnapped her?" Not waiting for an answer, Raphael pried in Callum's mind. "You believe she's your life mate?"

"I don't believe it; she is."

"Callum, this is against the rules; you've gone so far ahead this time even I won't be able to help you out of this one."

"I didn't plan it. It just happened."

"You didn't mark her, did you?" When Callum kept quiet, Raphael took his silence as the answer. "You did!"

"It just happened; I couldn't stop it. I didn't even know I knew the words."

"It is ingrained in our minds. When we find our mates, it just comes naturally. Now, this makes things more complicated. I meant it when I said I have to report it to the council. They have to know about her."

"They will kill her; you were ready to kill her once you found out what she can do."

"But I didn't because I could see how much she meant to you."

"Raphael, if anything happens to her, no one is safe. No one, not even you." Callum confessed the sincerity in his voice for his brother to hear.

"You're serious."

"I am."

"She is your life mate."

"Yes."

"Does she know?"

"No, she doesn't know that I marked her."

"Callum!"

"I had to; it was the only way. She's stubborn and different."

"It was the same thing with Priscilla, so you must tell her what you did."

"Priscilla knows our culture, and she came around; I'm not so sure about Rielle. She's so determined. She doesn't care that I'm the man, and if I say 'jump' to keep her safe, she should jump with no questions asked."

Raphael chuckled. "Mortal or not, women don't jump just because you tell them. Even our women. They know keeping them safe is our main priority, so when it comes to their safety, they do as we say. But trust me, brother, when I tell you that women ask a million questions before they jump."

"She thinks I'm charming."

"Oh, seven hells! You indeed have found your life mate. Now you're going to be a madder man than you already are. She's got spunk, that's what you need." Raphael smiled approvingly.

Callum chuckled. "Yeah, too much spunk, I think."

"What are we going to do? I'm not sure she's an enchantress. What she did just now, an enchantress doesn't hold that much power to do it," Raphael admitted, bewildered.

"Honestly, I don't know."

"We need to find Zachariah. If we find Luke, we find Zachariah. Maybe he will be able to shed light on all of this."

Chapter 11

The little girl ran; she was bleeding, crying for help. Rielle ran after her. She wanted to help her. *"I can help you, don't be afraid,"* Rielle screamed after her. She stopped and pointed her finger toward the deep end of the forest.

"He's here," the little girl whispered, crying.

"Who's here?" Rielle asked, concerned.

"The man in black, he's going to hurt me."

Rielle held her hands. *"Did he do this to you? Don't worry. I won't let him get to you."*

"You can't help me; no one can. He always comes back." The small child sobbed. A loud whistle echoed through the forest; she panicked. *"He's here! Please don't let him hurt me."*

Rielle pulled the girl behind her. She was surrounded by six individuals. No longer was it a day, as the moon was now dim above them. Their black clothing blended with the shadows, their faces obscured by their black hoods. "*You'll have to get through me to get her,*" Rielle said.

"*We already have her,*" one of them answered. The little girl was now standing next to them, crying for help.

"*Let her go,*" Rielle screamed, moving toward them, but suddenly her limbs became numb once they began chanting words. A sharp sting cut across her thighs. She looked down at her legs; blood poured on the ground. Searing fiery bursts pulsated around the wound, intensifying with each second, jarring and brutal. Another sharp pain cut through her chest. Blood seeped through her shirt as her pain amplified, and she struggled to move. Blood was slowly oozing out of numerous wounds on her body. The pain was like a knife being twisted everywhere on her form. It shot up fast, erasing every thought from her head and paralyzing her body. She screamed out before her consciousness receded. Black haze swirled at the edges of her mind.

Callum was in a deep sleep, and her scream awakened him. He sped to her room, sensing her discomfort. The moon shined inside of the room. The trees were whistling as if they were trying to say something. The smell of blood invaded his nose. Her fear hit him; he immediately knew. "No . . . no, Rielle! Wake up!" He compelled her mind. "You have to wake up." He shook her. His chest contracted to see the cuts on her body. She was bleeding everywhere.

Shortly, Raphael and Davide entered the room. "She's in a trance," Raphael uttered, stunned. "Callum, she's in tremendous pain. We have to wake her up."

"She's unconscious."

"If she stays unconscious for too long in the dream world while she's hurt, we might lose her. You have to wake her up," Davide uttered.

"I can't find her in the dream world, Raphael, Mierdei," Callum roared.

"They probably sheltered her; you have to try again," Raphael said.

"Rielle, wake up!" Callum forced himself into her mind, commanding her subconscious. Alarmed, Rielle woke up, letting out a struggled scream. "It's me. You're safe . . . you're safe." Callum kneeled by the bed, a troublesome look on his face.

"Callum—," she sobbed.

"I'm here. You're safe." He stroked her hair.

"They have her—I couldn't save her." Pain coursed throughout her body.

"Whoever she was, she wasn't real. You're alright," he said, his voice betraying his certainty. She tried to move, but he stopped her. "You have cuts all over your body. Don't move." Rielle didn't protest as her whole body ached.

"Can you tell me what happened in your dream, Rielle? How did you get wounded?" Raphael asked. Until now, Rielle wasn't aware of him or Davide in the room. She sent a pleading look to Callum as she squeezed his hands.

"We can ask her about it later, Raphael. She's in pain, and I have to heal her," Callum voiced quietly. Whoever did this to her, he wanted to give them a taste of their medicine.

"It's done, brother, nothing you could have done; they invoked her," Raphael communicated to him telepathically. Callum knew that Raphael didn't need to read his mind to understand what he was thinking.

"This is unfamiliar, Callum. Her wounds appear to be real. Trance or not, it still happened in the dream world," Davide rejoined.

Rielle looked at all three men in the room. Although they were calm, and she couldn't read their expressions, she knew that something was wrong. "Callum, what's wrong with me?" she quietly asked.

"Shh . . . I just have to attend to your wounds," Callum comforted her.

"I must heal her, and I don't want her to panic," Callum communicated to Raphael and Davide using their mental path.

"We'll get out of your way," Davide replied. Seconds later, both men left the room.

"This was more than a dream, wasn't it?" Rielle asked, scared.

"You were in a trance. Yes, it's more than a dream. Your body stays in this world, but your essence is in the dream world, that's why it feels so real. If your essence wanders for too long in the dream world without your body, you can get lost. It's what mortals call being in a coma."

"Why? Why are people after me?"

"I don't know. I promise I'm going to find out." He observed her. "I have to heal your wounds, Rielle. I need you to stay calm and not panic. I don't want to send you into a deep sleep, so you're going to be aware of what's going to happen, and it might be a little painful. Your body might reject the shock once my healing energy is poured into you."

"I think maybe we should go to the hospital."

"Mie cehia, no hospital. They'll ask questions, and your wounds won't heal fast. Though there is another way I can transfer my healing energy to you, it's better this way, and I don't want to scare you," Callum confessed quietly.

"I trust you."

Callum stayed quiet for a moment, his face restrained.

"What is it?" Rielle asked, now concerned.

"It's the way those of us with the healing gift attend to his or her life mate. It's the most effective way to heal someone, as you're not only losing energy, you're also feeding on them."

"Alright then, do it." Callum didn't answer her. The look on his face, the sudden tension in the air implied it all. "Oh—," Rielle whispered. A quavering sensation ran through her. Holding her breath, she shut her eyes tight, wheeling away the thoughts of his hand touching her everywhere on her body.

"Stay calm and don't move. I have to concentrate, or else I might hurt you." He climbed in the bed. Gently, he heaved the oversized shirt, examining the cut above her thighs.

Rielle gulped and opened her eyes.

Callum was looking down at her face. Her body temperature went from zero to ten immediately. She was hot in all the right parts of her body, the way he stared at her. The man was just too damn handsome. "Are we—?" She asked, not recognizing her voice. Callum's jaw muscles clenched, the tension in the room became palpable. "Don't answer that," Rielle smiled dimly, wanting to make light of the situation.

"Don't worry. I'll be healing you as if you were Davide or Raphael."

"I'm not worried." She jerked when he touched the wounded part of her thigh. "I'm sorry," she whispered.

Callum said nothing but continued with his inspection. "Are you in excruciating pain anywhere else besides your thighs and your arms?" he asked after what seemed to be like an infinite moment.

"My chest—I think the same cut is on my chest." She cleared her throat.

"If you were into a deep sleep, I'd heal you without having to make you feel uncomfortable. I'm sorry, Rielle, but I have to inspect your wounds first before I can heal you—"

"Just do what you have to do." She cut him off.

The silence felt in the room. Callum pulled the shirt higher. Adrenaline rushed in his brain and down to his groins when her perky breasts hardened. He groaned.

He needed to concentrate, or he might hurt her. "Anywhere else?" he cleared his throat.

"My side," she whispered, staring at his lips and then his face. The heat between her legs became unbearable. How was he so calm when she was feeling all kinds of feelings, and her body was aching everywhere for his touch, with him being so close. "I'm aching," Rielle quietly said, embarrassed of her confession.

Callum knew what she meant. He could feel her arousal for him; it was calling out to him. He ached for her, too, but he needed to control himself. "I know. but you won't be for long, I promise."

"Callum," Rielle softly whispered. Her eyes were pleading with him.

She made a throaty sound, Callum all but forgot his resolve. He bent his head and gently pressed his lips to hers. Rielle lips parted, his tongue gradually licked the opening between her lips and then slipped into her mouth to find her tongue. Removing his lips from hers, "It'll be quick, I promise." He watched her, unsure of what he was looking for, but whatever it was, he found it gazing into her eyes, having a non-verbal and non-mental conversation. "I am in no way calm in this situation. But mie cehia, your health is my priority right now, and I must heal you." A thread of hair fell in front of his face. With ease, Rielle set it behind his ears. "My instincts are screaming in need of you. Every time I'm near you, I ache for you too. I yearned for you. You can sense it, that's why it's painful for you. Its hell for me knowing, feeling, tasting, and smelling your desire for me. I'm lured by it. I want so badly to make every inch of your longing and wishes come true. I can't count how many instances I have imagined sinking into your trembling body and claiming what's rightfully mine, but I can't risk it with your wounds," he continued; his needs were on his face for her to see.

Rielle's lips parted, her breath shallow. Callum groaned, losing his resolve as he leaned down and kissed her earlobes gradually down to her neck. Rielle's nipples budded, pointing against his chest. She pushed her body harder into him, and a soft moan came out of her mouth. *It is just a hickey, Rielle, relax*, she reminded herself. Feeling stirred up more, he kissed that specific spot. Callum stopped kissing her and pulled back away from her. Rielle opened her eyes, wondering why he stopped. She watched him; in a blink of an eye, she was naked. Both her underwear and her shirt were on the floor. *How did he do this?*

"I just wished them away, the way an Arcadien would."

"How?"

"By focusing on the clothes. They're just matters, and I manipulate them."

Rielle tried to sit up but cringed at the sharp pain in her chest. "Stop moving, or you're going to hurt yourself more," Callum warned. Rielle frowned. She just wanted to help him with his clothes. Callum smiled, her thoughts conveyed to him. He removed his shirt the mortal way while her eyes focused on him; he loved the sparkling glint in her eyes.

A half-naked Callum was standing in front of her. Rielle was in awe of his lean, hard frame. She had felt his muscles before, but seeing and touching were two different things. Rielle tried to tear her gaze away from the outline of his magnificent form, but it was no use. His devilishly handsome features shifted into a grin as he watched her staring at him. He removed the rest of his clothes. Rielle smiled charmingly in return, speechless of his beautiful body. *What woman in their right mind would turn away someone who looked like this?*

Callum moved on top of her, easing his towering naked frame down on her.

He began to kiss her. He kissed her neck, her collarbone, then her shoulder. His hands roamed on her skin; he touched her breasts as he carefully bent his head, kissing her wounds. His lips were inches away from her nipples. They hardened for him, desensitized before his eyes. Callum flashed an arrogant and shrewd smile, loving his effect on her.

"Your body knows it belongs to me, *mie cehia*." He leaned down and wrapped his lips around one of her nipples, kissing and grazing all over it.

Rielle helplessly arched up, panting with pleasure as he continued his action. Her breath turned to a moan when he sucked it, hard, again and again. He did the same for the other one and skimmed his hand down her belly. She stiffened. A small amount of energy flowed to her once his fingers reached the wounded cuts on her thighs. Gently he kissed them. A cooling sensation swarmed over her.

"Do you trust me?" He telepathically held the sweet smell of her arousal that filled his head. Rielle nodded, lost in the emotions he evoked in her. Callum went back to her mouth as he kissed her again with an urgency that gave her no time to think of anything else but his tongue stroking hers as his hands threaded through her hair, pressing himself harder onto her.

Skin against skin, he was hard where she was soft, and rough where she was smooth. His mouth still on hers without breaking apart, he slid his hands down her body. He cupped her, finding her sex slick and ready. He touched and teased the pulsating throb in that specific area. Rielle shivered to her bone, and it wasn't from being cold. Stirred her in slow circles. She closed her eyes, her body melting under his touch. She arched beneath him, magnificently quavering.

Callum stopped kissing her, watching her. Lust, yearning, and needs on her face, he wondered if it was a mirror of his own. The way she looked back at him. *"Ilia mie,"* his voice slipped into her head as he played strings with her sex, avoiding her most sensitive part.

"Callum," Rielle moaned, whispering his name.

Positioning himself on top of her, he used his arms to stop from crushing her. He nudged her, Rielle tilted her hips, allowing him entrance. He rubbed against her folds and pushed in a little. Reaching between the two of them, he guided himself inside of her. Rielle moaned.

"Uhhh." Callum groaned. A feeling of belonging and possession filled his mind. His heart stopped. Rielle touched his biceps, and he trembled.

Resting his forehead against hers, he closed his eyes then gazed at her. Stunned, he began to move, silently reflecting that he had peeked into her soul. Her soul was pure fire, unlike his.

Her legs wrapped around his waist, Rielle moaned, feeling a sensation of voltaic magnetic force transferred from him to her. She felt his need for her, she also felt the darkness in him, and the tenderness in his restraint as if he didn't want to give control to that side of him. Even when his breath became ragged, he kept his thrusts smooth for fear of losing control. She didn't know how it was possible, but she was in his mind, and for a moment, she swore that her heart wasn't hers anymore but became his. She identified the loneliness in him. The responsibilities he bore, the guilt eating him, his resentment of what he was and what he became—her heart shattered in a million pieces. He wanted to give up—he had given up before. Rielle couldn't stop the tears coming out of her eyes. *"Callum."* Sorrow swarmed Rielle's heart.

"You're crying . . . shh . . . *Mie cehia* don't cry for me. I have something to look forward to now. I have you to look forward to now," he beautifully expressed, kissing her tears. He kissed her eyelids, her nose, and finally her lips, deep and hard. He thrust into her, taking his time, not wanting to rush, revering this moment, feeling the thickness of his body stretching her. He loved the feel and the smell of her, her soft whimpers a melody in his brain. Her head fell back. She closed her eyes; her hips continued to embrace and cradle his thrusts. Losing control, she squirmed and wriggled beneath him, desperate for more. Callum quickened the pace, giving her what she wanted.

Rielle whimpered in approval. The two of them together like this was glorious, it was enthralling, and it terrified her that she was giving herself freely to him like this. Having him inside of her made everything around her and in the world cease to exist; It was beyond anything she had experienced in her life. Right now, it was only the two of them and the tension and passion convoluting inside them both. Forcing her eyes open, she gazed hazily at him. She read control, power, and hunger on his face. His eyes were bright; the blue in them turned lustrous almost like purple. Inhuman, unholy, and just beautiful. They consumed her. One last thrust, deep and hard, and her entire body throbbed, shaking with passion. Rielle moaned out louder this time, her whole world exploded, leaving her drained and shuddering.

Callum moved to her side as he laid on his back and tried to recuperate his breathing. The two of them making love was the final step of tying them together and their bond. She was his—mind, body, and soul. It was complete, and she was his. Swallowing a groan, Callum turned to face her. Looking at her, his hands scanned her body. "Are you feeling okay?"

"I don't know," Rielle answered, her eyes closed.

"I think you are." He examined where her cuts were.

Rielle smiled. She didn't open her eyes, but her brows wrinkled. "Thanks to you."

Callum grinned and pulled her close, shifting her on top of him, loving the feel of her naked skin pressed into his skin. "This is the most effective way I've used my gift. I've never felt so vigorous after I healed someone." He was elated, surprised at the feeling.

"Hmm . . ."

"You're not going to open your eyes?"

"Not yet, I'm still not fully back to earth. I don't think I am," Rielle teased.

Callum buried his face in her bare neck, nibbling and kissing her. "Open your eyes. I want to see you." Rielle jolted, her skin leaping and heating at his touch. "Please." He ran his hand on her back until he found her rounded rear. He grabbed a cheek and pinched her hard.

Rielle surrendered. She opened her eyes to find crystal ones looking back at her. They were back to their natural color. Callum's head shot up. He captured her lips. Wrapping his arms around her back, he pressed her more into him, his erection soaring once again. He wasn't sure he would ever get enough of her and now understood why Raphael and some of the warriors were always in a hurry to get to their mate.

Chapter 12

$\mathcal{R}$ ielle woke up with a smile on her face. Feeling free and refreshed, she stretched out and glanced around the room, Callum's side of the bed was empty. Wearing the sheet around her naked body, she got up. The small bruises around her hips and her thighs were huge enough to notice. She blushed, recollecting last night's happenings and remembering his touch and him inside of her.

It was insane, she never gave herself so freely to anyone, yet she'd do it again given the opportunity. Everything between them was all too much too fast, and she needed to figure this whole thing out before anything else happened between them. After taking a shower, hungry, she walked to the kitchen, unsure if Arcadien people even eat.

Rielle opened the fridge, surprised to find it stocked with vegetables, fruits, and other ingredients. "I heard you mortals eat a lot, so I took the liberty to get everything," Davide's voice came from behind her.

"Good morning. Do you even eat?" Rielle teased.

"Let's say our diet is different than yours, but yes, we do eat. And no, we don't slaughter our animals to eat them. They are an essential part of our world and our life."

"Do you drink coffee? I'm going to make some. You might like it if you try."

"I don't think so." Davide made a face.

"I promise you won't be disappointed."

Davide looked at her as if he didn't believe her, then sighed. "Alright, I'll try it, but simply because I like you."

Rielle smiled. "Where are Callum and Raphael?"

"You should know where he is, you are his life mate," Davide answered.

"I'm his what now?"

"His life mate," he casually said.

"What exactly is a life mate?"

"It's one's lover, one's equal, a friend, one's soul mate, one's light. Without them, it's not worth living. Life doesn't make sense. So, you're his light and the only one who can help him. Arcadien men look forward to finding that one woman who makes them feel alive, giving them something to look forward instead of the ordinary and our curse."

"I'm not sure how you do things in your world, but around here before anything of this life mate affair takes place, people date and see if they are compatible with one another."

"But you are compatible with him; otherwise you wouldn't be his life mate, and he wouldn't be yours. You're in his mind as he is in your mind, that's how you know his whereabouts because you're his life mate."

"Always?"

"Always, you don't get a break."

"That's not normal."

"It is in our world."

Rielle handed him a cup of coffee. Davide looked at it, still uncertain. "Aren't you a big bad wolf? Try it," she mocked, watching him.

Davide lifted the cup to his lips. His reaction was priceless. "I like it." He smiled.

"Told you!"

"Something is different about you."

"I don't know what you mean." Rielle blushed.

"Yesterday you were tense, and you were wounded."

"A good night's sleep can do wonders, I guess. Plus, Callum used the weird thing that he does to heal me." She blushed once more. Liar, you know damn well you didn't rest last night, she said inwardly.

"Hence why I let you sleep in this morning." She choked, spilling the coffee in her mouth out on the table. "Are you okay?" Davide asked.

"Yes, it's just a little hot," Rielle lied.

"Boundaries, I was talking to myself. You can't just pop out into someone's mind at will."

"I'm in your mind, mie cehia, even when I don't say anything."

"Ok, this is just too much."

"It's not, that's the way it is. I'm sorry about last night." Rielle felt a slight ache in her chest. Did he have regret about last night? Why was he apologizing to her? *"No, mie cehia, I meant about your bruises and your bite marks. I saw your body this morning. I must have lost control without realizing it."*

Relief swept over her. *"Boundaries, we're going to have to work on that. And no apology necessary. I enjoyed last night."* She blushed. What was wrong with her? Did she confess to him she liked the sex?

"I loved getting to know your body, and I liked the sex too."

Rielle heard a chuckle in her mind. *"Boundaries, Callum, this isn't fair."*

"Our mind is one, Rielle. You must let yourself in my mind too if you want to know what I'm thinking."

"Are you with your brother?"

"Yes, we're looking at a lead. I'll be home soon. Round two?"

"I thought we already went for round three last night. I'm with Davide. I'm pretty sure he can make out the expression on my face."

"The power of recollection is his ability. I'm pretty sure just by looking at you he knows what we did after they left me to attend to your wounds," Callum teased.

Rielle coughed out loud. *"Oh my god, are you serious? No, don't answer that."* She heard his laughter in her head.

"Everything okay?" Davide asked.

"I have a migraine all of a sudden. I'm going to lie down a little," she said to Davide, bolting out of the kitchen.

※

Callum knocked on the wooden door; a tall man slightly opened the door as he stood behind it. "What do you want?" the man asked warily.

"Mr. Rue, my name is Callum Castallante, and this is my brother Raphael. We want to talk to you." Callum smiled politely, coaxing the older man's mind into letting him inside his home.

"Concerning what?" the old man asked sharply, then pensively said, "Castallante—you're Zachariah brothers, aren't you?" his eyes grew wider. He was alarmed. The older man glanced left and right, signaling Callum and Raphael to get in, closing the door behind him. "Did anyone see you?" He said, walking to a room where books of all sorts and all sizes were lying everywhere and anywhere. "Sorry for the mess; my cleaning crew quit."

Callum glanced around the room and could see why Zachariah took a liking to the male. He was as much of a *seckionei*.

"I know why you're here," the man said quietly.

"You do?" Both Callum and Raphael repeated.

"Yes, you're here for your brother. inquiring about his disappearance."

Apprehensive, Callum tapped into the older man's mind, reading him thoroughly. A mortal, and widowed, the man was a professor at the university. He knew who and what they were. "You know what we are?" he asked warily.

"Son, I research for a living, and my late great grand-mother was a custodian for your people when humans and the Arcadien lived close to another. We weren't so different from each other then.

"No, we weren't," Raphael reiterated.

"It was in the seventeenth century. Wasn't it? But then again, the epic battle took place, and everything changed. Your elders built this invisible force field separating your world from ours. It was the only way to protect your race and humans from killing one another. So yes, I know who and what you are. And I don't appreciate you in my mind, just like I've told your brother," the older man chastised.

Raphael smiled inwardly. He liked the man's spirit. "We found your name in our brother's note. We believed he was searching for something and came to you. Do you know if he found what he was searching for?"

"I don't know, but yes, I do know what he was looking into."

"What is it?" Callum asked.

"He wanted me to do research. Find out if it was possible for an Arcadien man to get involved with a human; can the woman give birth to a child, and what would happen to the child."

"What did you find?"

"It's not impossible, but it's not possible either."

"What do you mean?"

"It's one in a million for an Arcadien to have children with a human, it has never happened before, and I doubt it will. Your senses and your genetics are different than us and are five times stronger and more developed, enhanced than us. Not only would the woman die, but the child also wouldn't be able to survive as both genetics would try to extend beyond creating a genomic clash within the child."

"Did he say why he was looking into this?"

"No, but it seemed important to him."

"You said you had to meet him, where?"

"At a small café called Cuisine Douce, a young lady is the owner. Your brother was a regular. He said he felt more comfortable there. But I believed that he liked it there only because he liked to watch Rielle." The man smiled. "He was always watching her."

Callum felt a little cross hearing of his brother's fondness for Rielle. "Is there any reason in particular that he was observing her?" Raphael queried, watching silently.

"Things aren't what they seem to be around here. Your brother was onto something, but he didn't tell me what exactly. He was asking questions, people got suspicious, and he disappeared."

"What can you tell me about Rielle?" Raphael continued.

"The same thing I told your brother—she's a wonderful young lady and the niece of a friend. I wouldn't want her to get tangled in whatever is going on with your kind." Callum tapped into the older man's mind. He was telling the truth about Rielle being his friend's niece. But there was something else; it was elusive, and he couldn't get past it.

"Raphael, he has a defensive shield in his mind, the same as Rielle. I can't get past it."

"If you know something about our brother and the woman professor, you should let us know, as we're here to help," Raphael said gracefully.

"I'm sorry I've told you all I know."

Raphael tapped into the old man's memories. "A part of your memory is hidden; it's blurred and dark. There's something you don't want to remember. It's a spell. Someone locked that part of your brain magically."

"As I've told your brothers, I don't like your invasion in my mind," the older man admonished.

"Professor, please, this isn't just about finding my brother anymore. Rielle might be in danger, and I can't protect her or this town if you don't tell us what you know," Callum pleaded.

The older man heaved a sigh. They were right; she could be in danger. Finding out about the café caught on fire, he feared for the worst. He had promised her aunt he would keep an eye on her, but he had failed.

"Rielle is an enchantress," the professor confessed.

"I had a feeling," Callum added.

"She's not just an enchantress, son. Rielle is the last remaining heir of the Petion family, which means she's the last descendant of pureblood enchantress to be alive. Things are oddly bad around here. I'm certain it has to do with you two. Five women died; the town is on edge. People believe there's a serial killer on the loose, but I know it's not. Whatever is happening with your kind being here, you need to stop it before it escalates."

Callum's face went slack. His mouth slightly opened. Never in his years had he been so shocked. His body unmoving, he stared wide-eyed at the professor. As a child, he'd heard stories about the pureblood. They were fierce, everyone and anyone respected them. Until humans had accused them of witchcraft, killing them all. "She's a pureblood enchantress. Luke must know about her; that's why he had a watchdog in her restaurant. Zachariah must have been trying to keep an eye on her, that's why Luke captured him."

The older man went to his library and picked up a book. "I was twenty-seven when a woman showed up at my doorstep with a pregnant young woman, asking to use my phone because their car had broken down two blocks away from my house. The minute I saw the young woman and saw in how much pain she was, I didn't have it in me to let them spend the night out on the street, so I offered them to stay the night and check on their car in the morning."

"But something happened that night," Raphael cut in, staring at the older man.

"Yes, the young woman went into labor and was in excruciating pain; it was like nothing I'd ever seen before. It was painful to watch, and I just knew that she wouldn't make it, or the baby wouldn't make it. I'd never seen so much blood coming out of a pregnant woman. She was bleeding internally and externally. Her nose, her ears—it was just unnatural. Ellis was the name of the young woman. I wanted to call an ambulance, but I couldn't."

"What happened after that, professor?"

"Anais was chanting some words, but the young woman stopped her, shaking her head." The older man paused and walked to Raphael. "I remember Anais crying. You're going to die, she said. But Ellis was a stubborn one, it was apparent. I remember she closed her eyes and told her aunt that she was dead anyway without him. I assumed whoever they were talking about was the father. And then it happened—there was a white light around the young woman, separating her from the other one. Someone screamed no, the pregnant young woman pushed one last time, screaming in pain. She gave birth to a baby girl.

She whispered something in her aunt's ears. Soon after that, she died. I was furious and scared that a woman had passed away in my living room. I told Anais that I was going to call the cops if she didn't tell me what the hell had just happened."

"She told you the truth. She told you who you were," Raphael voiced.

"Yes, I thought it was insane. Those were my father's bedtime stories when I was a little boy. But then she used another spell, and I saw my father had died at the hand of a man who had the same character as you two, but his eyes were silver."

"Luke," both Callum and Raphael said out loud.

"I just knew then that there was this whole realm that humans didn't know. We aren't alone. So, I started researching the supernatural world. I became obsessed with the stories, seeking the truth. I found the war between humans and Arcadien. About the truce, the force shield, and how it was forbidden for your race to intervene in human affairs or for the two species to get involved with each other. Your laws, decrees, your elders deemed it a crime for Arcadien to father or mother a child with a human. It was all there in my father's study. Anais knew of the abilities of your people and others that could manipulate the mind, so she cast a spell on all three of us so no one would be able to summon up that night."

"Sorry for the letdown, professor. I'm sure it worked until now. But my abilities to summon up memories are greater than that of any supernatural, even my brothers."

"Do you know why Luke is after her?" Callum asked.

"Luke? Zachariah had mentioned that name. No, I don't know why," the professor said thoughtfully.

In the middle of their conversation, Callum felt a sudden emptiness; no soft intimate brush, just emptiness. A cold sensation blast spread through his body. His stomach strained to the point of pain—the urge to reach out to Rielle blatant. He brushed his mind against hers, needing the touch almost more than he needed anything in his life.

"Rielle." He heard nothing, and he felt nothing but emptiness. *"Davide! Check on Rielle,"* he instructed the warrior telepathically.

Davide shouted Rielle's name. Hearing the echo ring through the empty rooms, his heart sank. *"She's not in the house."* He communicated to Callum.

"Is the house secure?"

"Yes, we've been very cautious."

The warrior's words resonated in his head. For a moment, Callum thought a vise strained his heart. Real physical pain flashed through his chest. His gut twisted into hard, cramping lumps.

"What's happening?" Raphael asked, the aching of his younger brother struck at him.

"Rielle is gone. Davide can't find her anywhere in the house, and I can't feel her."

"Call out to her, don't reach out to her. She's your life mate wherever she is. If you call out to her, she must answer."

"Mierdei! Rielle! Answer me now!" The emptiness was eating at him. Callum took a deep breath, fearing for her. Angry at himself believing that she would be safe at the house, knowing that she was in danger, and trusting her life with others.

"Callum, what is it? I went to the boutique two miles away to get some clothes. I don't want to wear your t-shirt for the remaining days I stay at your place."

The sound of her voice brushed through his mind like a caress. Everything he felt moments ago almost disappeared. She was alive. They hadn't taken her.

His whole body went weak, something that had never happened before. *"I swear if in the next two minutes you're not home, Luke or anyone who's after you won't be able to find you."*

His voice turned hard as his heart and senses settled. She was going to hear the end of it, and it wasn't going to be pleasant—hells to her for giving him such scare, for leaving the house and shutting him out.

Rielle knew better than to argue. The icy cold in his voice warned her that Callum was beyond angry with her. Opening the small gate, she was in front of the house when he called out to her. Yes, people were after her. But she needed underwear and didn't want to keep wearing his oversized t-shirt. It was a couple of miles away; it's not like she walked there. She drove.

Davide stood in front of the door. But Rielle's gaze touched on the hard angles and planes of Raphael's face. "You're both angry with me?" She asked. Their eyes were warning her of the trouble she was in.

"I might be angrier than him." Raphael took her wrist and walked with her inside of the house.

"I just needed some air. I didn't think I was in danger; it was only a few miles away from here." Her breath hitched in her throat.

"You scared him to death. And I must confess I got a little scared myself."

Rielle looked at the man next to her who days ago wanted to kill her, but now was telling her that he was scared for her. These men were sure bipolar, she thought.

Suddenly her ears sensed a sinister and dangerous atmosphere lurking in the air. The minute Callum walked into the room, she knew. His eyes flashed bright with fire. He practically jogged toward her; she felt the danger closer and closer. That thing inside of him roaring with fear and anger; she felt it. Her heart pounded, feeling like a child about to get spanked.

"What were you thinking?" Callum roared and grabbed her arms. "You could have been abducted or, better yet, killed!"

"I didn't think—"

"Exactly, you weren't thinking! Shutting me out like this! Never shut me out, do you hear me? Never will you shut me out." He yelled

"I didn't, and I answered you. This telepathy thing is all new to me; it's going to take some getting used to."

"Next time you pull something like this again, you'll need some nice mortal cushion to sit on after I get through paddling your reckless and stubborn little rear," Callum continued, glaring at her while their audience watched with unmistakable fascination.

Rielle jaw dropped, feeling her heart skip a beat before racing on a burst of adrenaline. "What did you say to me?"

"You heard me. It isn't a game. People out there want you dead. You're a threat, and if Luke gets his hands on you, everything changes."

Someone made a choking sound, but Callum wasn't about to take his eyes off Rielle to see who it was. Waves of fear, not anger, rolled off him. Callum didn't even realize he was losing his temper. Lashing into a rage to keep from feeling the fear her desertion had caused.

"I'm a threat!" Rielle snapped, a pain shooting across her chest. There was the man she'd given herself to body and soul last night standing in front of her, and he thought she was a threat.

"Don't you dare!" Callum said, reading her thoughts.

Rielle caught herself, took a step backward, and stopped. "That's not what you said to me last night, last night you didn't think I was a danger or a threat."

"Should we do something before this escalates?" Davide murmured to Raphael on the other side of the room.

Rielle ignored their audience, too riled up now to care who watched them. He growled and took another step toward her. "You know that's not what I meant, and last night has nothing to do with you putting yourself in danger."

"I can take care of myself. I've been doing it for quite some time now." She was furious.

"I don't care if you can turn half of the fucking planet into ice, you're my life mate. Don't ever put yourself at risk. Ever. Never shut me out," he roared in tune with his dark possession, shocked that he'd used the expletive mortal word.

"I'm not your life mate. I wouldn't want to be, not the way you're talking to me right now. Certainly not when you think I need a cushion to sit when you are done paddling my ass," Rielle snapped angrily at him. Callum pinned her to the wall behind her, and she pushed against his shoulders. In a quick movement, he grabbed her wrists and pinned them above her head.

"Callum," Raphael shouted, unsure, afraid that his younger brother might do something crazy.

"Stay out of it, Raphael. This is between my mate and me," Callum cautioned.

"Brother," Raphael continued, using telepathy. "Clear the room. I want to be alone with my mate." Callum snarled.

Raphael reluctantly walked out. The room cleared out in three seconds flat. One thing he knew, he would have probably reacted the same way if Priscilla gave him a scare like this.

The sparkling flame in his eyes burning into hers. Rielle knew that their disagreement had taken another turn. Her heart was beating fast, and the buzzing in her ears wouldn't go away.

"Just because we had sex last night doesn't mean I'm your mate; people sleep with people all the time," she asserted.

Callum laughed, but he didn't sound amused. Shifting both of her wrists to one of his hands, he used his other hand to jerk her shirt aside until he could see his mark against her skin.

"You see this. It means that you're mine. As the mortals would say, this makes us husband and wife, baby, and last night was the final step to our union."

Rielle felt the spot aching and throbbing just from his looking at it. Eyes raging, he leaned down and drew his tongue in a long, riling caress over the mark. It may as well have been at the most sensitive part of her sex. Her entire body clenched in sudden need; a hungry moan broke through her lips. Her head fell back. Her breath shuddered out of her chest. The lick became a nibble that had her heart pounding, and the heat between her legs was too much to sustain. Her heart began to beat faster as the truth settled in her mind. He was telling the truth. How he do this to her, he didn't give her a choice, and she would never forgive him for that.

"How could you do this to me?" Sadness took over her. Rielle felt something dark enclosing in the pit of her stomach. "You took my free will away from me. which is the most important thing in my life." She couldn't breathe. Her head was spinning, and everything seemed foggy. "I will never forgive you for this. I'll always resent you for this."

"Rielle,"

"Let go of my arms. Let go of me," she screamed.

Seeing the hurt and the disappointment in her eyes, Callum let go of her wrists and moved away from her. The darkness and predator inside of him enclosing, ready to burst out. Before she could say anything else, he vanished from the room.

Rielle collapsed on the floor, crying. Angry—this isn't what she wanted.

Chapter 13

$\mathcal{R}$ ielle's words echoed in his head. Callum couldn't stop the tiny little stabbing wounds tearing his chest apart, and he didn't want to deal with the pain. Callum knew what pain was, even recognized it as his opponents breathed in their last breaths. But Rielle resenting him and rejecting him was the worst kind of pain he would endure. Bristled with fury, he wasn't in control anymore, he had given in to the predator and the darkness boiling inside of him. He would instead turn into the very things he hated rather than have her hating and resenting him for the rest of their lives.

Callum walked into the four-sided area, unsure of why he was at the place. The devil's playground was empty, the door unlocked. No security at the door, the area looked vandalized, and the smell of blood permeated the air. He used his enhanced hearing—a fight.

Focusing on the person's cries for help, Callum teleported to him. All eyes were on him—the man on the floor. He remembered he was the rebel who told him about Petrius, the conscious one whose life he spared the last time. The three men beating on him were also rebels, as enhanced as him, and the darkness in them was there to see. "One thing I hate is a bully," Callum scathingly uttered. "I think you guys should pick on someone your size," he continued softly. Too softly. The three soldiers winced at his tone, recognized it as being lethal.

"Callum?" one of them said. "You killed my brother; I can smell your scent."

"I've killed a lot of people, so my apology if I don't know who your brother is."

"Everyone knows who you are, so your chances of stopping us is none. Luke had prepared us for this day."

"And what day might that be?"

"We're going home, and when we do, we will enjoy killing everyone, and especially the council for banning us from our land—dumping us here. And so you know, when Luke is finished with Zachariah, it will be my satisfaction to kill him for what you did to Petrius. A brother for a brother." The warrior stood back and grinned as he pulled a knife out of his pocket.

Callum smiled wickedly. Using his enhanced speed, it looked like he vaporized from the room. One moment the warrior was standing there ready to fight, and the next, he slumped on the ground in a pond of blood, his throat slit. Callum stood next to the body, a menacing look in his eyes.

The next rebel ran toward him with speed. He faked a right punch, only to swing with a roundhouse kick. Callum blocked the attack and delivered a fist with the force of his enhanced strength as well as his body weight behind it. It landed straight to the man's face. The rebel staggered under the impact of the blow but regained his balance. He rushed toward Callum again. In a quick action, Callum pulled out his blade and thrust it into his heart. Blood spilled out as the rebel collapsed on the floor.

Fearful and not wanting to throw the first punch, the third man stood rooted, looking at Callum. "You have two choices. You either tell me where Luke is hiding, or you will be the third body to drop on this floor."

"I don't know where he is, I swear."

"Then you're no use at all."

"No, wait . . . I know where the lieutenant is. If you find him, you will find Zachariah, and you will find Luke."

"Keep talking."

"There is a gentlemen's club eleven blocks away from here. He usually goes there because he likes watching the girls dancing. He usually goes on Thursdays. He is a close friend with the governor, so humans and Arcadien alike are protecting him."

"His name?"

"Bartel, his name is Bartel."

"Bartel Peril, the council member who died in the war?" Callum asked, confused.

"He didn't die. It was part of the plan. Luke didn't kill him. He wanted our people to believe that he did."

Callum felt a sinister gloominess taking control over him as he saw red. He trusted the man, Bartel was their mentor. The man had taken them under his wing after their father died, teaching them the way of their people, teaching them how to be men and how to stay grounded, not lose their way. Enraged, a hunger for killing took center stage in his mind, lost in his head, lost in his obscurity. Callum walked toward the man and slit his throat. A pleasurable consciousness and thrill came over him.

"Give me one good reason not to slit your throat and finish what they started." He looked at the man on the floor.

⚏

The light clicked on; Davide entered the room, with no sign of Rielle. He called out to Raphael. "She's gone, she's not here."

"What do you mean she's gone?"

"She's not here."

"How is she gone when we have warriors standing outside of the house, I'm here, and you're here?" Raphael tried to hold the anger in his voice. Not liking one bit that she left, knowing that she was in danger. "She's probably long gone by now." *"Callum, wherever you are you need to come home now, Rielle is gone."*

In what seemed like zero seconds and a flash, Callum teleported in the room. His face hardened, his eyes bright with golden fire. He was watching Raphael with intense eyes. He was angry, and Raphael could smell sweat and blood on him.

"You idiot." Raphael swung his fist at Callum, a hard jab to the face. Callum barely slipped it and slammed both hands into his brother's chest. The blow rocked Raphael, but he stepped closer, not away, staring straight in Callum's eyes. "I swear to the gods I will kill you first before I let you give in to darkness." He felt the darkness in Callum for the first time. It was wicked and aggressive.

"Guys, can we maybe do this later, we need to find Rielle," Davide shouted.

Both glared at each other. Callum countered, "She shields me out."

"She's mad at you, make her come to you. It's not always a good idea to use mind control on your life mate, but in this case, you have no choice." Raphael said, still riled up, shocked, and afraid that Callum was closer to turning than he thought.

"She's just going to hate me more if I use mind control on her."

"Do you want her safe? I understand you don't want to use your gift on her, but you have no choice. You need to make her come to you, or I would have no choice but to do what is essential to keep our people safe."

"She's my life mate, so would you be willing to kill her." Callum snapped.

"She's also a pure, noble enchantress, which means there is a reason why Luke or anyone else wants to harm her. She could be a liability to all of us if we're not careful."

"She's my life mate, doesn't that count for something?"

"She's not like our woman, Callum. She will never understand our ways."

"What are you trying to say, Raphael?" Callum asked, wanting to hear out loud what his brother was thinking.

"You know what I'm trying to say—she's a danger to us all and especially to you."

"Are you asking me to give up my life mate? Is that what you're asking me?"

"I'm asking you to be realistic. I can smell their blood off you. I'm in your head; you felt nothing when you killed those rebels. You went out to look for trouble. And this is just after a disagreement between the two of you. I'm not going to stand and watch you destroy yourself; I'm not going to stand by and let our people die at the hands of Luke because your woman didn't listen to you."

Raphael meant every word. Callum was aware of it. If his brother was willing to harm Rielle to keep their people and their home safe, it was best to deal with everything on his own. He didn't want to fight Raphael, and he didn't want to put his people at risk, but he also knew that if anything were to happen to Rielle, no one was safe, and this was a fact.

Chapter 14

Rielle couldn't stop the tears rolling down her face. Her life had gone from being ordinary to have people wanting to kill her; being the life mate to a guy she desired but barely knew; having her restaurant burnt down, her house compromised, and creatures attacking her. She had no business and no home. She wanted to escape everything, to escape him. It was clear that this town was cursed, and she needed to get away from everything that was going on, start somewhere else.

She'd never felt like this before. Sorrow took over, and for the first time in her life, she felt alone. The further away she was from Callum's house, the more isolated she felt. At the thought of being away from him and never seeing him again, her heart shattered into a million pieces. Tears fell down her face, and she was gasping all of a sudden, trying to breathe. She couldn't breathe.

Fury swept through Callum. She shielded her mind from him. *"Now you've angered me."* He was afraid. Luke and his men could get hold of her. Another shadow walker could attack her. Even if she's able to kill or weaken the creature, she could be unconscious right now, making it easier for whoever was after her to abduct her.

"Mierdei! Answer me, Rielle." For the first time, Callum felt a near fright creeping over him. He was always cool under any circumstances. Nothing scared him. That's how he was able to do his job. But this was different. When he couldn't reach her, and she didn't answer him, he felt different. He panicked, and fear blossomed through him. He was terrified for her safety. On the side of the road if her car broke down, she couldn't get that far on foot, he thought.

The ground shifted slightly beneath his feet; the trees were shuddering in a warning trying to convince him to turn away, protecting her. Callum knew she wasn't far from here. *"Rielle, I need to know that you're okay."* He was shocked at the pleading pitch in his voice.

She ignored him still,

"You're ignoring me, and I have no choice but to do what I'm about to do, mie cehia." Using their summoning gift was one of the worst things a life mate could do to his partner.

Callum wandered into the wooded area. Standing next to an oak tree, he closed his eyes, letting his mind expand to take in the world around him. As an enchantress, this was her world, and she was a part of it. Freeing his mind, Callum became more powerful using his enhanced commanding nature. *"Rielle, come to me, you can feel me, I'm inside of you, come to me. You need me, so come to me,"* he conjured her; it became a tune, sending to her the command over and over.

The picture of her in his mind, Callum felt her soft skin, her body, and her hair. He knew every detail of her body, the small cut on her left thigh, her full lips, and his mark on her neck. *"We're one now. You're mine as I am yours, you need me. You urge to be with me, and you need to see me, hurry up, mie cehia."* Finally, Callum was in her mind, her defensive shield knocked down. She couldn't ignore him anymore.

He imagined kissing her, lying down on the grass with her under this moonlight, where he would have his way with her. Punishing her senseless and pleasurably until she begged him for mercy. Moments later, it became quiet. The trees were now calm and the wind silent.

Callum opened his eyes. Rielle was making her way to him. Her wild tumbled hair—he loved those curls that defied gravity and rules with uniform indifference. Her head held, she swanned with a graceful saunter. She took his breath away. All he wanted to do was make love to her right here. Rielle stood in front of him and lifted her face. He could see the tears streaming down on her face. She'd been crying, and she looked tired.

"This is what you want? Why did you mark me? Who do you want me to be? A mindless woman to obey you and be at your beck and call?" The spot where he marked her was burning. Rielle felt her skin flaming as if she was on fire.

Callum identified the ache in his heart. Nothing else mattered at this point. Seeing her crying like this was ripping his heart apart and turning him into an emotional man himself. He pulled her toward his chest, never once looking away. He held her gaze captive. Charmed by him, the pain in Rielle's heart had gone away. Her heart thudding, she was quivering. Too hard to hide it.

"I'm sorry." Callum bent his head and brushed her upturned lips. Once, twice. He wanted her to come to him but not due to his mind control. "I'm so sorry." Wiping her tears away with his finger, he kissed her face. His fingers tunneled in her hair as he pressed her closer to his hard chest.

"Callum!" Raphael burst through the forest, standing in front of them. Davide was next to him. It was a sharp command. Something he rarely did with his brothers, but Callum had him worried. With Rielle now being involved, things would be worse when it came to their curse and his brother turning.

"Tui Komeidente," Callum growled in their native language.

"Did you kill those two mortals down east of the forest?" Raphael uttered, his tone imposing and stately.

Callum tapped into Raphael's mind, appalled. "Why ask when you've already convinced yourself that I did it?"

"I can kill her right now and be done with it," Raphael threatened. "Quite frankly, the way you're going, there's no escaping the darkness inside of you, is there?"

"Don't tempt me, Raphael," Callum snapped.

In a blur, Raphael was behind Rielle, his blade on her neck. "You want to give in to it. You want to become the very thing that we're hunting. You want to let it control you; go ahead. But it's up to you if she lives or not."

"Take your hands off of her," Callum roared.

"Know that if anything happens to you, if you give in to the darkness inside of you, I will kill her myself. Do you hear me?" Raphael challenged.

His face darkening, Callum moved fast fluidly, a controlling fighting machine, his face dark with anger. He shoved Raphael aside, pushing Rielle out of the way. Rielle had enough of their testosterones power matched. To her horror, the men came together, faces hard, jaws set, gray-blue eyes as turbulent as a lightning storm. At that moment, both looked precisely alike, raw power, warriors of old, equally matched.

"Enough, you two!" she screamed. Both Raphael and Callum used their speed to move away as a tree broke in half and fell where they stood. All three of them turned to her, stunned. Her gaze went to both. "I'm tired of this power struggle between the two of you. And Raphael, this is the last time you will threaten me with your knife." She was frustrated. "Look, I get it. You don't know me, and you don't trust me, and I'm sorry for what I did to your mind. But honestly, I don't know what I did or how I did it. And you two fighting is not helping either one of us. I know you're worried about me being a threat to your people, and I don't understand your ways, but I'm willing to compromise because I want to know why people are after me, too, and I don't want to hurt anyone. So, stop using me as leverage to control and to tame your brother. Whatever it is that I must do, I will do. Are we clear?"

All three men were puzzled.

"I meant what I said, so control yourself, brother." Raphael's tone warned that he wasn't joking.

"And I meant what I said—if anything happens to her, no one is safe. Especially you." Both men measured each other up.

"Let's get out of here. The human police are close by." Raphael stared at Callum, knowing that it wasn't over between the two of them.

"Take Rielle with you. I'll be right behind you. Her car is not too far from here. I don't want to leave any trace of her."

❈

Zachariah awoke, ice water tossed over his head. His arms were hung high above his head. He was fighting against the darkness of the room to get his demeanors back. Thick metal bands locked him in place; a chain hooked to his feet kept him from doing more than just standing upright. Whatever spell the witch had used on him left him feeling weak and drained this time. The door popped open, and Luke strolled in. Zachariah had a feeling that his older brother enjoyed his little power pep talk more than he should. "Ready to talk, brother?"

Zachariah laughed coldly.

"Something amusing?" Luke inquired, moving closer to him.

"You. You amused me. You always have, you know."

"You were always a petulant little boy."

"And your sense of humor was always nonexistent. But tell me, brother, how does a witch end up doing your dirty work? I can't fathom in this life or the next how a witch is working with an Arcadien," he continued. A wicked smile spread on his face, his eyes sharp on Luke's face.

"You always thought you were so clever—so smart, little brother," Luke spoke calmly. The undertone of his voice said otherwise.

"Well, there must be a reason why you chain me in this godforsaken chamber and let your witch toy with me. I must tell you she is starting to grow on me," Zachariah sarcastically said.

Luke growled ferociously and grabbed Zachariah's neck, his nails digging roughly into his flesh, lifting him off the ground while tightening his grip around his throat, his brows furrowed. Zachariah read fury in them.

Zachariah tried to fight back. His hands restrained, the enchanted chamber confined his powers; there wasn't much he could do. Frantically he began to fight for oxygen. A smirk crossed on Luke's lips.

"See freio, your wits and touches of sarcasm are doing you more wrong than good. Because, as always, you irritate the hell out of me and murdering you is never far off my mind," Luke bitterly whispered and forcefully tossed him against the wall.

Zachariah felt his back crushed on the wall then landed on his side. The pain shot through him like a hurricane. Luke was always stronger than him, reminding him of the fact once again. "You're . . . not fighting fair, brother," he coughed, mending his lungs.

"Have you learned nothing from me? Fighting fair never wins battles," Luke snapped harshly.

"What . . . you're afraid of a little competition?" Zachariah grinned, knowing he was getting to him.

"That's the problem. This world and the otherworld are ours for the taking. We are powerful magical beings. We shouldn't have to compete with anyone or hide from others. And until you open your eyes and follow me to the light, you will always enslave yourself. Now enough of your game. Tell me what I want to know, or my blade goes straight to that soft heart of yours." Luke approached him.

"Go ahead, do it." Zachariah threatened, his voice cold.

"We both know what she is, but there is more."

"You should ask your witch as she's the one that's feeding you facts."

"Our father must be very displeased at how his sons came out. Parasites who aren't embracing their true selves and the gifts he bestowed on us."

"No, our mother must be rolling in her grave how her second son has turned into dishonor and a murderer." Rage fueled over Zachariah. "Kiss my ass as the mortal says. So, go ahead, kill me."

"You're pathetic!"

"It's just a matter of time."

Luke watched with mock amusement on his face. "You think Callum or Raphael are going to find you here?" Luke's laugh echoed maniacally through the room. "You are more pathetic than I thought. My witch is not just a witch. She has blood mage running through her veins. Why do you think your telepathy connection is severed here, and neither Callum nor Raphael can get in touch with you?"

"Maybe you give your witch too much credit," Zachariah said dubiously.

Luke moved closer, his eyes hard on him, then maniacally laughed. "You had me there for a minute, kid. Don't worry, even if they do find you, I guarantee you'll be dead by then because your time is limited. I'll make sure the witch pays you a visit. You need some motivation." He walked out of the room.

Zachariah knew that it was a matter before Luke figured it out. Although he couldn't speak to Callum or Raphael, he could feel their presence, as their bond was that strong. He was hopeful that his brothers would find Rielle before Luke did.

Chapter 15

*C*allum sat on the edge of the veranda, unsure if he should go in her room or not. Rielle was still upset with him, that much he knew as her emotions were palpitating all over his brain. "If you don't go in, the angrier she'll be with you," Raphael said behind him.

"Why do you care?" Callum snapped at his brother.

"First, your shield isn't up, so your worries are quite annoying. Second, it's amusing to see you sulking, mostly pathetic."

Raphael, what if I can't control myself, like father?"

"You're in charge, so of course, you can control yourself." Raphael paused. "Why didn't you tell me?"

"I didn't want you to worry."

"You're my little brother. Of course, I worry. I worry about you and Zachariah all the time." Raphael stayed quiet for a moment then asked, "How long?"

"Two full moons, since after Luke it's getting harder for me to control it . . . I struggle, so I find it easier just to let it win," Callum said, remorsefully. "I'm going to need your help. If, after all of this, she wants nothing to do with me, you're going to have to stop me from hurting her."

"She is your partner, your equal, and she is part of you. She won't survive without you as you can't survive without her. So she will follow you wherever you go."

"You have to promise me," Callum begged.

"You won't hurt her Freio," Raphael rejoined though Callum believed himself to be a monster; he always protected those he cared about.

"The killer inside of me won't let her go. I felt the rage inside of me brewing when the officer hugged her . . . just like him. Raphael, you have to promise me."

"You can control it; it doesn't control you," Raphael firmly said.

"Promise me, brother," Callum opened his mind to Raphael, so he had a peak of the darkness he hid so well inside of him. There was sincerity and a plea in his voice.

"Just go, apologize to her. It makes a lot of difference, trust me," Raphael said in disbelief. What he'd just felt inside of Callum alarmed him.

"Any particular words I should use?"

"Sorry is the first word." Raphael patted his back, then walked away.

Callum's mind could hardly function through the waves of pain, confusion, and fear that Rielle was feeling. Bound to one another, her anger and emotions were consuming him, making it almost impossible for him to think. He walked into the room. On the bed, she tensed up once she sensed him in the room. Callum couldn't help but think that this wasn't going to be easy. He walked to her and sat down, wondering how long she was going to ignore him. *"Just apologize."*

"Stay out of my head."

"I would if you kept your shield on and stopped sending me those blue waves. Wait till I tell Zachariah how the bad wolf is a puppy." Irritated, Callum shut Raphael off, putting his shield back on.

"I can't be your life mate, Callum, I know you believe me to be, but I can't be." Rielle faintly said, not looking at him. "I'm not the woman for you, Callum. I'm not what you're looking for."

"Yes, you are."

"Why are you trying to change me then? You keep taking away my free will. How am I supposed to be with you when you want to treat me like your property?" A soft sob came out of her mouth.

"Amorei mio, you're the most important person in my life. I'm sorry if I make you feel like that. I want to keep you safe. Although you'll probably resent me for the rest of your life for what I did, for binding us without your consent, I don't regret doing it because we belong together, and I won't survive without you."

"I was angry; when people are angry, they say things."

"I'm just figuring this out now." He wiped her tears away with his finger. "I'm sorry I frightened you." He kissed her face. "I'm sorry." His hands stroked caresses in her hair as he continued raining kisses over her face and licked at the tears in the corner of her eyes to stop them.

"I'm scared."

"Of me?" Callum brushed more kisses down her face.

"I can't cope with these extreme emotions of not being able to function without you. I don't know how to be in something so intense, so fast." He kissed the corners of her mouth. "I don't know why I'm still crying," she confessed.

"It's my fault." Callum pushed the hem of her shirt as he bent his head and kissed her. His hands went to her stomach, he unbuttoned the shirt, letting his hand roam around her breast. In a matter of seconds, he was towering over her. Callum looked at her, her eyes so dark with anger, her expression eager and hungry. Kissing her neck, he made his way to her breast, teasing along her skin, caressing her as he moved over her. He noticed his mark on her skin still, and it sent a rush of heat surging through his veins.

"Forgive me," he whispered as he wished for his clothes off. Magically, they did. Bending down, he took a hardened bud in his mouth.

Rielle closed her eyes. A soft moan came out of her mouth.

Holding his head, she ran her fingers through his beautiful hair. He owned her, body and soul. She couldn't deny it whether she wanted to or not. She might think that she didn't need him, but she did. She needed him just like he needed her. They were now attached. That was true. She felt it in her core, and it terrified her to death.

His thighs pushed hers apart hard, He thrust into her, aggressively with vibrating need driving through tight velvet folds, feeding his manhood into her, forcing his entrance as deep as possible, needing her to take every inch of him. Her taut body slick and welcoming, Rielle moaned, her muscles clenched around him. Callum needed to possess her.

Her eyes glazed with fire, her curly hair wild on the pillow added to his excitement. She was a sight to behold. "Wrap your legs around my waist." Callum loved her body, and he loved her perky breast, not too big but not too small, just the right size in his mouth. He loved her flat and long torso, and her tiny waist fit utterly in his big hands, but mostly he loved the little soft sounds she made as her body became his.

Bending forward, he kissed his mark on her neck, the action deliberately producing electrifying friction over her core. Callum sucked on the little pulse beating in her throat, dipped lower to find her breast again, and did the same thing. Rielle relaxed, her body welcoming all his manhood, and she took all of him. Callum moved slowly, testing her response.

Rielle wrapped her legs around his waist tighter. She was impatient, pushing against him with eagerness. He continued his stroke as slowly as possible. She needed to learn to be patient.

"Callum," she pleaded

That ragged little plea was all it took to shatter his control and to steal his heart. "Do you deny the attraction between us?" He wasn't sure that he could slow another stroke, teasing her into compliance. To show her that things would be done his way, at least in their bedroom. He managed one more. "Answer me," he growled.

"No . . . no," Rielle groaned out beneath him, locking her fingers on his shoulders. He caught her hips and jerked her forward and up into him, angling her body to take more, take him fully. He wanted to bury himself into her, merge them so close that no one and nothing would ever be able to untangle them. He slammed into her, driving home. He was pushing her beyond every sexual limit she had even conceived of, bringing her again and again to the peak of release. "You are mine, Rielle, fate never gets it wrong."

Rielle moaned out his name and yanked at his hair. She quivered under him, her legs locked in a tight grip. She met each stroke, crying out, driving him crazy. She had invaded every cell of his body, every organ, and every bone. No matter how long he lived, she would be the only woman he would ever crave.

One last thrust, a current of pleasure swamped his nerve ending and ripped through his body. Rielle screamed and buried her face in his chest to muffle the cries as her body rippled and pulsed, shuddering with a feeling so cosmic it sent waves through her body.

They lay together. Rielle kept quiet as a million questions were going through her mind, but she didn't have the courage or the strength to ask. Rielle kept her eyes closed; she needed some barriers, and keeping her eyes closed was the best she could manage.

There is no space or wall between life mates. The words resounded in her mind, and a shiver ran down her spine. She was his life mate. What was she going to do? What would happen to her now? She could never be what he expected her to be. What if this was a mistake?

"You have to talk to me instead of making your mind go crazy."

She ignored him; her eyes still closed.

"You can pretend I'm not here if you think it will help," Callum spoke so softly she thought she was deaf. Rielle turned her head away, and her eyes squeezed shut. "But I'm not going away, and you are everything I want and more. You are my life mate, and I'm not going to apologize for marking you." Callum traced a fingertip over the mark at the side of her neck, playing with her skin. "First, there is no point because I can't undo it, second because I don't want it undone, and third because it wasn't my doing. But I will apologize for not telling you about it."

It didn't matter that she couldn't see him; she could hear the superiority in his voice. "It seems to me you knew a hell of a lot what you were doing. You didn't even ask me or tell me," she said curtly.

At least she was speaking to him now even if it was to blame him. "The mark, yes, is my doing, but the reason I did it without asking your permission isn't so much of my doing." She kept silent. Callum heaved a sigh and continued, "It's just instinct when two Arcadien find out they are each other's life mates. The need and the urge to be together is unfathomable, instinct kicks in, and you never want to be apart from that person. Everything changes, you know you just fit with the other person, you see what you crave and have been missing, and you seize it so you don't lose it. I wouldn't be able to stop myself even I wanted to, Rielle, and I didn't want to."

"What if I wanted to?"

"It might have been fun to watch you try, but it wouldn't have worked even if I didn't do it then. Eventually, I would have done it because neither of us has a choice."

"That's ridiculous. What about free will and consent?" Rielle frowned.

"It's always been like that. That's the way things are."

"But I'm not Arcadien, and I didn't decide on anything," Rielle persisted.

"I know that you didn't decide—that's where this came in." His hand stroked over her bare skin as he pressed a kiss to the mark on her neck.

Her eyes opened enough to scowl at him. "What does it mean?"

"The mark?"

"Yes."

"It's there to prove that you belong to me."

"How dogmatic and cavemen." She rolled her eyes. "Does every woman have one when you men claim them?"

"No, some mates never get them."

"How come I got it?"

"The ones who need proof get marked." He was drawing little patterns on her belly until his hands reach between her legs. "When two Arcadien mate, no one gets marked. There's no need. We all are aware of what's happening. But if one mate is reluctant or unwilling, the other marks her or him."

"What if the mate has good reason to be reluctant? What if she doesn't like the jerk that marked her? Is she forced to stay with him?"

"No need to force her, even if she is reluctant. They are fated to be together. The two of them belong together and will never be happy with anyone else."

"No one ever leaves?"

"No, because one can't live without the other—see how you felt empty and miserable and sad when you shut your mind to me and tried to run away from me? It's much worse. Some mates fall to madness because the pain is too much to bear." He moved up his hand little by little until he reached the most sensitive part between her legs. He gently touched her there. She tensed in his hand as the tight outgrowth clenched.

Rielle took a deep breath, trying to overcome the heat between her legs. "Well, that's not normal . . ." he began circling the tight bud with his thumb. She let out a little gasp. "No . . . no one should depend . . ." He continued his little action, enjoying how confounded she was. Maybe this should be how he shuts her off from now on, Callum thought. "Depend emotionally on someone else like that." She moaned out the last word and turned her face to him.

"Hi," Callum smiled at her charmingly.

"I can't talk to you if you're making my body feel like this." She tried to scowl him, but with no success as her voice was soft and stimulated. "According to you we are married, yet we've never been on a date."

"Like the human does? It's pathetic how humans waste their time trying to impress each other on dates." He pressed hard on the pulsating part.

She bit her bottom lip and whimpered. God damn it, this felt too good. "That's not the point," she panted out.

"Then what is the point?" Callum was amused. And it was such a turn on watching her face and her expression. Though overly enthused, she kept berating him. Maybe this wasn't enough, he thought.

"The point is, this is too soon and too fast. I get it that you did what you did, and we can't undo it. But we have to get to know each other bet . . . better." He flicked the spot that was so intense. Rielle closed her eyes and rolled her head back.

"You do know me."

Rielle sighed in frustration. She tried to sit up. Callum draped a heavy arm across her waist, pinning her in place. "We can't talk like this; I can't talk to you when you are doing things to my body."

He moved over her, looking down at her face. "You belong to me as I belong to you. End of the story," he said, matter-of-factly.

She stared up at him, feeling her heart clench inside her chest and remembering what it felt like when he buried himself inside of her, how everything seems okay when he's around. Her entire world had changed, and no matter how desperately she wanted to deny the truth, she knew she couldn't go back to how things were before him. They would never be the same.

She would never be the same. But that didn't mean for him to get away with acting like a controlling freak and a barbarian. Rielle breathed out loud. She told herself to be firm. Then when she spoke, she could hear in her voice the echoes of soft unfamiliar emotion she had been feeling and that was currently stirring in her chest.

"I'm not certain I understand all of this, and I need time to process all of it. We need to make some changes on both our parts for this to work. I get it; it's your instinct to keep me safe and protect me, but you must understand, you cannot dictate to me. Tell me when you're concerned about my safety. Don't just order me around and make decisions without telling me. I'm not your child, so don't boss me around."

Callum met her gaze for a long moment before he gave a brief nod. "I'll try mie cehia, but I can't promise anything. I can't make my instincts go away."

She looked up into those warm eyes. "I mean it. The moment you start taking over my life, making decisions without my input, I will walk away. No matter how hard and painful or miserable it might be."

"I'll do my best." He brushed a soft, lingering kiss against her lips. His hands gripped the curve of her bottom. He turned to his back. Shifting position, now she was on top of him, straddling him. He clasped her hip to guide her, easing her body forward until her breast was just over his hungry mouth. Then he worked her back down. Forward and back. Rielle didn't take long to take over. Rocking him for her pleasure, Rielle arched backward. Her hands were behind her on his thighs, her hair was sweeping over his legs. Callum growled. Seizing her rounded rear, he lifted her and pulled her down back on his shaft just as he bucked upward and thrust up again. Rielle closed her eyes, groaning with pleasure.

Locked in each other's arms, Callum woke up in the middle of the night, his body covered with sweat. He kept his hand in her hair, his fingers lazily massaging her scalp while his heart quietened and felt strangely at peace for the first time in a long time. She was asleep. He shifted his body to take his weight from her reluctantly, leaving the warmth of her body. He draped an arm around her, bringing her onto her side, facing him. He loved the way her nipples erected and were so hard just by touching her, and he wanted her again all of a sudden. Softly he brushed a kiss to her lips as he watched her sleep. Until his dying breath, he would do everything to keep her safe.

Chapter 16

"I'll say the apologies went well because your pathetic rants stopped buzzing in my head after a while," Raphael said, keeping a straight face, but Callum was no fool, familiar with his brother's mocking tone. Davide grinned suspiciously.

"In case both of you forget I'm still a cold bastard without a heart, don't tempt me."

"Yeah, that was then, brother," Raphael chuckled. "How's she doing?"

"I think she's trying to come to terms with the recent happenings."

"You told her?" he asked.

"No . . . I haven't. We didn't have time to ponder—I mean talk about it." Callum avoided looking at their eyes, aware of how he sounded.

Davide snorted while Raphael held in his laughter. In all their life he'd never seen his younger brother turning red. From time to time, he'd felt Callum's despair and loneliness and was sure it was why his brother camped in the deep end of the mountain. Although Rielle was probably a significant threat to them, Raphael was grateful he had found his mate even though she was mortal and was as stubborn as him.

"What?" Callum laughed.

"Nothing. You have to tell her; she deserves to know where her abilities come from."

"I will," he agreed. "Now, on a more serious note, Bartel is alive."

"What?" Raphael asked, all trace of amusement gone from his face. "How do you know?"

"The rebels I encountered before I went looking for Rielle— one of them confessed. He didn't know where Luke was, but implied that if we find Bartel, we find Luke and Zachariah."

"I saw him dead . . . How?"

"He planned it with Luke."

"I trusted the man," Raphael said, disconcerted. "He was like a father to me, to us. I buried the man," he continued, feeling the anger coming over him.

"Father always said when it comes to power, trust is a mere sign of faith."

"If it weren't for me, he wouldn't have been in our lives."

Callum saw the guilt in Raphael's eyes. "Don't you dare feel guilty. I say, let's visit him and get our brother back," Callum coldly said.

"Yeah, but leave Bartel to me," Raphael said, equally deadly.

⊰⊱

Rielle quickly packed a bag of clothes and her aunt's diaries with the pic of the two of them together. Earlier she had to put down her foot and threaten Callum to let her come pick out a few things. Yeah, Arcadien people were trying to kill her, though she was grateful for him trying to keep her safe. That overbearing macho attitude he had going on was enough to drive any sane woman crazy. The front door knocked. She became still, apprehension hit at her. "Who is it?" she screamed.

"Rie! It's me. Open the door."

Relief swept over her, Rielle opened the door. "Where the hell have you been? I've been calling you and Jao too. I swear we were about to put out a missing person file if you didn't open this door." Syrah reprimanded, making her way in. "You just disappeared. I know you wanted some time after what happened to the café, but you got me worried. You could have let me know you were ok."

"Sy! Breathe!" Rielle smiled. "I'm ok. I promise. It's just a lot has been happening lately. I'm sorry if I worried you."

"You should be sorry. I thought something had happened to you, or worse."

Rielle was remorseful. "No, nothing happened . . . well, something did happen, or things have been happening, but I'm ok."

"Of course something happened—your restaurant got burned down. Jao is still looking into it, but he told me they don't have any leads yet. That we probably left something on, or a gas leak—"

"I'm seeing someone, Sy!" Rielle blurted out to her friend.

"Wait—what did you just say?" Syrah's eyebrows furrowed, a perplexed look came on her face.

"I'm seeing someone, and I've been staying at his place the past couple of days."

"Ok, who are you? And what the hell did you do to my friend?"

"I didn't want to say anything because well, you know me, and it's new," Rielle admitted, feeling bad and not wanting to scare her friend or tell her what's been happening.

Syrah mischievously smirked. "You slept with him, didn't you?" Rielle nodded, feeling flustered. "Oh. My. God! No freaking way," Syrah teased, laughing. Rielle joined her in laughter. "I have got to meet him! He must be some man. Oh man, Jao is going to be devastated." She continued to laugh. "So, tell me about him, what's he like? Where did you meet him? How was the sex? Leave out no details!"

The front door burst open. Three men barged inside the living room where they were sitting. "What in hell? Who the hell are you guys barging in like that?" Syrah uttered.

Their eyes fixed on Rielle. They had that same confident and deadly quality as Callum and Raphael. "Sy, we got to go!" Rielle quickly grabbed her friend's hand and the bag on the floor, dragging her running to the back of the house.

"What the hell is going on? Who are these men? Why are they after you?" Syrah asked frantically.

"Syrah! Not now," Rielle snapped at her friend. Seeing the fearful look on her face, Rielle retracted. "I promise I'll explain everything to you later, but right now, we have to get out of here." Syrah nodded.

Rielle locked the door behind them, knowing that was not going to stop these superhuman men. She had to get her friend out of here. She didn't need to be involved. "Sy, can you jump over the fence? I'll give you a hand."

"What about you? We should call the police. What have you got yourself involved with, Rie?"

"Trust me. The police are no match for these guys. Here, come on." Rielle pulled out her hands so Syrah could get over the fence. Rough hands grabbed her, throwing her on the wall. Syrah fell on her face. The same man walked toward her quickly. Rielle crawled in opposite of him, her back facing the wall. "Who sent you? And why are you after me?" she asked.

"The commandant, and you know why we're after you, don't you?"

"What do we do with the simple mortal woman?" the one holding Syrah yelled.

"I don't care! Compel her to do whatever you want. We have who we came for," the bigger man standing in front of her said.

"I have an idea," the other one said. "Let's just make her our flavor for the day." He tried to kiss Syrah, but Syrah slapped him.

Rielle felt the aggravation coming from the man; it was different. These men were different. They didn't have the warmth that Raphael or Davide had. She felt the same darkness in them as Callum, but there was something else uncouth about them. She had to do something. "Let her go!" Rielle yelled,

"Or what? You're going to chant a spell turning us into toads?" the man sarcastically said. "Well, sorry, sweetheart, the witch already took care of that. Now get up!" he grabbed her by her hair, pulling her up. Rielle screamed in pain. "I'm ready for a show. Are you ready for a show?" he asked proudly. "Guys, give us a show of the mortal."

All of them roared with laughter as the one who tried to kiss Syrah pulled her hair out of her bun and ripped her shirt off. Something akin to fire burned inside of Rielle's heart. Her face contorted in a fit of all-consuming anger—her nostrils flared, her eyes flashed and closed into slits. "I said, let her go," she repeated, feeling like a volcano ready to release its pent-up emotions into the world. Suddenly something unleashed within her. A blowing wind whipped toward them, howling all around them. Dark thunder clouds all of a sudden formed over their heads. Rielle stared at them defiantly, challenging.

Thunder roared in the distance. Soon after, lightning flashed. She whispered to herself. The storm clouds shifted uneasily, letting out another violent torrent.

Shortly a lightning bolt struck the rebel in front of Syrah. His clothes started to burn, and he caught fire. In a jiffy, a rebel was onto her. He grabbed her neck, lifted her, throwing her against the wall. Rielle yelped in pain, incensed.

She felt an overwhelming urge to make him suffer. With one hand, Rielle pointed at the rebel—"mouri a mort nouvo." She repeated, unable to stop the words coming out of her mouth. The rebel crouched down holding his chest, pain consuming him. He yelped.

Syrah watched on the side, dumbfounded and scared. Choking, blood was coming out of the rebel's nose and mouth, and Rielle was the cause of that. Three other men out of nowhere surrounded them. Where in the hell did they come from? Did they fly here? No, humans can't fly. Syrah tried to make sense of it. They were calm except for the one with the shoulder-length hair approaching Rielle. "Hey, get the fuck away from her!" Something was wrong with Rielle, but no way she was going to let these men hurt her friend. "Now!" Syrah screamed, threatening, and grabbed the stick in front of her. The shorter man smiled warmly at her.

"We mean her no harm, little one; we're here to help her."

Syrah didn't know why, but his voice was so clear and resonant that she found herself smiling at him too. She snapped out of it immediately. Who the hell was he calling little? And why the hell did all three of them look as if they just stepped out of a fashion runway? More significantly, what in the hell was going on?

Callum was in the small library dent with Raphael, searching for the research the professor confessed that Zachariah was working on, when he brushed her mind but couldn't sense her. Wanting to compromise like they had agreed and boundaries as she had asked, he wanted to prove to her that he wasn't mainly a caveman as she called him many times. But hours later he tried again, vowing to have a lengthy conversation with her about shutting him out completely; that's when he sensed her panic, her fury manifesting over him. Immediately he knew something was wrong.

The storms happening on this side of the town, Callum realized, had to do with her waves of anger—overpowered with it, the angrier she was, the more the weather was gloomy as if nature was following her lead. But what stunned him was the rebel agonizingly suffocating on his blood, yet she wouldn't let him die. Callum stared at her, unsure. He was proud of her. At the same time, scared that her powers were coming to her too fast.

"Rielle," he softly whispered her name. She wasn't herself. Whatever she managed to unleash wasn't so pure. It was dark. Calmly, he advanced on her. "Let him go; you've protected your friend, she's safe." "*Let him go, mie cehia, you're scaring your friend.*" He slipped into her mind, the seduction in his tone for her to hear.

Her brows puckered.

Rielle glanced behind him. A frightened Syrah was watching her with concern. Raphael and Davide were also watching her, a stoic expression on their faces. "I can't help myself. I don't know how to stop it," she uttered, the need to harm the man kneeling in front of her compelling.

"Look at me, mie cehia."

She did. The warmth and adoration in Callum's eyes calmed her down. Rielle took a deep breath, letting her hands fell on her side. Fast, Raphael grabbed the man. The other rebel was being held captive in Davide's grip.

"Don't come any closer," she warned Callum stepping closer to her. "I don't want to hurt you."

Callum took her in his arms and held her tightly against his chest while whispering words of reassurance in her ears. Rielle wrapped her arms around his back, pressing herself more into him, grateful that he was here. "I don't know what came over me. Is he dead?"

Her body tensed. Callum kissed her hair. "No, he isn't. Arcadien only meets death by the blade, and now lightning bolt apparently." He raised an eyebrow.

"I'm sorry. They were going to hurt Syrah. They wanted to . . . to . . ." Rielle panicked.

"Shh . . . you did well. Your friend is safe because of you." He tipped up her chin to look at her eyes. "You did good, but do you think you can let go of your anger so the storm can weather a bit? We don't want the humans to start freaking out about the weather." She nodded. Callum smiled at her, a quick peck on her lips.

"You guys think you can stop with the public display of affection for a minute and check on her mortal friend? She's scared to death," Raphael reproached.

"Hold your horses," Callum responded to Raphael. "You should probably talk to your friend, or I can ease her mind of what happened today," Callum said to her.

"No, I'll talk to her." Rielle let go of his embrace and walked toward Syrah.

Callum joined Raphael and Davide, all three of them unsure of what to say. The rebel lay down on the ground, barely breathing. The other one looked at him, scared. "Where were you taking her?" Callum asked the man calmly but deadly.

"We were following orders," the man replied.

Davide gripped the man's shoulder harder, almost crushing his bones. He squealed in pain. "That's not what I asked you," Callum said.

"We were supposed to wait at a rendezvous point. A car is coming for us."

"Is Luke waiting for her at the rendezvous point?" Raphael questioned, his voice bold and commanding, reminding the rebel who he was.

"My liege! I don't think I've had the pleasure to meet you in person before," the rebel answered, bowing his head to Raphael.

Raphael raided his mind, even planted a false narrative in his brain. "The next twenty-four hours, I urge you to seek Luke out. And contact Zachariah. Do whatever it takes to make contact even if your life depends on it. Now go to your rendezvous point and tell them what happened. Tell them what she did. But you manage to escape." Raphael compelled him.

"Yes, my liege," the man answered and walked back inside the house.

Raphael looked at Callum, then asked, "What?"

"You can't do this to me. Right? Tell me you have never coerced my mind me like this. Because you know we're brothers, and that would be against everything we stand for."

Raphael smirked devilishly. "Why do you think you were at our last summit despite your convictions not to attend?"

"You're joking. Right?" Callum was dubious.

"What are we going to do with him?" Raphael changed the subject.

"Simply kill him, although death is too much of a good thing for him right now," Callum spat without hesitation and plunged his blade into the rebel's heart.

Chapter 17

"You're not mad at me?" Rielle asked, hoping that this wasn't the end of her friendship with Syrah. They grew up together, and she was the only person she had that was close to a family.

"I am mad at you for keeping it a secret from me. Why didn't you tell me? You're like a sister to me, don't you trust me always to have your back no matter what?" the disappointment in Syrah's voice was there for Rielle to hear.

"I didn't want you involved in all of this or get hurt because of me . . . or think that I was crazy."

"Crazy? For months things have been weird around here; those dead creatures were just the tipping point. We grew up together, Rie, we all know your aunt did things that were odd to most people around here. Healing Mrs. Juniper, finding

Rhiannon when he got attacked. I just never thought that you were. I just thought that it was herbs and luck."

"I'm sorry, Syrah. I should have told you about everything. I didn't know I could do any of these things until a couple of weeks ago. I don't know how I'm able to do these things. I hope you can forgive me."

"Forgive you! Rie, you're my family, and you saved my life. Nothing will change that," Syrah smiled. "But we'd be square if you hook me up with one of those gorgeous men. Jesus, what are they eating on that other side of the world. Even the thugs looked good."

Rielle laughed out loud. "You're impossible."

"Well, your man is yummy; a little scary but yummy. Are you sure you're safe with him and not under his penile influence? Because he looks like he's about ready to devour you every time he looks your way. Jesus Christ, he makes a girl want to do dirty things to him."

"Sy!" Rielle laughed out.

"We are feeling so out of our comfort with your friend objectifying us like that," Callum brushed her mind.

"Oh, really, you guys love it!" Rielle teased.

"Davide loves it indeed, as he can't stop grinning from mouth to ears." He heard her soft laughter in his mind. *"Is everything ok on your side?"*

"Yes, we're fine. But I need a favor from you."

"Anything, mie cehia."

"Can you compel her to take some time off from here for a little while? At least until we figure out everything, and she's not in danger because of me?"

"Are you sure?"

"Yes, I'm sure."

"Stay safe, ok!" Syrah uttered. "I think I need to clear my head of all these magical kinds of stuff happening, and I don't want to become a liability to you. So, I'm going to cayes town and stay with my aunt a bit."

"I understand, Sy. I'll see you when you get back." Rielle hugged her.

"Thank you." Rielle sent out to him. Callum smiled warmly. The prospect of him kissing her played in her mind.

Chapter 18

*C*allum woke up in the dark. Rielle's small frame pressed tightly against his chest. His fingers grazed across her lower back and up. Rielle's body shivered against him. Even in her sleep, she was responsive to his touch. *You are nothing but a killer; it's just a matter of time before she realizes what you are. You are your father's son. Sooner or later, she'll be miserable and leave too.*

The words echoed in his head; he buried his face deeper into her frizzy coiled hair, willing his thoughts aside as his hand carefully moved down the line on her back and slowly across her thighs. With all the care in the world, he glided his hand, slowly up and down her leg, going closer to her sex with every upstroke. Rielle was in a deep sleep still.

Without hesitation, Callum slid his hand further up, his palm resting on her pubic mound. He kept his hand there as he watched her chest rise and fall. With his fingertip, lightly Callum stroked her as he kissed her neck, deliberately licking and nibbling the spot he had marked her.

A soft moan escaped Rielle's mouth. Reluctantly, she opened her eyes. "I need to sleep," she said, half asleep as he turned her around to face him. His hands cupped the sweet curves of her buttocks, squeezing her firm flesh. Rielle ground her groin into his.

His dark possession awakened, Callum made a low throaty sound. Immediately his hungry mouth descended on hers. Rielle wrapped her arms tightly around his neck. Her small breasts pressed against his chest. Callum growled as he deepened their kiss and spun her on her back, his erection pressing against her.

"Hi," she smiled at him, drinking him in. His hair fell in deep waves to the line of his strong shoulders, his mouth and eyes were a sinner's sin. He was just too good looking. Without breaking eye contact with her, Callum slowly entered her, pushing himself deeper inside of her, stretching her around him.

"Tui aparatenie a mie." His lips raggedly took hers, and passion ignited inside of her. Her hands clutched at him. Rielle dug her nails into his skin as he began to move steadily, picking up the pace, fighting with himself to be gentle. But the sudden yearning and longing for her made it impossible to slow down. *You're your Father's son.* The words lingered in his mind.

Rielle whimpered. The soft sound echoed through his head, pushing his demons aside. He buried himself deep inside of her with ruggedness, feeling his heart bolstered of coldness, yearning, and longing for the fire inside of her. Callum began to pace faster and harder, moving in and out of her deeper and harder. He needed to be closer to her.

Rielle closed her eyes, quivering beneath him. Her muscles taut, her body surrendering gradually to him. Gone was the gentleness in his body. Now replaced by sharp and intense movements, her body tried to ease the discomfort, as his body rode hers with increasingly powerful thrusts that reverberated through her. But the pleasure was so great and so good. "Callum . . . ," she moaned and opened her eyes.

His eyes closed, his brow furrowed.

Callum quickened his pace, getting more excited. She consumed him, needing to move faster and harder, her small moans driving him insane. He growled, urging to move deeper, harder, and ruthlessly into her.

"Callum," Rielle moaned, feeling him growing bigger inside of her. Her body tightened, she screamed, struggling against the pain and pleasure of the fullness he created inside of her. She knew when he lost control of whatever he was fighting inside of him, as she felt a melancholy and multifaceted sensation reaching out to her heart, wanting to release it from itself. With each plunge, her heart intertwined with his. Their souls seemed to join. "Callum," she softly whispered. His eyes shut, he growled, still pounding inside of her, hard.

"You are mine," he groaned, pumping into her, the length and level of his arousal now brutal. "Mine," he growled, pushing harder into her. His movement hastened to give her full, hard, painful thrusts.

"Callum, please look at me," Rielle pleaded in his mind.

Unable to resist her drowsy voice like a caress on his brain, Callum reluctantly opened his eyes. The blue in them turned green and purple. Rielle had seen his eyes like this before. She slightly touched his face, running her fingers through his hair and gripped a significant amount, pulling his head down to her. She kissed him with everything that she was feeling. "Whatever is inside of you is a part of you, and I accept it because I accept who you are. I'm not afraid of it. I'm not afraid of who you are." Callum pumped into her harder, his grip on her hips strong, crushing her bones. The slight pain was beginning to be a little unbearable.

"Mine." He repeated, still pushing hard into her as if he couldn't stop.

Rielle put her left hand on his chest beneath her palm. His heart thumped, uncontrollably but constant. She removed a thread of hair out of his face, then gently touched his arms, reaching for his hands intertwining their fingers together. It seemed to work, as she didn't feel the coldness in him as much. She wrapped her legs tightly around his waist, and deepened his thrust inside of her. Clenching her muscle she held him there still, wrapped tightly against her fold.

Callum growled loudly. The sound was almost animalistic, and his breathing hardened. A sense of comfort swept over Rielle. The feelings were more of him than her. His strong arms circled her waist. He moved his hands under her backside as he pulled his body toward her head, his pelvis now slightly higher up her body grinding against her pelvis, rubbing against her.

"Lo aparatenie." He slid his hands beneath her rear, tilting her against him, changing the angle. His pelvis bumping her mound with every thrust, the intermittent pressure pushing her higher. Rielle screamed, crying for release. She wrapped both her legs around his back, pulling herself onto his lap. Callum thrust into her once, twice, three times his senses intensified. One final thrust deep inside of her, he filled her up, his naked body joined with hers.

Waves of pleasure consumed their bodies. A pulsating feel took over her. Her head was spinning. Her body was shaking uncontrollably as a volcanic sensation erupted inside of her. Callum groaned, and she moaned out loud. Holding onto him, she pushed herself more into him as she stretched around him.

Callum held her tight in that position for what seemed to be a long time.

Then, gently, he pulled out of her and rolled on his back next to her—neither of them spoke.

Quivering and shuddering, Rielle felt a pulsating pulse in her center still. Out of breath, it would be a while before she composed herself.

"I bruised you." He towered over her and examined her body. The marks on her thighs and around her hips—a solemn look fell on his face. He flipped her around. Small bruises were on her back. His handprints were on her buttocks, and a reddish mark was at each side of her waist. Callum tensed up. "I shouldn't have lost control with you. I just—," he whispered. Shame encompassed him, whirling her on her back again.

"Shh—," hearing the distress in his voice, Rielle pushed herself into him. Her breasts gently caressed his chest. "You're not a monster, Callum. Why do you keep making yourself believe you are one?"

"I don't believe, mie cehia, I know," he groaned. His voice was unfamiliar even to his ears.

"What does this tattoo mean?" Rielle touched his left arm.

"It's a mark. I got it when I was a decade and seven Foremoons. It means the guardian of the people. To protect and to guard."

"Does every Arcadien have one?" Rielle's fingers trailed his left arm and up to his chest.

"No, only the one fated to serve," Callum answered. Soft hands went up to his shoulders, and into his hair; it sent electricity to his body.

Despite his apprehension and worries, Callum's senses ignited, and he couldn't think straight. He leaned into her. Softly, he nibbled at the mark on her neck. Rielle let out little whimpers of anticipation. Callum worked his way back to her lips and rolled her on top of him, changing their position. She was now lying on top of his firm, muscular body. She ran her lips up to his neck, then she kissed his chest, sucking on his nipple. Callum groaned, his hands into her hair, and pulled her back to his lips. "I have to take care of your bruises."

"I'm fine," Rielle said against his lips. He hardened beneath her. "I'm not as fragile as you think I am, besides lots of people have rough sex," she teased.

"I'm not lots of people, mie cehia. I went too far with you," Callum muttered a throaty sound. He flipped her around so that he was now on top of her.

"But you didn't," she replied.

Callum observed her, wondering if he'd have the strength to let her go when she realized what he was and wanted nothing to do with him.

She can never; she belongs to me.

You're your father's son. The words echoed through his mind.

"What's on your mind?" Rielle asked, alert of the tension in his body.

"Nothing."

"You're worried about something. your pupils darken when you're angry, worried, and apparently when you're lying." Callum ignored her, kissing her passionately.

"Kissing me doesn't let you off the hook," Rielle scolded. "What is it?"

"Mortals burned down your restaurant, I'm not sure if they found about your abilities or if they were compelled or spelled, but your restaurant burning down wasn't an accident. Davide had found the word witch written on the wall," Callum said. It was better just to let her know what was going on instead of telling her that she was glued to him forever, whether she wanted it or not.

"What?" Rielle pushed him off her. She wrapped the sheet around her and jumped off the bed. "You've known it all this time. Why didn't you tell me?"

"I didn't want to scare you," Callum confessed.

"You can't keep things from me for the reason that you don't want to scare me. You have to tell me what's going on. That's why you didn't want me to go home, didn't you?"

"Yes, and I was trying to keep you safe."

"By hiding things from me," Rielle snapped.

"Yes, and when it comes to your safety, if I have to hide things from you, I will, always."

Rielle read his face. He was unapologetic. "This isn't a dictatorship, Callum." She was furious.

"But it is, baby, it is. Your safety before everything else. We can argue about this for the rest of our lives, but when it comes to the matter of keeping you safe, nothing will change. Especially when I have one brother who won't hesitate to kill you and another that's interested in you for God knows what," he roared at her.

"What?" she said, confused.

Callum ran a hand through his hair, taking a deep breath. "You have more powers than you can imagine, mie cehia, even for an enchantress."

"An enchantress? You mean like a sorcerer or a witch?"

"No, an enchantress is one who chants and speaks magic. They see the good in people, and they help out others. They practice magic, use the supernatural, but for the greater good. They're in touch with nature, like you are. The elements such as water, earth, air, and the wind and sometimes even fire are within them and obey them. An enchantress can manipulate a shadow walker into doing his or her dirty work, they can control the creature, but they can't kill it. Only a pureblood one could kill a shadow walker. We thought they all died centuries ago until you. You are the last pureblood enchantress alive."

Rielle stared at him, not wanting to believe a word he said. "This can't be, my mother died giving birth to me, my aunt was a hippie. Yes, she loved nature, but that didn't mean she was a witch or an enchantress." She remembered how her aunt would heal sick people among other little things she used to do. "This can't be," she said to herself more than to him, realization hitting at her when she remembered the journal. The blank journal her aunt had left her before she passed away.

"You have descended from a family of pureblood enchantresses; they were the first ever with the gifts. You are of pure blood, which is why you were able to kill the creatures or manipulate the weather as you did."

"The chant that came to my head . . ."

"It came naturally because that's who you are. But I'm guessing your aunt has taught you about your magic but just locked that part of your brain each time."

"How?"

"I don't know, but professor Rue is a custodian and was the one who confirmed my belief about what you are."

"Professor Rue?" Rielle asked, shocked. "My aunt's ex-lover? He knew about me? He knows about what's happening?"

"He's a custodian *ino*. In other words, he's the librarian of the supernatural world."

"So my mother and my aunt were of the supernatural, my whole family was, and I'm the last? Is that why I can talk to you and can hear you in my mind?"

Callum saw the panic in her eyes, and his protective instinct told him that he shouldn't tell her anything more, but she was right earlier, they were partners, and for them to work out he shouldn't hide things from her. "No, that's not why."

"It's not?"

"No."

"Callum?" She pushed.

"I don't know why. Enchantresses have never been telepathic, even pureblood ones."

Rielle felt sick all of a sudden. She sat down on the edge of the bed, unsure of what to feel. Was her father even a soldier? Did he die in a war? So many questions, she was on a whirlwind trying to solve the puzzle of who she was. Her hands on her face, she closed her eyes, trying to make sense of it all.

Immediately, Callum was next to her, sending his calm energy to her. He pulled a thread of hair behind her ear as he caressed her back. "Hey, look at me." She did as he asked. "Your aunt was probably protecting you for the same reason Luke or anyone else is after you. There's a reason why he had a rebel pretending to be a cook at your restaurant, and there's also a reason why those rebels came after you at your place."

Seeing the fear in her eyes, Callum kissed her fast and light. "I will fight everyone tooth and nail for you, even my brothers. I will die first before I let anything happen to you." He smoothly stroked her face.

"What are you not telling me? Why is Luke after me?"

"If Luke is after you, it's because he knows about you and whatever he's up to involves you. But Zachariah knew, which is probably why he crossed the portal, and whatever it is, it can't be good."

"And Luke has him?"

"Yeah."

"Something happened between you and him, didn't it?" Rielle asked. Callum's guilt and regrets hit her at once.

"We should go back to sleep," he ignored her question. If he told her what happened between Luke and him, he'd also have to reveal the kind of monster he was. Although she was aware of it, he wasn't ready for her to walk out of his life.

"Callum, you can't hide things from me if we are to try this."

"I promise I'll tell you anything you want to know, but right now, let's get some sleep." Rielle pushed past him, and her frustration hit him all at once. "Please," he implored. Rielle hated the way he looked at her as if his world would fall apart if she walked away. She loathed that terrible knot brewing in the pit of her stomach for making him feel this way.

"Please come to bed," his seductive voice pleaded in her head.

"Fine, only because I'm tired. But I meant what I said Callum. We only work if we are open to each other."

Her warning more of a threat than anything, Callum grinned inwardly. She was, indeed, his mate.

Chapter 19

Zachariah lay on the ground, his face closed in grimace, a painful thrust in his heart. Every few minutes, he would hear her scream, see him stand over her body, the blade he drove into her heart in one hand. The bruises on her face and arms from when he had fought with her. He'd felt her pain then, and he sensed it even worse now. He had never told a soul what he did to their father, not even his brothers, and the witch was using his demons to torture him. It was working this time, he was feeling her suffering with a raw quality, and the realness of it consumed him with an agony that knew no end or limit. Bitter blasts cut right to his bones and gripped his brain fiercely. He'd do it again in a heartbeat.

"You can make it stop," the witch walked in the room in gratification.

"You're wasting your time, witch, if you think using my memories against me is going to get you what you want."

"You and your brother aren't so different. Except you act as if you are above the moral compass," she smirked.

"You don't know anything about me," Zachariah's voice ominous challenged her.

"Oh, but I do. You let it happen; you were there that night. You knew what would happen. Still, you let it happen, and you did what you did, not for her but for yourself."

"You are nothing but Luke's disposable piece in a game of chess, and once he's finished with you, he'll get rid of you. That is, if I don't kill you first," Zachariah growled.

The witch moved closer to him, gripped his face in her hand, whispered close against his mouth. "You have to give me more credit than that. He has his end game, I have mine."

"If you believe any of the promises that Luke has made to you, then you are a bigger fool than I give you credit for."

"Your brother is about to change our world as we know it, and I want to be by his side when he does. I need to deliver that witch to him so things can go back to how they need to be."

"And you believed him?" Zachariah crackled out loud. "Luke has never been about anyone but himself. He's using you, sweetheart, why do you think he's after Rielle?"

"I need her blood."

Zachariah chuckled. "He's not going to kill her if that's what you think. He needs her, and she's a pure enchantress.

He can turn her dark. By her side, he would be unstoppable. What makes you think he's going to give that up?"

The witch looked at him dubiously. "He wouldn't. Your brother and I are one, bonded by mage blood and magic."

"You don't know Luke if you think any of that means anything to him."

Angrily, the witch pointed at his chest. Immediately, Zachariah felt a sharp pain in his chest as if his heart was coming out of his chest. He screamed in agony.

"Tell me what I need to know." She made a fist with her hands, and the pain amplified a thousand more.

"Go to hell," Zachariah screamed, his nose bleeding.

"That's where you are headed." The witch continued her rituals.

Zachariah coughed, and maniacally started to laugh. "I'm already there, sweetheart."

"Maybe a little bit more motivation." She called out to the guard outside, signaling him toward Zachariah. "Our prisoner needs a little motivation; thought you might be able to help," she smiled.

"Yes, ma'am," the rebel said, and struck Zachariah in his chest.

"I like his pretty face, so make sure his face stays intact."

⚜

"How did this happen?"

"I've never seen anything like it. Zen was choking on his blood, and she wouldn't let him die. The only reason I'm alive is that my liege wanted you to be aware."

"Your liege?" Luke grabbed the rebel by his neck, throwing him across the wall. "You're telling me I sent three of my best fighters to acquire one little enchantress girl and she managed to kill two of them without the blades, and my older brother is the one who spared your life?" he roared, seething.

"I'm sorry, my commandant, but her powers aren't little. She killed Benetti with a flash of lightning, and it came out of nowhere."

"You're worthless! All of you are." Luke paced around. "We're running out of time. Get me the witch, and no one goes near our prisoner until I tell you otherwise."

"Yes, my commandant." The rebel stood rooted in place.

"Out of my sight, you *imebecilai*! You're lucky you're one of my best. Otherwise, you'd met the same fate as the others."

Luke paced around the room.

No enchantress held that much power. There was more to her. Her family lineage was strong and powerful, but his witch had taken care of the aunt with no problem. He was missing something.

"How dare you send your goon to fetch me in the middle of an interrogation?" The witch walked into the private room furiously.

"Need I remind you of your place?" Luke threatened, his caustic and disdainful tone sending shivers through her spine.

"I'm not one of your goons, Luke. I would think I've earned your respect by now after everything I've done for you," she uttered.

"Maybe you're not what I think you were because your potions or spells haven't worked on any of my men. And an inexperienced enchantress just killed two of them. We are Arcadien. We only meet death by the blade, yet she killed one of my men with lightning, and another choked on his blood."

"Maybe you gave your men too much credit because my spells work. I've proven that to you many times. If they let one novice enchantress end their lives, maybe you need better warriors to fight for you," she rebuked.

Luke approached her. Scared, she walked back until her back was against the wall. Slowly his hands ran up her arms until they reached her neck. She heaved a sigh.

His eyes were cold, the anger in them warned her of the looming threat.

"We are bound by mage blood. Anything you do to me you do to yourself too," she faintly said. Luke ignored her warning as he encircled his left hand around her neck, then gradually made it through her hair, harshly and forcefully yanked her hair and brought her face close to his. She yelped in pain.

"Three times now that novice enchantress has not only beaten you but has completely humiliated you. So, no, I don't need better fighters; I need a better witch." His voice was eerily calm. "And have I ever given you the impression that your life, bonded to mine, has any value? I'm the angel of death."

"Luke, please, you're hurting me," she pleaded.

Releasing her, he walked away from her. "Have you gotten anything out of Zachariah?"

"No, but I'll go back and . . ." She looked at him, scared.

"You're not to go near him. We've tried it your way; I'll get my brother to talk. Just stop that *noirei* from using her magic. Now out of my sight," he spat angrily.

Chapter 20

*C*allum woke up. Sorrow filled his head. A painful current ran over his body. He looked on the left side of the bed. Rielle was sleeping peacefully. *"Raphael."*

"I feel it too. It's Zachariah."

"They're torturing him. I swear to heavens and hells, I'll rip Luke's heart out with my own two hands."

"You'll do no such thing. I can't afford you turning. We'll bring Luke to the mountains, and the elders will see to Luke's comeuppance," Raphael casually said. His worries filled Callum's head.

"We'll get him back. I vow my life on it."

Raphael was silent for a moment. *"I promised mother I'd keep an eye on all of you, and so far, I've failed."*

Callum felt the chagrin in Raphael's voice. Rarely did Raphael let himself be vulnerable with them like that. Always his demure, practical, and modest self, he hid his pains and his melancholy well. The burdens of their people and their survival rested on his shoulders, he was trying hard to be the best leader their people deserved. *"Mother would be proud of the job you've done and how well you've taken care of not only us but also our people. Give yourself some credit, freio. We will rescue Zachariah and end Luke's terrors once and for all."*

Raphael went silent, then continued, *"It's the rebel. He's made contact."*

"With Zachariah?"

"Yes, I can sense him, but not telepathically. I need you to merge your mind with me, Callum."

"Can't you do your mind control tricks?"

"He's too far. That's why I need you to merge with me, and whatever you see, stay focused."

⊰⊱

"If you've come to torture me more, you might as well just kill me, witch," Zachariah whispered once the door opened and someone walked in.

"Zach."

Painfully, Zachariah rested his body against the wall, staring at the rebel in front of him. The only people who called him Zach were his mother and brothers. The witch was getting to him. He chuckled. "I'll say your witch is no quitter. Using my connection to my brothers to get me to talk, that's the best she's come up with thus far."

"Zach, it's me." The rebel approached him. "Look at the rebel in his eyes, Zach, I'm in complete control over his mind, and we haven't got much time. It's me—well, it's us. I know you can't sense us telepathically. Something is cloaking me, but we found your notes and professor Rue."

"I hid that part of my brain. Surely she couldn't have known about the professor or my notes," Zachariah said out loud.

"We did, and we know she's a pure enchantress. She's under our protection—well, Callum protection mostly, but we got to her."

"Raphael?" Zachariah whispered.

"Yes, brother, now we need you to hold on just a little longer before we get to you."

"If you only knew what I did, Raphael, you'd let me die. Luke holding me hostage is God's way of punishing me," Zachariah barely whispered. "He's in me, Raphael, I see him. I sense him."

"He's in all of us." Raphael knew what he meant. "And whatever you did, little brother, I'd never leave you to die, mother would never forgive me." Zachariah's guilt and remorse ate at him. "Now I need you to try your best to connect with me. Our bond is stronger than any magical spell. We sensed your anguish earlier when you tried reaching out."

"I don't have the strength. The witch, there's a magic cloak," Zachariah faintly whispered.

"I need you to try, freio."

A bang on the door. Luke walked in and grabbed Zachariah by the neck. "Come on, little brother, tell me what I want to know, and this will all go away. I know you're hurting."

"Go . . . to hell," Zachariah slowly uttered.

Luke pressed his shoulder, a cracking sound, and a loud pop sounded in the room. Zachariah screamed in pain. The rebel took a step toward them. "Get out," Luke snarled.

Rooted, the rebel's hands turned into a fist. He advanced on them. "Did you not hear me? Get out! And secure the door." Distantly the rebel shook his head and followed Luke's order.

"Kill me. Get it over with."

"No, freio, not this moment but in due time. Tell me how this novice enchantress can kill one of us without the blade?" Luke pressed harder on the broken bone. "It's ruptured; the bones are disjointed. In a moment, you might lose the arm, so tell me." he pushed his blade in the shoulder then pulled it out quickly.

Zachariah grunted in agony, blood pouring out of his shoulder.

"I assumed you didn't want me to kill the mortal because you knew my plan to reverse the magic of the portal, but it's much more than that, isn't it?" Luke knelt in front of him. "We might not be as close when it comes to our connections, but we're still brothers. The link between us is not severed. I can feel what you're feeling, freio. You're afraid. What are you afraid of?" Luke stared, forcefully merging their minds. Though weak, Zachariah tried to shut him out, "You're afraid she might turn." A unique look on his face. "This is going to hurt a little, brother." Luke's hand ripped into his chest, slashing his flesh apart to get to his heart. An outpouring flow of blood pumped through his veins, and it stopped through his heart as Luke held his still-beating heart. An excruciating pain took over his heart and body. Zachariah shouted. He wanted to die.

"Father taught me how to stop the bloodstream from the heart—just right, without stopping the heart. But I'm losing my patience." Luke gritted his teeth.

"She's half Arcadien," Zachariah painfully blurted out. The pain was unbearable; it intensified. He couldn't fight it, fight Luke.

Luke removed his hands out of Zachariah's chest, stopping just in time. "You're telling the truth?" He fascinatingly queried. Pacing around, he wondered how it was possible. Then he remembered Gabriel. The night he killed Gabriel, the guardian didn't put up a fight. It all made sense now. He was protecting whoever was in the house; giving them time to escape. He did sense others in the room that night, but his men didn't find anyone. "She's Gabriel's daughter. That's why you crossed the veil. Your finding out about my plans was just pure coincidence."

"You will never get to her." Zachariah spewed blood out of his mouth.

"You were fine to worry, brother, but I won't send the witch to see you tonight. You deserve a break."

"You're better off getting rid of me. When I get out of here my face will be the last thing you see before I kill you myself," Zachariah threatened.

Luke laughed maniacally. "I had the shivers—I almost believed you there. You don't have it in you, little brother. You're weak just like father believed you to be."

His face contorted. Zachariah's brows furrowed. "If he did, he sure thought otherwise moments before his death," Zachariah coldly said.

Luke stayed silent for a moment and shook his head unbelievably. "No, you didn't," he leered, "You? You killed our father?" recognizing the darkness brewing inside of Zachariah. He beamed in admiration. "Little brother, maybe you have it in you after all. The bastard deserved to die. Seven hells, I would have killed him myself sooner or later, the way he treated our mom. The difference is, I'd feel at peace doing so."

"You don't know me, Luke, you have no idea what I'm capable of, which is why I'm warning you to get rid of me now, or you'll wish you did when you had the chance."

Luke chuckled and walked out of the room.

Chapter 21

"*W*hat in the hell happened? We had him."

"*You happened. I told you to stay calm under any circumstances, and you didn't. Your wanting to beat Luke to a pulp took over my mind. I had to pull out, or he would have figured it out,*" Raphael chastised.

"*Did you not sense Zachariah's pain? He's giving up. Luke broke him,*" Callum hurled, throwing himself out of bed, walking around. "*We had the bastard. We had him.*"

"*And you think the rebel was strong enough to take out Luke even with me taking over his mind?*"

"*Mierdei, we must get him out of there. He won't survive another day,*" Callum said, frustrated.

"*I agree, which is why we're going to get him out. Leave Luke to me. You get Zachariah out, no matter what.*"

"*Sorry, I can't do that, freio. You leave Luke to me and get our little brother out, no matter what.*"

"*Callum, I'm not asking you.*"

"*Neither am I. You're the leader of our people, and I'm your guardian. Besides, what will I tell my nephew if anything were to happen to his father on my watch?*" Callum retorted, not backing out.

"*Or niece, we still don't know the gender.*"

"*Did you get a precise location of where they are?*"

"*Yea, I retracted it from the rebel mind. I say we move at sunrise. Davide will stay behind with Rielle. How is she taking all of this?*"

"*I don't think it's easy finding out that you're not who you thought you were, but she's managing,*" Callum answered, looking in her direction.

"*Yeah, it can't be easy.*"

"*I can't tell her about that night. I just can't.*"

"*You must. She must understand why we are the way we are. I found out the hard way that women do not like it when we keep secrets from them. And especially your mate is a spirited one. I doubt it'll go well for you.*" Raphael said trying not to laugh.

"*You're enjoying this, aren't you?*"

"*It's not every day the big bad wolf is afraid of a little lamb. So yes, I am.*"

"*It's not easy to tell anyone what our father did,*" Callum admitted.

"*I know, but you can't keep it a secret from her.*"

"She's my mate, Raphael. She's mine. Fate decided she was the one, and I can't lose her."

Raphael heard the possessiveness in Callum's tone.

"I'm not questioning that she is. You two were fated to cross paths. And yes, she is your mate, but pride, possession, and love are different. I want you to make sure which one you hold high when it comes to your bond. If love, you need to tell her and let her make her choice." He could sense his brother's doubts, and he understood the apprehension. The bastard died, but he was within all of them in some ways more than others. *"Get some rest. We're on a mission early morning."*

Callum kneeled in front of the bed, watching Rielle sleep.

Raphael's words were getting to him. His connection to her was intense. It was raw, and he didn't want to go back to feeling empty or alone now that he knew what it felt like being with her. Were all these feelings purely physical because they were magically chemically paired, or was it love, he asked himself. His possessiveness was at an all-time high when it came to her. He wanted her all the time. The thought of another man with her drove him mad, but the idea of her walking away from him drove him even more insane. Raphael was right. He had to know the difference between love, pride, and possession. Did she love him? Did he?

Their mother, falling out of love with their father, drove the man mad.

What if it was purely flesh between them? Fate brought them together and their connection, but what if she decided that she deserves better? His parents weren't so lucky, fate did bring them together, and that didn't turn out well for either of them.

Not every Arcadien was fortunate to find their mate, but most were lucky to find someone to pair with, and the elders give their consent.

You're your father's son.

The voice nagged in his head. I am my father's son.

"No, you're not. You wouldn't harm me," Rielle softly spoke. She picked up on his feelings.

"Did I wake you?"

"Yea, when you abruptly left our bed. And this buzzing sound in my head, whatever is upsetting you." Rielle opened her eyes, staring at him, "Does it ever stop?"

"No, but you get used to it in time. I'm sorry. I should have shielded you out," he apologized. Callum stared at her, wondering how he was ever going to let her walk out of his life.

"You want me out of your life?"

Her telepathic voice, like a drowsy caress in his mind, sent a shiver through his heart down to his groins. Callum wasn't sure he would ever get used to it, loving how it was becoming easier for her now to slip in and out of his head. *"No, but you would if you knew what and who I am."*

"How about you tell me and find out?" Rielle shifted her body toward him. "Your father—does he have anything to do with that thing you're fighting inside of you?" she asked out loud.

Her dark brown eyes piercing into him, Callum concluded that she was bewitching him without even knowing it. "He was a good man at first, then he became something else. It's our curse, mie cehia."

"He hurt your mother? Is that what you're afraid will happen to me?" She touched his face. "I don't believe you would hurt me, Callum. You might be a Neanderthal at times and bossy, but you wouldn't hurt me. You said it yourself. I'm very good at reading people." She smiled.

Callum felt touched the way she was trying to reassure him, but she didn't know the truth, and once she did, she might see it differently.

"He killed her," he grimly said. "He killed her because he was a possessive, jealous man who was scared of her leaving him for another." His voice was raw even to his ears. He waited to see the horror and the disgusted look he usually got when people brought up their father and mother. But instead, he saw sadness and compassion in her eyes. He continued. "I am exactly like him, Rielle. I feel the same sentiments he did toward her. Concerning you."

Rielle sat up straight, holding his face in her hands. "Why do you persist on seeing yourself as a monster?"

"I need you to understand what and who I truly am."

"I know exactly who and what you are. You're bossy, and you like things your way. You're charming, and you have a good heart." She gently stroked his face. "I had a peek in your heart. You burden yourself with a lot so that people can feel safe. You've given up on who you are so that people can be safe. You think you're this jealous guy who will harm me, but . . ."

"I am that jealous guy. When that officer hugged you, I wanted to make him disappear. The thoughts of another man touching you drive me crazy." Callum squeezed his eyes shut. "My father was so jealous that he couldn't stand my mother talking and laughing with her brother. He fought her every time a man glanced her way, or he assumed she was going to leave him, which was often. You belong to me, and the idea of some man holding you in his arms, kissing you, sharing your body . . ." Frustrated, he heaved a sigh, running his hand through his hair. "The thought of you not wanting anything to do with me after all of this, or leave in the future maddens me, and it feels intense." Ashamed, he moved away from her.

"Callum."

He ignored her and stood in front of the window, turning his back so that she couldn't see him. He didn't want to and couldn't look her in the eye. "That morning, when we argued, I felt your emotions when you found out I bonded us. It made you sick to your stomach how I reacted and what I said. You were afraid of me. I saw it in your eyes. But I could do worse, Rielle, I'm capable."

Rielle walked up to him and wrapped her arms around his waist. "You're not your father."

"I've killed countless men; I almost killed my brother. I am as much a murderer as he was. I honestly don't know what I'd do if you decided not to go home to the mountains with me. This thing inside of me—it's part of me, it's another side of me, and I can't always control it. It knows you, it recognized you, and it wants you. You belong to him as much you belong to me." His voice was cold, unattached, and emotion-less.

Sadness encompassed Rielle, aware of how much Callum was fighting the demons inside of him. As a child growing up, the death of her parents saddened her. But she had her aunt Anais, and her aunt loved her unconditionally. Not knowing her parents was hard, but witnessing your father beating and killing your mother was worse. It must have been hard for Callum growing up—hell, it would be hard for anyone to live with that. She could feel the echo of the love his mother had for him and his brothers. So Callum had known love. But he was holding on to the memories of what happened. It made him afraid of himself, and it was eating him inside. His past had turned him into this, reliving it over and over, unable to let go.

"Callum . . . ," Rielle whispered. It troubled her that he hurt so bad and he didn't even know that he was. He wasn't aware of it; the only thing he knew was the fire of rage or the ice-cold deep inside of him. It was all or nothing with Callum. Fury or ice.

"Don't!" he cut her off sharply. It was the third time she was crying for him, and it hurt as much as the first two, if not more. No one had ever cried for him.

After his mother's death, and Luke turning dark, the rest of the world looked at him and his brothers like monsters that their father had created. Especially him.

"I meant it. You tear out my heart when you cry. Just stop, mie cehia, I can't change what I am. I might try to for you, but I can't deny what I am." He spun around, facing her. His thumb brushed at her tears.

"If you were your father, you would have killed Jao back then at the café," Rielle said, quietly compressing the sob trying to escape from her mouth. "You wouldn't feel how you are feeling right now."

Callum picked her up, walking back to the bed. He sat with her legs straddling him. "I wanted to." He brushed kisses along her face, kissing her tears.

"But, you didn't," Rielle persisted.

"No, I didn't. But mie cehia, I'm not a charming man. I'm not as good as you believe me to be. I've carried out a lot of things in my past that are scarily horrifying, and I would do them again in a heartbeat. I need you to know that and not deceive yourself about me, so when you see that side of me, you're not frightened."

"I've sensed danger in you, Callum, since the first time I've met you. I know you're not a saint, but you're also not a monster."

"I can be, with you," he replied, knowing it would be a matter of time before she realized that she would not put up with his constant need to protect her, to dominate her, and it would tire her. Callum groaned softly. He'd seen firsthand how stubborn she was. He knew the kind of woman that she was. She would want her freedom, and eventually she would leave him and never want to look back. He also knew that wherever she went, he would follow.

Rielle reached up to trace his lips with the pad of her finger. She heard the ache in his voice. "Well, I'm telling you differently, Callum Castallante."

There was silence, his arms tightened even more around her as if by crushing her to him and nuzzling her neck, she was right, and he was no monster. The thought of him putting her through the ordeal that her mother went through was crushing. It tore up his insides until he could barely think straight. He needed to talk about something else. "We've found Zachariah's location. We're moving in on Luke before sunrise."

"In a couple of hours?"

"Luke is torturing him, and he's giving up."

"He is your brother, no? Why would he want to hurt you guys?"

"He gave in to his darkness. Our powers are also our curse. Luke believes our abilities make us above everyone, but our parents' death changed him for the worse. We didn't know how much. It changed all of us."

"Davide briefly mentioned Zachariah to me. Why is Luke holding him hostage?"

Callum heaved a sighed. His body stiffened. "Raphael is the oldest, and then there's Luke, Zachariah, and me. After our father died, one of us was to lead our people. Being the oldest and the wisest out of all of us, the council and the elders chose Raphael. Luke was the head of the army at that time. He was adored and loved by everyone. His skills and abilities to keep us safe distinguished him from everybody else, even Raphael. But he wasn't humble.

"Though he did things his way, everyone respected him. He was loved all around, but the glory got to his head. Once he found out the elders and council chose Raphael as our leader, he became enraged. Engrossed with anger, he resented those who voted against him. He thought of them as disloyal. So he started to plot to overthrow Raphael, killing whoever got in his way.

"It turned into a civil war. A lot of people died, mostly children and women." He tightened his grip on Rielle. "I had never seen him this cold and heartless. It was horrible.

"So I dealt with it myself. We were once close. I knew I would have to be the one to stop Luke. I tried, but I came short. I couldn't kill my brother, so I turned him in. I betrayed him."

She saw the guilt in his eyes. Callum sat frozen from anger and resentment. He blamed himself for Luke's losing his way, and it pained her to know that he shouldered all these burdens.

You did what you had to do to stop a war and saved the lives of many.

Rielle slipped into his mind, leaning into him and resting her forehead against his. She wanted to make him see what she saw. Feel what she felt when she was around him. A caveman, he was, but a monster he wasn't. Slowly, Rielle ran her fingers through his hair, kissing her way along his earlobes. Callum closed his eyes, his breath hitched.

Tracing her tongue to the back of his left ear, Rielle heard him quietly moan. She smiled inwardly. She needed him here present, not lost to the anger and guilt brewing inside of him. "Merge your mind with me," she whispered in his ear.

"Rielle . . ." Callum countered, his voice low and husky. A chill ran down his spine.

"That wasn't a request. Now merge your mind with me," Rielle charged. His pupils dilated. She swore a halo flash sparkled around his iris.

Her voice alone appeased his tensions. But her commanding tone sent current to his brain down to his manhood. Aroused, he merged their minds. Callum feared he would explode in his pants with her thoughts and the images she was conveying to him. In a speed of seconds, she managed not only to obliterate every thought in his mind but had taken over his mind. His desire to touch her, to feel her softness, and to give her everything she wanted was going into overdrive, and until he did, the throbbing pain between his legs would not cease.

Rielle kissed his lips, pushing herself more into him as she ground and rocked her hips against the erect bulge in his shorts. Callum cursed at the pieces of clothing serving as barriers between them, wishing away both her underwear and his shorts the Arcadien way. Gently, he tunneled his fingers through her wild hair, the other hand caressing her back.

Her tank top was still on. It was too much of a barrier between them. Callum's hands drifted to her side. He ripped it apart.

"Do you always have to be in control?" Rielle pulled back at his hair harshly, to look into his eyes.

Callum grunted. The slight discomfort made him chuckle. Gently, he touched her face. His thumbs traced her lips, her neck resting on her collarbones. He pulled her into a fiery and passionate kiss. Her naked breasts against his warm chest were perfection. Must she be so perfect? He inwardly said, holding her gaze. His breathing quickened, as did hers.

"You make me feel alive," he breathed, nuzzling her neck with delicate kisses. So faint, they were like whispers. His fingers gently ran up and down her spine, his need for her intensified.

Rielle ground her hips against him, holding on to his shoulder. She lifted her body, and with one hand, slowly guided his fully erect shaft inside of her. Just barely taking in the tip and relishing the sensations, teasing him agonizingly slow, and giving him just enough to want more. Enough to make him shiver. A pent-up frustrating sound came out of his mouth, and Callum thrust inside her. She withdrew. A sexy smile curved her lips

"Should I make it clearer for you that you're not in control?" Rielle blew in his ear, leaning more into him, keeping their bodies close.

"Keep this up, and you might find yourself tied up," Callum protested. He needed to be inside of her so intensely his lower body ached. Driving inside of her with force, he closed his eyes and stifled a groan as he put a hand around her waist, adjusting their angles. She stopped teasing him, moving up and down along the length of his shaft. Her slightly tilted hips pushed down, and she began to rotate in deliberate slow circles like a very long drawn out crescendo.

Rielle was in control, staking her claims, keeping them steady, altering her movements so that he didn't get too excited.

Her sensual body, her flowy frizzy curls tumbled over her shoulder down to her back. Bliss and desire churned inside of Callum. She enchanted him. Body and soul, and the thought of another man who would ever dare see her like this, possession rapidly crawled inside of him. She was his life force, and he wasn't going to give her up. "Bellasimai . . . ile mio." He took her breasts in his mouth. Rielle tugged at his hair, rotating her hips like a dance. Rocking, grinding, bouncing with shallow strokes and deep thrusts so that his length slipped in and out, working him, proving to him that he wasn't in control. At her whims, he moved with her and upped the pace, clutching her hips and ass. He rocked her back and forth, pushing his pelvis toward her while she pushed down on him.

Rielle closed her eyes. She arched her back, moaning sensually, the friction hiking up her excitement. She pushed him on his back, her stomach clenched. Callum wrapped his arms around her waist, thrusting, filling her up. His body tensed; he squeezed her, driving into her one last time.

Loud moans rung the room as they both came simultaneously. Rielle fell forward, feeling him throbbing still inside of her. He held her tight, their heart dancing to the same rhythm. "You will be the death of me."

"I hope not. this life mate thing is starting to grow on me," Rielle teased.

Callum quietly laughed. "Promise me you'll be good and won't leave the house. Davide will stay with you, but you have him wrapped around your fingers. I'm afraid he'll do anything you ask him to. I can't be worrying about you and trying to rescue my brother."

Rielle grinned. "I'll be good."

He quickly whirled her around. She was on her back now with him looming over her. "I mean it, Rielle. I need you to stay here safe, or I won't be able to protect myself or my brothers, worrying about you."

She licked his lips, removing a full amount of hair fallen over his face. "I promise I'll be here, safe." Callum moved. She watched him lie on his back.

He wrapped his arms around her waist. "Good," he whispered into her neck, pulling her closer into him, inhaling her scent. Rielle wiggled her butt into his groin. A mischievous smile snuck to her lips, hearing him grunt, "We should get some sleep."

"Yea, we should," Rielle said, disappointed, all of a sudden wanting to feel his hands on her, touching her and caressing her. She had turned into a sexual being concerning him. *What is wrong with me? We just had sex, yet I want more.*

Hearing her thoughts, Callum smiled, amused. Arcadien did have a higher sex drive than a human mortal, but she was his mate, so maybe it was perfectly normal for her to mirror his sex drive. Slowly he moved his right hand down her hips across her pubic bone, sliding it down. He slipped his fingers between her fold.

Immediately she was aroused, her too eager body welcoming his touches. Stroking his fingers through her labia, Callum whispered in her hair, "Nothing is wrong with you. Your body knows it belongs to me. Besides, I can't let you go to sleep dissatisfied." Rielle sighed, unable to keep it in any longer. She felt raw, exposed, and damped. "This is mine," Callum croaked, inserting a finger inside of her. Rielle gasped in pleasure, and then disappointment read on her face once Callum removed his finger. He spun her around. She was now on her back once again. He towered over her. "Say it," he uttered as his finger continued his actions.

Rielle quivered, the pleasure starting to intensify as he worked her up. "God."

"No, mie cehia, just me." Callum grinned. Tightly, she clenched around his finger. The faster he went, the tighter she gripped. "Say it," he kissed her neck, his mouth slowly going down. He gently sucked on her breasts. He toyed with her nipples. An electric wave surged through her spine. Rielle tugged on his hair.

Callum slowly kissed her body; his mouth made its way to her hips, abdomen, and her navel until his mouth rested between the center of her legs. With all the care in the world, he kissed her slit. Slow and deliberate he took his time.

A faint moan escaped her. Rielle couldn't deny that she didn't see herself with anyone else but him. She couldn't imagine anybody else's mouth or hand pleasuring her like this but his. A warm sensation, the feel of wetness between his hands and her tender skin with the way he was kissing, savoring her, Rielle felt helpless to the exquisite feeling and the erotic sensation of him trying to subdue and coerce her in such way.

She should be mad that he thought he could make her do anything just by touching her and with sex at that, but she wasn't. Her most sensitive parts being overpowered by his kisses and touch, was something to look forward to.

"Callum," Rielle whimpered. She needed him. She wanted him. She never had this visceral physical need for a man every time he touched her.

"I'm yours, and I will always be yours, just say the words." He picked her on her thoughts, teasing her, lightly stretching her, licking and sucking on the hood in long strokes. His tongue driving her insane. It was too much for her. Darting his tongue in and out, gently he nibbled, bit, then sucked and tongued at the same time, Callum was punishing her into submission. That much she knew. Rielle squirmed, ready to combust.

Callum wrapped his hands under her legs and pulled her into his tongue as he kissed slower and sucked harder. Rielle closed her eyes. Her head rolled back as she gripped the sheet. Groaning and moaning louder as the sensation intensified, she couldn't fight it anymore. "I'm yours," she gasped out loud.

Callum quickened his pace, licking, flicking, kissing, biting her softly but at higher speed, holding her hostage under his tongue. Rielle moaned out, panting, breathing hard as her legs shook and her whole body shuddered. Jerking his hair, she tried to pull him away, but he held her hands, pinning them over her head as he moved up on her kissing her passionately. "Yours. I will always be yours." He, too, repeated the words to her. A burning sensation jumped into her chest; her heart clenched.

Chapter 22

allum glanced up at the swirling dark clouds obscuring the stars and noted the shadows of the trees close to the hulking building, inspecting the building for any indication of someone sneaking or coming through the darkness out of the building. "Are you sure this is it?" He voiced to Raphael. His gaze kept straying back to the large hunting cabin a couple of feet away from it.

"Yes, this is what I retrieved from his mind."

"You think you can do your mind control trick again, so he opens the door? I'd rather not kill anyone, so we don't sound any alarm."

"It doesn't work like that, and I won't be able to fight if my head is exploding."

"You are to never try this on me, Raphael. God, help me, I will hurt you if you ever do."

Raphael laughed. *"Brother, you wouldn't know even if I did."*

"I mean it. Does Zachariah know about this ability of yours?"

"No, and I'd like to keep it between the two of us if you don't mind. I don't want to hear Zachariah lecturing me about it."

Callum smiled. *"He does like to give his two cents, doesn't he?"*

"Yea, he took after mother. Wait, someone is coming out of the building."

"On my right or left side?"

"The right side stays put." Callum held his breath, trying to disappear into the dark as much as he could. *"Alright, clear."*

"If I don't come out in precisely thirty minutes, I need you to shoot or burn and ask questions later," Callum whispered.

"And have your mate come after me? No, thank you, until I know how she's able to do what she does. I'd like you very much to be alive, so she doesn't burn down half the world with her grief."

Callum chuckled. *"I mean it, Raphael."*

"No, I'm not burning down the place with you and Zachariah in it. If in thirty minutes you're not out, I'm coming after you. Now you have twenty-eight minutes."

"Must you be so pragmatic?" Callum chastised.

"And must you be so Neanderthal?" Raphael mocked.

Callum growled. *"I hate that word. And how did you know that? Ok, never mind."*

"You don't shield me out, brother, you must know we're in each other's mind all the time. Besides, you guys aren't necessarily the silent type. Not when you guys are discussing your issues and especially not with all the sex that you guys keep having. I swear to the gods you guys make me sick."

Callum couldn't stop the laughter coming out of him, hearing the disgust in Raphael's voice. *"Hey, I sucked it up with you and Priscilla at the manor, so it's only fair."*

Raphael was quiet for a moment.

"I'm glad you found her. She's fierce, precisely what you need."

"A little too fierce," Callum smiled. He was in front of the door, surprised to find no guards. Callum opened it.

"Twenty-six minutes," Raphael emphasized.

A door left ajar cast a white beam into the sultry night. Callum found it odd no rebel was patrolling the hallway, and another door was wide open.

"Raphael," he reached out telepathically but couldn't feel their connection.

He walked inside the gate. Two rebels were playing Carte. Before they could do anything or realized they weren't alone, Callum broke their necks instantaneously. The killer in him roared in approval.

Footsteps echoed through the hall. Callum hid in the shadow, his hands on his blade. He felt sorry for whoever was coming his way, because he wasn't going to ask questions. A woman walked in. Callum steadied himself. "Is someone here?" she queried.

Callum came out of the shadow behind her. "I don't want to harm you," he whispered. The woman shook her head; she was human. "Where's everybody?" Callum asked.

"I don't know. I just maintain and clean the rooms," she said in fear. Callum realized that not only was she compelled, but Luke's man abused her, too, and she had no idea.

"Where's the prisoner? Take me to him."

"Malone forbade me to go to that side of the building. He will get mad if I do," she panicked.

"You're with me, so it's fine. I'll tell Malone it was my idea."

Callum found it odd that there was no guard around even in front of the chamber. Either Luke was slacking, or this was a trap. The latter resonated true in his mind once he realized he couldn't even use his powers to open the cell. The human ran, Callum stood trying to find the key to open the prison cell. A rebel walked in, holding the key in his hand, a smirk on his face.

"You thought it was going to be that easy," he sneered.

In a nanosecond, Callum was behind the rebel. His blade bored through his heart. The rebel thumped on the floor; he was dead.

"It was." Callum took the key and opened the cell. It was a trap. He had to get Zachariah out. Without his power, he couldn't teleport, so this was going to be a brutal one.

Zachariah was lying on the floor, his shoulder bleeding. Callum felt a sharp current in his gut as he kneeled in front of him; he was unconscious. "I need you to fight with me, freio." His voice choked up, inspecting the wound. The infected areas deduced this wasn't a fresh wound and that Zachariah must have been bleeding for days. "Mierdei."

Callum face hardened, a slow burn rising to the pit of his stomach. "Come on, brother. I know you think it's easier to give up, but I'm not ready to let go yet. Mother's ghost will haunt me if I let anything happen to you," he said, frustrated, unable to heal him on the spot. "I need you to wake up. Come on, Zach, wake up!" Callum pressed on Zachariah's chest. The panic in his voice startled him.

Several attempts later, Callum felt a slight rhythm under his hands. "Here we go, keep fighting," he encouraged and ripped the shirt apart.

The bruises on Zachariah's chest—Callum's nostrils flared, his brows furrowed, and his breathing hardened. "Come on, Zach, I need you to wake up, or I might end up killing a lot of people. You don't want that, do you?" Callum pumped his chest, breathing into his mouth.

A long moment after, Zachariah exhaled. "You always have to be so dramatic," he barely whispered. He coughed, his eyes slightly opened.

Callum chuckled, relief swept over him. "Do you always have to get yourself in trouble where I have to save your behind?"

"You're my older brother. It's your job to save my ass." Zachariah forced a smile as he grimaced painfully, holding his shoulder.

"You want to tell me why this place is empty?" Callum asked.

"Luke knew Raphael had compelled the rebel. He knew you guys were coming. It's a trap."

"I can't teleport us out of here. My powers aren't working in here, so we have to go through the entrance door. Are you able to keep up?" Callum heard feet walking and stomping in the hallway.

"It's the witch. She cloaked the entire space with dark spells. Help me get up."

"Witch? So Luke is working with a witch. That explains the shadow walkers after Rielle."

"Not just any witch. She's a mage too."

"That explains the Encenzia near the portal. How unoriginal." The door flew opened. Now surrounded by rebels, arms in hand. "Good for you guys to join the party. I was beginning to get bored," Callum uttered, shielding Zachariah behind him.

"It's seven of us and one of you," a rebel spat out condescendingly, looking in Zachariah's direction.

"I'm guessing you're the one in charge," Callum said, a deadly grin on his face. "I don't like your tone very much."

"I don't care what you like," said the rebel. Using his enhanced speed, he leaped toward them, throwing a blow in Callum's direction.

Callum missed the blow, spun around, and stood behind the rebel. In a fluid movement, he ripped the man's heart out his chest from behind. "You should have learned your math better. It is two of us, and now six of you," he sardonically said. "But also, not fair, you get to use your powers, and I don't." The rebel fell flat on his face. Stunned, everyone stood quiet.

"You mind warning me first next time?" Zachariah complained, breaking the silence.

"Sorry, little brother . . . how about you close your eyes right about now?" In a speedy blur, Callum went around the room, and bodies thumped on the floor one by one. "I don't want to hear it," he warned, looking at Zachariah, wiping off the drops of blood on his blade.

"Your speed?"

"I don't need my powers to be fast, I've always been faster than you guys. I just let you guys win the races. Can you walk or do I have to carry you out of here?"

Zachariah gestured. Callum laughed. "Luke." His mood darkened all of a sudden

"In the flesh, freio." Luke walked inside the cell. immediately surrounded by a small army of rebels and a woman next to him. "You didn't think you'd get out that easy, did you?"

Callum's heart pounded, rage brewing inside of him.

"We are outnumbered," Zachariah warned under his breath. He'd seen once how dark Callum could go, and he recognized the killer inside of Callum risen.

"Listen to our little brother Callum, especially when your powers are useless here, thanks to my witch." Luke pointed out to the woman next to him. "You see, I knew Raphael wouldn't let my man go without compelling him, and when he attacked me, I knew it was a matter of time before you guys showed up here. I'm guessing Raphael is somewhere around the bushes keeping guard and must be worried sick right now that he can't reach you. I'm expecting him to join us in a matter of moments. Killing three birds with one stone."

Callum growled, taking a step toward Luke. "That's what he wants you to do, so don't fall for his bait!" Zachariah screamed at Callum. "He needs me to open the gate, so he won't kill anyone."

"You're right Zach, I need you, but I don't need him, or Raphael. Thanks to whatever bond you guys still hold on, they are now leverage. So, you will open the gate if only to save one of them," Luke smirked.

Unable to control his actions or his instincts, Callum flung toward Luke.

"Is that the best you can do?" Luke laughed and tossed him around the room. Without his powers, Luke was faster and stronger than him. "You're still weak, still in your head, still feel guilty." Using his speed, Luke picked him up. "You're a disgrace," he angrily roared as he hurled Callum to the table. The table broke in half.

He grabbed Callum by the neck, lifting him. He dropped him hard on the floor. The floor cracked. "You disappoint me, Callum, I figured you'd bring your all out. It's in there, I can feel it. You're angry at me, you hate me, but you won't use that anger to fight me," Luke said, and headlocked him.

꒰꒱

Rielle paced around, her heart pounding hard against her chest, and a sadness encompassed her. Whatever it was that made her so anxious, she feared it. The only time she had felt like this was when she ran away trying to escape him. She brushed his mind for the umpteenth time. Sadness took over her mind. She didn't like it. *"Why can't I feel you?"* Rielle walked out of the room to find Davide. "I think something is wrong," she said.

"Please tell, my lady." Davide mocked.

"It's Callum. He's not in my mind. I mean, he shuts me out. I can't feel him."

"He's protecting you. In battle, he can't have you experiencing whatever he is experiencing. He's fine," Davide reassured.

"No, he's not responding to me, and I have this uneasiness that I can't help."

"It's normal to feel like that when he shuts you out. That's how he felt last time you shut him out."

"Please, I need to know that he is ok."

Wanting to reassure her, Davide reached out to Callum but hit a blank wall. He did again with no success. Callum would shut Rielle out but not him, especially when he had entrusted him to watch Rielle. Not wanting to panic, Davide smiled at her. "No need to panic." He reached out to Raphael. *"Raphael, what's going on? I can't reach Callum. Do you need backup?"*

It took a moment before Raphael answered, and by the tone of his voice, Davide knew something was up. *"He's inside the building, I can't reach him too. The place is spellbound so Luke is probably working with a witch."*

"Rielle is having one those episodes when your mate senses that something is wrong."

"*If she is, then something must be wrong with Callum. I must go in,*" Raphael said.

"*No, all three of you can't be trapped inside. If Luke is working with a witch, we have an enchantress here, and her mate is inside of that building, whatever spell they did. She can break it,*" Davide looked at Rielle.

"What is it?" Rielle asked, perplexed. "It's Callum. Did something happen?"

"*Yes, and I need you to get in contact with him.*" Rielle heard the unfamiliar voice in her head as another buzzing sound that wouldn't stop. "*Rielle, it's me, Raphael. The place is spellbound, and it seems that telepathy doesn't work once you're inside as if there's a cloak. You're an enchantress, and Callum might be trapped inside, so I need you to get to him.*"

"*He shuts me out.*"

"*He didn't, and he wouldn't. He would shield you from experiencing what he's suffering, but he wouldn't shut you out.*"

"*What do I do?*"

"*Concentrate on him and reach out to your mate. He might be in danger; that's why you're feeling what you're feeling right now.*"

Rielle tried again, but with no success. "*It doesn't work. I can't reach him.*"

"*He might be dying in there, Rielle. Imagine a world without Callum in it, imagine his suffering as he tries to get back to you.*"

"*Stop it!*" Rielle snapped.

"*He's dying, but he's still fighting to get to you.*"

"No, I said, stop it!"

Davide saw the conflicting pain in Rielle's eyes, tears coming out of her eyes. *"Raphael, you're scaring her, whatever you said to her."*

"I know what I'm doing, warrior. I need her to tap into whatever it was when she killed that rebel; that's the only way."

Rielle felt like the world was slowly disappearing, and she was fading away. At the thought of Callum being dead, her empty burning lungs and her heart hit her chest so hard she thought it would break her ribs and rip apart her skin.

Picturing him hurt created a void inside of her and a black hole in her head. Deep inside, her soul, slowly swallowing all her hopes and dreams in a world without Callum in it. *"Find him, Rielle, find your mate before it's too late,"* Raphael pressured her mind.

"No!" She called out to him. He was dead. He had to be. Sorrow filled her heart. She screamed out the pain of him being dead too monstrous to endure.

The windows broke, the glasses shattered as if a bomb had gone off in the house. Davide leaped toward her, crushing her on the floor so she didn't get hurt. Sudden inky darkness covered the sky, lightning burst on the house and streets, steadily making its path from one end of the town to the other.

Amazed, Davide looked outside of the broken windows as flashing bolts came and went. *"Raphael, are you seeing what I'm seeing?"* Davide asked in awe.

"Yes, it's a bolt of pure energy flashing around where I am, and it's standing long moments around the building." Raphael felt Callum's anger and Zachariah's pain, and relief swept over him. *"She did it; She broke the spell,"* he said, stunned.

Chapter 23

*A*ll at once, despair hit at Callum. "Rielle," he whispered.

Something was wrong with her; he had to get to her. Enraged, anger boiled deep in his system, as hot as lava. It churned within, hungry for destruction, it was too much to handle for him. In a frozen second, his eyes flickered. He wasn't in control anymore.

Callum stepped a foot back behind Luke's foot, locking in his leg, feeling his speed back to normal. Callum bent his knees, getting out of the headlock as he pulled Luke diagonally across his body and threw him on the ground with force, his hands around Luke's neck. He had him in a chokehold.

The rebels all at once ran in their direction. Forgetting the injured shoulder, speedily, Zachariah ran toward them and plunged Callum's blade into their hearts one by one.

"The cloak, the spell is broken," the witch said, bemused, as she started to sing another spell.

Zachariah leaped in her direction; his hands squeezed around her neck. "I warned you."

"Both of you get out of there. You're better than that," Raphael chimed in, using their mental path.

"All the shit that witch did to me, she deserved no mercy from me," Zachariah reacted through gritted teeth.

"Not today, brother, more rebels are on their way to you guys. Just leave now."

Raphael felt both Callum and Zachariah's anger manifesting all over him. *"Rielle broke the spell, so teleport out of there. Callum, she needs you."*

"You've imagined this day. Fight me! Do it! The killer in you wants it!" Luke yelled.

"Don't listen to him, Callum, I promise you this isn't the way," Raphael worried. If Callum gave in, it would be the end of him and Rielle. Just like their parents.

"Stop fighting who you truly are. We are the same. I can feel it inside of you. It's who you are. It's our essence," Luke continued. "We are our father's sons; we are exactly like him. Our people are not cursed; we are the angels of darkness. Just accept it, brother. It is in you."

Callum growled. His hold strengthened around Luke's neck.

"No, you're not. You're more than our darkness, Callum. You are nothing like our father. You have a beautiful woman who's your mate, and she just proved to me that she would burn

the world down for you, to keep you safe. You ought to look forward to this life," Raphael countered in Callum's mind, showing him what Rielle had done.

"I feel sorry for you," Callum said to Luke. Tension left his body. He released Luke but not before he punched him with his enhanced strength, sending Luke through the wall. In a blur, he teleported with Zachariah out of the room.

"I hope your great plan worked," the witch warily said, catching her breath.

Instantly, Luke was on her. He pinned her against the wall, hard. "How did she break the spell?" his voice seethed with anger.

"I don't know. Luke, you're hurting me," she yelped, frightened.

"Maybe I don't need you after all to open the gate, or your spells. Your magic is no match for her. She'll do it on her own."

"You need me, if only to turn her. I can turn her dark. Please, Luke," she pleaded.

Luke released her, his thumb tracing her face, then whispered in her ear, "You have one last chance—you turn her or you die. I know you think that we bonded by that blood magic of yours, but I've been alive long enough to know a thing or two about spells. So I reversed it. Your life means nothing to me, and I won't hesitate to end it." Shocked, his eerie tone sent shivers to her body.

All three of them teleported to the house. Immediately Callum went to Rielle. She was on the floor, unconscious.

"My god, Rielle, we're going to have some ground rules about you using your powers. I can't have you falling into unconsciousness every time." He stroked her face gently.

"She did all of this?" Zachariah asked, amazed.

Davide nodded. "I've never seen anything like it."

Zachariah made a painful growl as more blood was coming out his shoulder. "Guys, If I lose any more blood . . . I . . ." he laid back on the floor, weak and dizzy.

Raphael approached Callum, a hand on his shoulder. "Heal our brother before he loses any more blood. I've got her." Reluctantly, Callum left Rielle's side and went to Zachariah.

"Is she okay?" Zachariah faintly asked.

"She will be; she loses consciousness every time she uses her magic," Callum said, unable to stop being worried despite knowing she was going to be okay.

"When enchantresses use too much of their magic, it weakens them, and she's half Arcadien so it would make sense for her to fall into unconsciousness as her genetics are trying to overlap each other at that moment," Zachariah casually said.

"What?" Callum uttered.

"What did you just say?" Raphael walked toward them.

"She's half Arcadien. Gabriel is her father." Zachariah scowled as the pain in his shoulder intensified. "Callum, anytime now to start healing me, or should I go to a mortal hospital?"

"You're serious?" Callum was dumbfounded.

"As the pain eating me on my shoulder. Of course, I'm serious. That's why I crossed the portal. I found his testament in our library asking father for forbearance and leniency from the council as it was fate's doing that he had fallen in love with a mortal on his mission."

"So father knew?" Callum asked,

"What mission?" Raphael cut in.

"I don't know what mission, but I don't think the council knew about it either because it's not in the books. I think it was between father and Gabriel. Those two were close, remember."

"But how? We've learned of Gabriel's death before Father turned," Raphael continued trying to make sense of it all.

"That was a lie because Luke killed Gabriel. He told me himself while torturing me. It's against the law to be familiar with humans, let alone falling in love with them, so either father faked Gabrielle's death, or the elders found about his testament gave him an ultimatum—his duties or his love for the mortal, and he chose the latter. Hence he stayed in the human realm."

"That explains her telepathic abilities," Callum said, more to himself than to his brothers. "But the professor told us about your findings that mortal couldn't birth a child with Arcadien. That the child and the mother will die."

"Her mother was not only a mortal, but she was also a pureblood enchantress, so fate figured it out. She's the key to the portal for Luke. And if turned, with her magic, we are all screwed. Luke doesn't know that she's the key to the portal.

He thinks it's her blood and some spell. He knows what she can do, although she doesn't know how to control her powers yet, and while torturing me, he picked it from my mind. Rielle can turn dark because of our curse, half Arcadien."

"Then we can't let him get to her." Raphael pronounced.

"No, we can't. Luke will be unstoppable, and once an enchantress turns dark, the more magic she uses, the more darkness seduces her. The more she loses herself in the process. It's worse than a witch."

Callum growled—the thought of her turning dark scared and worried him. "She's my mate, we're bound, wouldn't that stop her from turning? She stopped me from turning."

"She didn't stop you from turning. She makes it impossible for you to lose whatever humanity you have left in you without thinking of her, that's why our mate is our light," Raphael rejoined, thinking of how close Callum was to tap into his darkness when Luke was instigating him. Both his brothers picked on his thoughts.

"Raphael is right. But she'll fight it."

"How?" Callum asked, fear enfolding his brain.

"She will have to fight it just like you. As long as she has you, you make it impossible for her to lose herself. But once she gets exposed to dark magic, there's no turning back. Luke wants her. He wants to kill everyone on the mountain. He's manipulative, and he'll find a way," Zachariah responded.

"I can't lose her to darkness, to Luke or whatever else. I simply can't." Callum's emotions and plea filled both his brothers' heads.

"We won't lose her," Raphael uttered firmly. "Our people's lives depend on it, and yours too. I say we ready ourselves for war now that we know what the threat is."

"Alright . . . but before we get ready for war, do you think you can alleviate me of this pain?" Callum nodded.

"So, you mated with her?" Zachariah asked.

"It just happened," Callum defended.

"I should have known something was up once you were making jokes; I don't remember the last time you did. And now that I can smell, you reek of honey and flowers."

"Do you want me to heal you or not?" Callum threatened.

Zachariah chuckled, "Oh, now the wolf is out. A moment ago, I could have sworn you sounded like a puppy."

"I need to concentrate," Callum grinned.

"I can't wait to meet the woman who saved my brother's life," Zachariah said. Callum knew what he meant, as Zachariah was the first one who had a glimpse of what he was capable of.

"Just a warning—she'll have you wrapped around her little fingers just like Davide if you're not careful." *"I'm happy to have you back, nerd."*

"I'm happy to be back."

Much later, Callum had sent Zachariah into a deep sleep, and Raphael magically restored the shattered windows. Never in his life had he been apprehensive about anything, but now he was, concerning Rielle. As a guardian, his job was to protect his people, do anything to keep them safe, yet his mate was the one entity who could destroy them all.

He'd sensed the darkness in her. She had opened that box. He saw what she could do, and yet she didn't entirely come into her powers. Having Luke next to her molding her, there would be no stopping her. "I'll kill him," Callum said out loud, running his hand through his hair.

"And I'll help you kill him this time," Raphael slipped in his mind.

"You were right; she is a danger to us all," Callum confessed.

"No, I was wrong, brother. She's your mate and the daughter of Gabriel. She's part of our world, and we make sure she doesn't turn into Luke's pupieteio." The sincerity in Raphael's voice was there for Callum to hear.

"She needs to know the truth about her father. She's a noble too, and she's not just an enchantress."

"A noble Arcadien and a pureblood enchantress—no wonder she was able to get in my mind, that's a feared combination right there. One should wonder if the war was the only reason why humans and Arcadien sheltered themselves from one another. Or was the cause of the war what we know."

"I believe our pasts documented to deify the people, our basis, and powers. We will never know the truth, and we'd be foolish to think the elders would tell the reality of the happenings of that period. But one must wonder how we went from coexisting together to fighting each other."

"If you were to choose to stay in this realm with your mate, I'm with you. And if you decide to come home, I'm with you too. Together we'll fight any laws or decree. I give you my word."

"I know." A faint sound brushed his mind, his heart fluttered. Rielle was awake. Instantly he teleported to her. She watched him, unsure. She leaped out of bed and jumped into his arms; her legs wrapped around his waist. Callum smiled, wrapping his arms around her, holding her tight, pressing her body to him. "I thought you were . . ."

"I know, and I'm sorry." One arm held her to him. The other one cupped her face. He kissed her eagerly.

"Don't you ever scare me like this again."

"I give you my word." He kissed her again.

"Zachariah and Raphael?"

"They're ok."

"But . . ." Rielle felt his apprehension.

"I found out about your father," Callum confessed.

"You did?" Rielle unwrapped her legs around his waist slowly; she pulled herself down.

"Yes, he wasn't a soldier like you thought. Well, he was, but not in the human sense. He was a guardian like me." He held her still in his arms, watching her face, waiting for her reaction.

"A guardian? So he wasn't human; he was an Arcadien."

Callum rubbed her back. "A noble, a respected warrior, and exceptional guardian. He was a very close friend of my father."

Rielle moved away from his embrace; her back to him, she stood in front of the large windows. Callum couldn't read her emotions. "Don't shield your feelings from me, Rielle, it's ok to be angry, mad, sad, or disappointed." She ignored him, staring out the window. "Your aunt was trying to protect you, and for a good reason," Callum continued.

"What reason is that? Depriving me of knowing who my father was and making me believe that he was a soldier who died in the war," she snapped at him.

That's good, Callum thought. At least she was angry. "He was a soldier," Callum emphasized.

"You're defending her actions? I deserved to know the truth. I deserved to know about my heritage from both my parents. She had no right hiding things from me and using magics to manipulate my mind. How did they meet? Were they in love? How did they die? I deserved to know."

"I'm sure she had her reasons, and they were valid."

"Leave. I want to be alone right now." Her clipped tone conveyed she was feeling more than she was letting on.

Callum wanted to force her shield down, but understood she needed to process it on her own. He marched to her and wrapped his arms around her from her back. Rielle's body stiffened; she was shaking with anger. He kissed her hair.

"They were in love," he whispered.

"You don't know that."

"Gabriel gave up our world to be with your mother. The only way a man gives up his duties, his people, for a woman, is if that woman becomes his world. So yes, I think they were very much in love." Callum took her hand in his and intertwined their fingers.

"Why didn't she just tell me the truth?"

"You have every right to be upset. But you also must understand why your aunt kept it a secret from you. You are a half Arcadien and the last pureblood enchantress. These are two powerful entities combined in one. If people had found out about you, we wouldn't be here. Believe it or not, even my people would have found a way to get rid of you. Human and Arcadien signed a treaty a long time ago before our times to keep the two realms safe from one another. But your father chose your mother instead of our world. Your powers are great, and they can also be a great danger if you don't control them." The tension left her body. Callum turned her around to face him. "I would have done the same thing your aunt did, if only to keep you safe." He held her face in both hands. "You have to forgive your aunt."

"I understand, but I still deserved to know."

"Well, you do now, and your aunt probably left you something or told you the truth but locked it in your mind, too, just like the spells."

Rielle's eyes widened. Something clicked in her head. "The blank diary." She quickly ran to the bathroom, looking in her duffel bag. The small book was in her hand. Callum was behind her. "There is such a thing as a safeguard spell, you have to figure out how to reverse it. You're an enchantress. You can do this." He wrapped his arms around her stomach.

"Stay with me."

"I'm not going anywhere, mie cehia."

Chapter 24

*R*ielle turned on the coffee maker and grabbed a cup from the glass cabinet. The sun was out, birds were singing—she loved that side of the kitchen. Trying to figure out a way to read the journal, she didn't get any sleep, and Callum had fallen fast asleep. It was eight in the morning; she grabbed another cup, expecting Davide any minute now after his morning meditation. "You're late," she loudly said, hearing the feet walking along the hallway.

"Am I?" Rielle turned around, staring at the man standing across the room, taken aback at how much alike he looked to Callum but with Raphael's mannerisms, only friendlier but with an edge. Medium length auburn streaks hair, they fall around his face like rope strands, he had an oval face and a wicked smile. His snow-white silver silver eyes were small and evenly apart, sitting below trim eyebrows. He was as handsome as his brothers. She also was grateful that at least he didn't pull a knife on her as Raphael did.

"Forgive my brothers. They can sometimes be a little hot-headed," Zachariah smiled, picking on her thoughts, surprised he could get into her head so quickly compared to the first time he saw her at the restaurant.

"A little?" Rielle raised an eyebrow.

"You're right; they're complete animals," Zachariah joked.

Rielle smiled, liking the fact that he had a sense of humor.

"Is my brother still getting his beauty sleep?"

Rielle cleared her throat. "Yes, we didn't get any sleep last night." A mischievous smirked cornered around Zachariah's mouth. Rielle realized what that must mean. "Not like that . . . I meant we were up late trying to . . ." Zachariah raised an eyebrow, grinning. Rielle felt flustered, her face giving away her embarrassment. "We didn't, you know . . ."

Amused, Zachariah marched toward her and held his hands to her. "Zachariah Castallante. It's nice to meet you, Rielle, officially."

"You too," she shook his hand.

"So you're the reason my grumpy brother is mellow these days."

"I guess so," Rielle smiled. "How are you feeling?"

"Great. Actually, thanks to Callum, but a lot hungry." He moved away from her and opened the fridge.

"I could make you some breakfast. No one ever really eats here besides me. It would be nice to cook breakfast for once for someone other than me." Rielle continued, "I know your diet consists of greens and vegetables, so I'll make us something to eat."

"Are you sure?" Zachariah asked, pleased.

"Yes. it's the least I can do." Rielle smiled at him.

"Professor Rue told me once you offered non-carnivores' options at your restaurant the first time we met; I didn't believe him."

"Did you know about Rue?" she asked.

"Yes, I did know that he was a custodian," Zachariah said, taking his time to look at her.

Rielle felt under a microscope all of a sudden.

"You visited my café?" Rielle asked, aware he was staring at her, and that made her feel a little uncomfortable.

"Yes, only one time. I wanted to make sure that you were who I thought you were." Zachariah continued, "And that day, Rue confirmed it to me. He was too protective of you, warning me off, and you both had the same mental block, so I knew."

Rielle stayed quiet, thankful that he had searched for her. Her thoughts conveyed to Zachariah unbeknown to her.

"Callum needs to teach you how to shield your mind better," he smiled. "But your father was an excellent man and did a lot for our people and our home, so finding his daughter was the only reward I thought he deserved."

"It's a little hard to get used to," she smiled in return. "What was he like?" she was curious.

"I was merely a teenager when I knew him, but I remember him as being brave and kind and a wicked good guardian. He was respected widely."

"Does he have any extended family left?" Rielle handed him a plate.

"Yes, you do. You have an uncle who is an Elder and part of our council. Your grandparents died in the Civil War when Luke went dark." He took a bite of his breakfast. "Mierdei, this is delicious," Zachariah uttered a satisfying low sound.

"And smelled delicious." Davide walked in; Raphael followed.

"I made plenty for everyone if you guys want to eat, and coffee for you, Davide."

"My morning would be dull without you feeding me coffee, my lady," Davide teased.

"Thank you, Rielle," Raphael said to her. Rielle knew he wasn't thanking her for the food but rather for what happened with Callum. She nodded. "I'll have a plate too," he smiled at her.

Moments later, Callum walked in, confused. "What's all the fuss about?"

"Sleeping beauty, it's nice you finally joined us," Zachariah taunted.

"Rielle made us breakfast," Davide grinned.

"No, she made me breakfast. You guys are just benefitting from it," Zachariah voiced proudly.

"She makes me coffee every morning, so you're not that special," Davide hit back.

"Mie cehia, you don't have to feed these guys. That's not your job." Callum joined her behind the counter and kissed her. Their audience made approval noises. "Grow up!" Callum laughed, gesturing the three men. Rielle was sure it meant something rude.

"Don't tell her what to do," Zachariah said, mumbling his words with his mouth full.

Rielle chuckled, "Want a plate?"

"I'll have a plate, please." Callum looked at her. Pride gleamed in his eyes, and his heart filled. He gave her a peck.

Moments later, Rielle joined them at the table, sitting across Callum, next to Davide.

She couldn't stop smiling, watching the four of them. They were genuinely enjoying her breakfast, and it wasn't even her best. These men had taken her under their protection when they didn't even know who she was. They had put themselves at harm to protect her, and to cook breakfast for them was the least she could do.

Observing them, she had never seen Callum or Raphael so relaxed. Zachariah was the glue to their bond, and they fed off his outgoing and friendly personality. Staring at the three brothers, Rielle acknowledged how close their relationship was. And although they shared some similarities, they were also different, even Davide.

Callum laughed a deep laugh at something Raphael said. Rielle turned her attention to him. Watching him, her heart skipped a beat. His hair tumbled all over his face. He ran his fingers through them, removing a couple of strands out of his strikingly beautiful face. Rielle smiled inwardly, focused on his lips. She reminisced about the time when he mouthed her into submission.

Those lips, magical as those fingers—she wanted to kiss him right this moment, letting his ample sensual mouth do away with every part of her body. A low sexy growl ringed in her head; a jolt of energy ran through her body. Rielle grinned. He picked up on her thoughts.

Engrossed in the conversation with his brothers, Callum didn't realize she was staring at him or that she shielded him, until her mind conveyed and painted a perfect picture of her thoughts to him. Her flushed cheeks, her shortness of breath—he took a longer than necessary look at her rising and falling chest. Aroused, her desires of his mouth doing away with every inch of her body not only tempted him, but he was also in full erect mode.

"Rielle," Callum called out her name, seductively low, his eyes holding her gaze.

At the sound of his voice in her head, Rielle nipples erected under her top. She bit down the lower bottom of her lips.

A low growl escaped Callum's mouth. He had completely forgotten about the others in the room; he cleared his throat, a strain on his face, sure that his brothers and even Davide would make out his painful hard-on, if not careful.

Rielle stayed quiet, avoiding Callum's eyes, pretending to tune in the conversation. Mischievously she smiled, wondering how far she could take it. The guys resumed their conversation. She was aware that Callum was watching her like a hawk. Her fingers slowly played with the cup in front of her. Sensually she brought it to her mouth. She sipped her coffee, making eye contact with him. The cup lingered on her lips. Callum's pupils dilated when she swallowed and licked her lips. Another growl escaped from his mouth. This time everyone looked at the two of them, an amused look on their faces.

"What do you keep growling about?" Zachariah eyed the two of them impishly.

"I don't know what you mean, brother," Callum answered. *"You're so going to pay for teasing me so hard,"* he warned Rielle.

"You can't say hard, then I want to touch, see, and feel."

"Oh, you will feel! I'm going to bury myself so deep and hard inside of you, you will beg me for mercy." Rielle coughed out loud, choking on her coffee. Her head down, she didn't dare make eye contact with any of them, but she sensed Callum smirking.

"Mierdei brother, we're so used to being into each other's mind that you don't even know you didn't shield us out," Zachariah teased. *"I don't suppose any of us needed to hear that."*

"I, for one, sure didn't," Raphael uttered.

"I'm sorry, guys. Habits," Callum apologized. He didn't want his brothers to hear that.

"Yeah, you're not doing a good job," Raphael continued.

"I said I was sorry. Now can you guys get out of my head?" Callum grinned apologetically.

"Are you ok, Rielle?" Davide asked, concerned, getting her a glass of water.

"Yes, just choked a little." She avoided Raphael and Zachariah's eyes, certain that they were aware of their little banter.

"*Your brothers are looking at me differently, and it's all your fault,*" she scolded him.

"*Mie cehia, my brothers are the least of your worries and are the sole reason you're not on this table right now with me on top of you sinking balls deep inside of you.*"

Everyone at the table groaned in revolt. "You two are like rabbits," Raphael scorned.

"I just lost my appetite," Davide laughed.

"Shield, you two! Put your shield on! All that sexual tension between you two is already in our faces. Now we don't want to hear what you guys want to do to each other. And, especially on the table, we eat." Zachariah threw his spoon at Callum and walked out of the kitchen.

"Get a room," Raphael scoffed and shook his head.

All three of them left. Callum laughed and winked at Rielle.

Chapter 25

*R*ielle shook her head quietly. She'd been here before. The forest seemed gloomier, the little girl playing with the bunny she'd seen her before. *"Again, do it,"* the voice in the shadow sternly said. *"But aunty,"* the little girl cried out. *"It's for your good. I need you to know how to protect yourself,"* the woman pressed.

"I can't do it, aunty, I'll hurt it." The woman came from behind the shadow and kissed the little girl's hair. *"Yes, you can."* Rielle watched as the woman disappeared and was now standing in front of her. *"What are you waiting for?"*

"Aunt Anais." Was this another dream? Rielle heaved a sigh. It wasn't real, Callum had told her before. How could it be?

"Aunty, are you real?" she asked the old woman standing in front of her.

"*As real as your consciousness wants me to be.*" the old woman replied, hugging her.

"*I've missed you so much.*"

"*We don't have much time.*"

"*Am I dreaming?*" she asked.

"*You're in a trance. I'm so proud of the fierce woman that you have become. Your mother would have been proud too.*"

"*Why didn't you tell me?*"

"*I couldn't. I made your mother a promise, and I didn't want to lose you.*"

"*Were they in love?*"

"*They're here. You have to go.*"

"*Who?*"

"*You have to go now. Protect yourself . . . protect yourself.*"

The forest became pitch black; her aunt's eyes were bleeding. "*Aunt Anais!*" Rielle screamed, holding her hands. "*Leave now! Protect yourself,*" the old woman flicked her hands. Rielle felt a rush of wind around her, pulling her.

Shaken, Rielle was startled out of her dream. Her cheeks were wet, and her body covered in cold sweat. The sheets were tight around her limbs. Her heart pounded against her chest. Rielle trembled. The dim light enhanced the room. She carefully rolled onto her side and looked at Callum. His features were softer in his sleep. He looked peaceful. Slowly she got out of bed, cautious not to wake him. She walked to the corner of the room and retrieved the journal from her bag. "What am I missing?" she sat down on the chair next to the window and opened the small book, going through the pages. The little girl from her dream, her aunt. "Trance?" she repeated. "The bunny . . . jasper?" She whispered.

Rielle closed her eyes, reminiscing of that day in the forest when she saw the bunny. Her aunt smiled at her and told her that she had done an excellent job. Rielle remembered she had kissed the small animal. *It's all better now.* The sound of her voice echoed in her mind. "I remember, I remember," Rielle said out loud.

The bunny, its legs were injured . . . she healed it. Sharp pain in her head. Rielle winced. Everything started to come back to her. Her aunt, teaching her about spells. Syrah's bullies and how she scared them in the bathroom. Rielle opened her eyes, shocked. It was all in there.

The journal, her aunt's handwriting, the spells—she could read them. She turned to the last page of the journal, and in big letters, it read; *I love you. If you're reading this, it means you have reversed the forgotten spell, so protect yourself.* Rielle traced the letters with her fingers. A small sob came out of her mouth.

All this time, everything her aunt did was to protect her. She wasn't allowed sleepovers, or going to camp with Syrah— it was all for her protection.

Waking up from his sleep, Callum looked around the room and saw her in the corner. Pulling the duvet off him, he sauntered to her.

"You broke the spell." He kneeled in front of her.

Rielle nodded. "It's all there, all of it." A blinding flash was followed by a sharp and quick blast. Callum instantly pulled Rielle on the floor, shielding her body with his. The windows shattered into millions of pieces.

"We are under attack," Raphael slipped into his mind.

"Are you ok? Zachariah? Davide?" Callum called out to them.

"It's mortals," the young warrior said. Gunshots cracked into the air, the bullets flying everywhere, piercing every inch of the house.

"These bullets are engineered to kill us, so stay alive," Zachariah warned.

"Are you okay?" Callum checked Rielle's body, "I need you to stay close to me, mie cehia, and whatever it is you can do to protect yourself, do it, no questions asked." Rielle nodded, still shaken. *"How many of them?"* Callum sent out

"Too many to count. I say, let's have our feast in the living room. I single-handedly picked every furniture in these rooms, and I don't want blood on every one of them," Zachariah replied.

Another blow sounded. It shook the entire house.

"Anytime now, Raphael! Get them in the living room," Callum rejoined.

"I can't. Their helmets are shielding them."

"Now you believe me when I told you they have declared war on us and have been studying us?"

"It doesn't matter; we have a truce," Raphael uttered, irritated that Callum was right.

"How did they find us? I've guarded this place from mortals," Zachariah asked.

A small device was thrown inside the room. Just in time, with Rielle in hands, Callum teleported them out of the room and in the library. It was another blast. A fist of orange flame pushed its way from the bedroom. The walls shattered. Smoke and fire rushed out. Thousands of pieces of glass and steel. The roof collapsed. Alarms, piercing and loud, erupted.

A big piece had come out of the side and the roof of the rooms. Callum had seen the size of the device and was surprised that it did so much damage. "Don't move," he ordered Rielle, and disappeared. *"I've had enough of this shit,"* he communicated to his brothers, his irritation riding high.

"Disarm and wipe their memories. No killing," Raphael specified.

"Mierdei, Raphael! they want to kill us and brought the fight to us, they are militarized and ready for battle, yet you want us to wipe memories."

Soldiers walked inside of the house. "We've got you surrounded. Come out and surrender yourselves," a voice commanded.

"No, Raphael is right. We can't kill them. I have an idea. Just be ready when I tell you," Zachariah sent out to them.

"Well, whatever it is, do it fast because I'm sick of this do-nothing bullshit." Callum trippingly walked to the hall. A bullet flew past his ears.

"I'm coming down, don't shoot, I surrender," Zachariah yelled. He saw Callum's shadow in the corner of the hall and signaled him to stay put.

"Don't do anything stupid, Zach."

"It's ten of them in the house and seven of them outside. Raphael! Stay ready. You too, Callum." Zachariah walked down the broken staircase.

"Or we can rip their weak little hearts out of their chest in two seconds, three max." Callum's voice was hollow and laced with impatience and irritation.

Several guns pointed at him. The soldiers geared up from heads to toes. "Gentlemen, is this necessary?" Zachariah quietly put his hands behind his head.

"Where are the others?" Zachariah took a step further in the middle of the room. "One more step and my men won't hesitate to blow your brain out," the soldier rumbled.

"That would be a huge mistake, officer," Zachariah nonchalantly smiled. "You see, I'm trying to save yours and your fellow officers' lives. I have one brother who is very impatient and eager to rip every one of you apart, and that would enthuse him to beast out."

"Get on the ground. Now! I said get on the ground!" the man shouted.

"If only you asked nicely—" In a blink of an eye, Zachariah teleported out of the room. Guns fired; screams broke out.

"Yellow 5 yellow 5," the officer spoke to his radio transmitter, shouting orders. The men outside rushed inside. Gunshots cracked into the air, as loud as thunder.

"Callum, let's take their toys away from them, now!"

"That was your great idea?" Callum snarled, eluding bullets while molding a quick visual shroud around the armed

soldiers. Speedily he ran a circle around them, removing their weapons from their hands one by one, while Davide promptly went in a circle, punching everyone out of their helmets. *"Now, Raphael,"* Zachariah instructed.

Immediately Raphael took control of their minds. Coaxing the men on the ground, placing their hands behind their heads. "These are some pretty sophisticated weapons." Raphael strode around the room.

"That liquid in the bullet, it's the same thing they injected into Alessio. the same thing Callum had to heal me from." Davide studied the shot.

"We need to bring every weapon home so our researchers can figure out what's in them. How did mortals get hold of something that can kill us?"

"They've been studying us. With Luke and the others abusing and using our gifts against them, it's no surprise they have decided to protect themselves. I'm positive the four women who jumped off the cliff, they were compelled. Unusual things have been happening in their town, and they took the matter into their own hands," Zachariah disclosed. "What do we do with them?"

"Wipe their memories so they don't remember anything. And compel one of them to destroy their lab." Raphael bent down, looking at the handcuff attached to the hip of a soldier on the floor. "This is like our gilt cuff. Where have humans found the rare metal that is forged in our home to create their version of restraints to attack us?" he glared at both his brothers.

"Luke. His men had the same weapons when they attacked me at Devil playground." Zachariah felt his whole body tense.

"Could it be Luke is working with the human? One rebel confessed to me that Bartel was alive and is friendly with the governor." Callum noticed the tautness in Zachariah's jaws.

"Bartel is alive?"

His acute hearing picked on two feet. Callum shifted his attention. "Someone is still out there," he warned. Dread crept down his spine like an icy chill. "Rielle?" He called out her name and rapidly ran in the library. Her journal was on the floor with the rest of the destroyed books, but no sign of her. Adrenaline flushed over his body. Callum reached out to her, using their mental path. Either she was asleep or was knocked out—the last rang truer. Angst looped around in his mind. He bolted out of the room, his disquieting nerves getting the best of him.

So focused on the mortals attacking them, he had forgotten and was arrogant enough to leave her by herself when the attack could have been a distraction all along. Concentrating on her, Callum ran into the woods to the main road. He found a crashed car on the side of the road.

"She was in the car." Davide stood next to him. The young warrior opened the door, summoning what happened. "She's unconscious. The mortal injected her with something."

Sweat drenched Callum's skin. Pure rage vibrated in his veins. His fingers curled into a fist. He couldn't hear his rapid breathing but could feel the oxygen flooding in and out of his lungs. Fast, he ran back to the house. With one hand, he gripped the ranking soldier with his enhanced strength and hurled him on the ground. The man's bone splintered. Both Zachariah and Raphael stepped aside. Davide entered the room, out of breath.

Callum dropped to his knees and seized the man's face. "Where is she?" his voice shattered the silence in the room, rumbling, trembling, almost deadly.

The soldier gasped in pain. "I don't know. We were following orders."

In a tight grip, Callum squeezed his neck. "Where is she?"

"He's telling the truth, brother, I read all of their minds. They were following orders to take us out. They believed we're responsible for the murdered women and three mortals who died in the forest." Zachariah tried to pacify Callum's anger.

Callum squeezed the man's neck, daring his brothers to get between him and the male in his hold. "Who gave the orders?"

"Jao; he is our sergeant. He gave the orders."

The name lingered in Callum's mind. Anger churned inside of him; he released the male who was gasping for air, his face red. He should have killed the officer when he had the chance to.

Chapter 26

Rielle cracked opened her eyelids, and it took her a few seconds to focus on the white ceiling above her. The sun lighting up the room, it took her a minute to figure out where she was. Someone was already in the library when Callum left her. They had attacked her from behind. Turning her head to the other side of the room, she sat upright, moving too quickly, feeling fuzzy from whatever they must have injected into her.

Rielle groaned, wincing at the sudden pain in her head. A shadow was outside the room. She rose to her feet, hiding behind the door. As soon as the door opened, without hesitation, she threw a sucker-punch.

"Son of a bitch, Rielle."

"Jao?" Rielle ran to him and hugged him. "Am I glad to see you. I'm so sorry you got involved in this. I promise we'll find a way out of here."

"Is it you in there? Do you remember who I am?"

"Of course, what are you talking about?"

"I had to get you out there. I'm so sorry I didn't come for you sooner." He pulled her in and embraced her, kissing her temple.

Rielle pulled out of his arms. "It was you? You attacked me?"

"I didn't attack you. I just injected you with a sedative. I didn't want to take any chances of him tracing us."

"You ordered the attack?" Pacing around, Rielle ran her hands through her hair. "You have no idea what you've done. They will die, Jao. All of your men are probably dead by now."

"I did it for you. I saved your life. When you didn't come home after the café burned down, I just knew that something was wrong. But Syrah convinced me that you needed some space. I'm sorry, Rielle. I've let you down, I was careless. You're safe now. He can't get to you here."

"He?" Rielle asked, confused.

"That abomination, that thing that kidnapped you. I warned you to be careful, and things were happening in Kannan. You should have listened to me. I was so focused on other things, I've left you vulnerable and unprotected." He moved toward her, and slowly, he touched her face.

"Jao, I wasn't kidnapped."

"Shh . . . shh . . . it's ok. I know you were under this demon influence like the governor's wife and the other women. Even with the sedative, it's going to take a while before you get back to yourself."

"Callum didn't kill these women, nor am I under his influence," Rielle defended, walking to the other side of the room. Her instincts were screaming danger at her.

Jao frowned. His cheeks turned red. "You mean to tell me you fucked him of your own accord?"

Shocked at his tone, Rielle gasped. "Excuse me, who I sleep with is none of your business."

"Two weeks ago, we had an anonymous tip about a house on the hill where four people who fit the profiles of those who have been terrorizing our town reside." He took a couple of big strides in her direction. Rielle forced herself to step back. He was that menacing. "Imagine my surprise watching him fucking you on that kitchen counter when a couple of officers and I went to check it out. I told myself that it couldn't be. You must have been under his magic tricks like the many whores who fuck these freaks at the gentlemen club. So I went to your place and waited for you. I kept going by your place, but you never did come home." He kept advancing on her. "How could you do this to me? To us?" He howled.

Alarmed, Rielle didn't recognize this man in front of her. The Jao that she knew was caring, sweet. This man was anything but. "There was never an us."

"Whose fault is that?" he yelled, irritation on his face. "I've given you plenty of time, I've done everything to hint at the two of us, and never did you take a chance on us. This freak came out of nowhere, and you fucked him like a cheap whore without even knowing what and who he is."

Rielle's hands cracked across his face hard, causing his face to reel. A flicker in his eyes, she knew that she had made him angrier. Scarily, he towered over her. "Jao, you're my friend, and I don't want to hurt you." Anger boiled inside of her.

"Hurt me!" He laughed as he grabbed her wrists. His hold was firm. Rielle tried to pull free. The entrance door kicked down. Feet walked toward them. Jao looked at her, a smirk on his face. "I'm sorry, Rielle. It's for the good of the town."

"What are you talking about?" Rielle's eyes widened. An army of Arcadien rebels walked into the room, armed. "What did you do? Jao, what have you done?" A tall, good-looking man walked into the room. Rielle wondered why he seemed familiar.

Deep-set piercing eyes, He had the same build as Callum, nearly the same facial expression and the same eyes. His hair was cut shorter. His eyes zoomed in on her; they darkened, and his brow creased. Fear swept over her.

An evil look split across his face. He had no warmth to him, no emotions, and it sent shivers down to Rielle's spine; it was soul chilling.

"Such a small human, yet yields so much power." He walked around her as if studying her.

"What do you want with me?"

"My brothers didn't tell you?" he grinned. "It is so like them to withhold the truth from people they say they are protecting."

"Well, I'm asking you." Rielle held his gaze.

Luke scowled, intrigued at her courage. She was scared, yet daring. "Help me change the world."

"And what if I refuse?" Rielle continued.

"You have no say in the matter. You never did." Luke looked at his men, then back at her. "Take her."

Protect yourself, her aunt's voice echoed in her head.

Two men approached her; survival mode kicked into Rielle. She flicked her hands; both men went flying on the wall, stunned that she did that. "Not without a fight." She stared Luke down and saw a hint of approval on his face. Two more men approached her. A chant came to her mind. Holding her hands in front of her, she sang the words in her head.

Luke stood rooted in place, amazed. Watching all five of his rebels choked, gasping for air, blood coming out their mouth. He smiled. "Kill them, kill them all," he encouraged her.

Rielle felt a buzzing in her mind. It was nefarious and terrorizing. *"Kill them."* His voice in her head was ominous. *"Kill them, Rielle. Now!"* Rielle shivered, a fragment of her mind fighting to give in to his demand. A warm sensation coursed through her mind. She recognized it. It was Callum. She felt his worries and his fears. The feelings were too great to ignore.

Eyeing Luke, she focused on him. "Lachan ale ate," she whispered.

Immediately, Luke was on his knees, coughing. "Fascinating." A deafening diabolical laugh bellowed through the room. In a speedy blur, Luke stood in front of her. His fist connected to her face. The force of his blow caused her head to reel as it slammed her into the wall behind her. Rielle fell hard on the floor, unconscious. "Take her to the car!" Luke roared. Her fierceness appalled him, and that she was able to bring him down on his knees.

"You said you weren't going to hurt her."

Luke shifted his attention to the corner of the room. He had forgotten about the mortal man. "Your work here is done," he growled.

"I did what you asked me, now it's your turn. Release the governor from your mind control. And while we're at it, you and your kind can get the fuck out of our town," Jao scorned. In zero seconds, Luke was towering over him and thumped his head to the wall. One . . . two . . . three times.

Chapter 27

*C*allum picked up the large bed and threw it against the wall. He was a ticking time bomb. The more he couldn't reach out to her or sense her, the more he was ready to explode. He needed to fight something or someone. He craved to kill someone, anyone. For the brief second, she was in his head. He'd picked up her distress, and it led him here. "We're too late." He punched the wall. There was a cold burning to his rage, and it scared Raphael. He'd seen that look before in their father's eyes. *"We need to wheel him in, or this is going to be bad for the two of them,"* Raphael communicated to Zachariah, shielding Callum from their dialog.

"Cut him some slack. You'd react the same way too," Zachariah rolled his eyes. The look on Raphael's face indicated that, as always, he had to take one for the team.

"Callum, you heard Davide. She brought Luke to his knees. She's not only beautiful, but she's also fierce, your mate. Besides, the mortal is dead," Callum growled; his fiery eyes met Zachariah's. His pupils dilated, the iris around them flashed purple. "Oh shit!"

Callum leaped to him, adrenaline pumping through his veins. "You dare call my mate beautiful." He gripped Zachariah by the throat, closing off his air and almost crushing his windpipe. "How dare you? Are you challenging me?"

Zachariah made a choking noise. His face was turning red. Fighting back was not an option as he didn't want to incite Callum. *"Now would be the time to do your calming tricks, Raphael. But no pressure. Our brother is just choking the life out of me."*

"I told you we should have wheel him in," Raphael scolded. "Callum, listen to me! She's alive, and now is not the time to beast out on us."

Callum set his jaw, fighting to get himself back under control. *He wants her. Jealous. Mine.* He sucked in deep, exhaled, and inhaled again. Zachariah was his brother. His baby brother. He still couldn't release him.

"Callum!" Raphael used the deep, commanding tone he rarely did with his brothers. "Let him go. Now!"

A growl. Reluctantly, Callum released his hand. Zachariah crunched over and coughed. He choked and spluttered, his hand clutching at his neck. "Seven hells, I'm done taking one for the team."

"You shouldn't have called his mate beautiful, knowing he's a mad man in heat," Raphael rebuked, his eyes still on Callum.

"Hell to you both," Zachariah managed to choke out, his words rough, grating.

Still, on edge, Callum stepped away. "I'm sorry, brother, I don't know what came over me."

"We need to find your mate, so I need you to control yourself, guardian. Can you do that?" Raphael said, still in a commanding tone. Callum nodded. "Good. The mortal is dead. Luke killed him, so he paid for his actions. Now we find Bartel, we find Luke, and we get your mate. If not, then the gods help us all because it will be the end of us."

Chapter 28

A large canvas hung on the walls; The bar rounded into the room, with a high wooden stool enclosing it. A jazzy tune was playing in the background. Luxurious high ceiling lights dangled over each table in the almost filled room, creating a dark, intimate atmosphere. A few men sat down in a remote corner, with women practically hurling themselves at them.

"It seems like this is the place to be if you're a big shot in this town," Zachariah slipped into his brothers' minds.

"Evening, guys, how can I be of service?" a young dark-haired woman wearing a revealing two-piece set smiled and approached them.

"Bartel is mine." "Take us to Bartel," Callum growled, eyeing the room.

"I'm sorry, sir, there's no one under that name here." Her eyes gave away the false sincerity in her voice.

"This wasn't a request." Callum's eyes narrowed on her, rigid, cold, and hard.

"No need to scare her off, brother. You can ask nicely." Zachariah smiled charmingly at the woman, compelling her. She smiled at him and bit her lips. "Right this way, sir."

"See, a little bit of flirting does the trick. Rielle is a saint for putting up with that barking of yours," he mocked. Callum growled, his eyes shooting daggers at him.

"Stop provoking our brother, or next time I'll just let him choke the charm out of you." Raphael queued in behind Callum as they followed the young woman to an elevator.

The elevator had grey marble walls and floor, a wooden railing, and three pushbuttons. The young woman pushed the second button; it activated the elevator. The door slid shut, and the elevator rose to the third floor without stopping.

"They know we're here," Raphael uttered.

The elevator door opened. Four Arcadien rebels stood in front of them, their guns pointed at them.

"Thank you for the lift. Now you can get yourself out of here with the rest of the people downstairs." Zachariah pushed the woman behind him, compelling her once more. She smiled, promptly hard-pressed herself into him, and kissed him.

"Zachariah!" Raphael snarled, stepping out of the elevator. "Our trouble is not with you. Drop your weapons. We are here to see Bartel." He continued raiding their minds, realizing their weapons were the same as the ones with which the mortals attacked them.

In a blurry flash, Callum went around them. One by one, a thumping sound, as each one fell on the floor. "Speak for yourself," Callum said, a blood-spattered heart in his left hand. He dropped it on the ground and kneeled, wiping his hands on one of the rebel's face. He stepped over the lump of bodies on the floor and strode to the door across the hall. Raphael and Zachariah glared at each other, following his lead.

Callum opened the door, and immediately guns blazed at him. A bullet grazed his left shoulder. Instantly he curved to the left side of the door. Pain ran through his upper body. *"They weren't joking about these bullets,"* he raged, adrenaline running through his veins.

"Take cover!" Raphael screamed. In seconds, he was next to Callum. Bullets flew all through the wall and over their heads. *"Mierdei,"* he scolded, surprised that Callum was bleeding.

"It's just a scrape," Callum breathed and disappeared. Moments later, the gunshots stopped. Silence fell inside of the room.

"He's going to get himself killed," Raphael grumbled, walking inside of the room. Three mortal men were on the floor. Dead.

"I don't want to hear it," Callum warned, and sauntered into the next room. Four enhanced Arcadien stood around Bartel.

"At last," the grey-haired man with brown eyes said, nodding.

Callum took a step forward, but Raphael stopped him. "Patience, brother." In a frozen moment, his eyes flicked from the rebels to Bartel. "I don't want to kill you. Rebels or not, I'm responsible for your lives as your leader. Surrender yourselves, and I'll show you mercy." Raphael's voice shattered the silence in the room, rumbling, almost dangerous. His face was unreadable, mystifying, warrior of old, and king. Nervousness read on the faces of the rebels as they recognized who stood in front of them. Unsure, they looked between Raphael and Bartel.

"What are you waiting for? Kill them," Bartel yelled.

At fast speed, the enhanced rebels leaped toward them. Immediately all four of them froze in the air. A quick second later, in a ghostly crusade, Raphael's blade cut through them. One by one they hit the ground. Raphael soared on Bartel, pushing him against the wall and gripped him by his shirt. "You've betrayed our people. You've betrayed me," he said angrily.

"I'm freeing our people. We are powerful, but we hide. Why do we hide, who we are, and our gifts, when we have the world at the tip of our hands?" the older man puffed.

"I trusted you. I mourned you like a son mourns a father. We all did. We buried you," Raphael thundered.

"You call it nobility, but I call it naïveté. You were always too naïve to understand what's going on. Open your eyes, son; this isn't about Luke being a ruler or betraying you. It was never about him. This is about us taking over as we reigned centuries ago before we had to share the world with the humans and others, before we went into hiding."

Raphael's eyes widened. "We?"

The older man chuckled, a mischievous smirk on his face. "I warned you about trusting them." Puzzled, Raphael invaded his mind at full force using his gifts. "Did you think Luke could escape on his own?" the old man laughed.

"No," Raphael said dismayed, releasing his hold. He stepped away and stared at his brothers. Tremor filled his brain.

"This is bigger than you. Neither your brothers nor you can't stop it."

Callum's qualms went into overdrive. The defining silence of Raphael alerted him that things had taken a turn for the worse. With force, he snagged Bartel up and rammed him into the wall. He didn't have time for riddles and certainly not for Bartel's divinity speeches. Not when Rielle was in danger, could be in danger at any given time.

"My brother is indeed noble, but I am not. He is too merciful to rip that traitorous heart out of your chest, but I am not. So you will tell us what you know. Starting with, who are we? And most importantly, where Luke is hiding?"

"You've always been the mongrel of the pack. No discipline, no self-control, a violent dog."

"Is that so?" Callum's hands were around his neck; he squeezed, choking him. Bartel's eyes became round as he panicked for air, his desperate arms flailing, clutching at Callum's hands.

"Callum, we need him alive." Raphael said aggravated. "A few members of the council are working with Luke. His escape, Bartel's death, it was all planned. War is what they want. Mortals or Arcadien, it doesn't matter. They want dominion, and Luke as the head."

"All the reason why we should just kill him now." Zachariah cast his eyes on Bartel.

Eyes once filled with admiration and reverence that was now replaced with disdain and dislike. He had looked up to the old man while growing up.

"We kill him now. We won't be able to locate Rielle. I didn't get it out of his mind."

With force, Callum threw Bartel on the ground, his foot over his head. "You said it yourself I'm the mongrel of the pack. So you know I'm unfamiliar with my brothers' moral compass, always have." He pressed his foot harder. "I won't hesitate to crush your skull with my sole foot. By the time my brothers get to you, it will be too late. So I'm going to ask you one last time—where is Luke?" his low guttural tone emitted a thrilling vibe in the room. Both Zachariah and Raphael were afraid of what he might do next.

"Callum," Raphael pleaded. As much he wanted Bartel's head, this wasn't the way. Justice needed to serve, the council members needed to be outed, but Bartel was the key to do that.

"You won't find her," Bartel hissed. "By now, I'd say he was having his way with the *Hafei*. She's an abomination to the natural order of our people, but she has a purpose until we get rid of her like her traitorous father."

"He knew," Davide calmly said, putting two and two together, and looked in Zachariah's direction. "Bartel knew. They knew about Rielle. Finding Gabriel's letter in your father's study was a setup. They knew your curiosity would drive you to the mortal realms, and they were confident Callum and Raphael would cross the realm looking for you." His eyes rounded; he raised his brows. "Unless . . . they needed you guys out of Arcadin. But why?" the young warrior continued.

"Speak." Callum roared his foot, pushed harder against the old man face.

"Leverage—without their guardian and their leader, our people won't want to fight back. Not when they know they won't win the war without the three of you. And the soon to be the heir and their mother is of importance," Bartel yelped.

In a nanosecond, Raphael snatched Bartel from Callum's foot grip and heaved him against the hedge of the upper tier of the room. His clenched jaw and hunched form displayed an ill feeling that was frightening and forceful. "You dare threaten my unborn child and my mate?" Raphael gritted his teeth; his face was harsh with suppressed rage.

"She's my niece. I would never harm her," Bartel admitted "But they would, if only to make you understand that this is real, and you can't stop it."

"Leave us," Raphael blurted out

"What, Raphael, no."

"Leave us! It isn't a request. It's a command," Raphael roared, his eyes fixed on the man in his grip. The last time he felt ire and resentment churning inside of him like this was the night their father killed their mother. He didn't want his brothers to see him in this state. He urged to rip Bartel's eyeballs out and putting it on a display for those who betrayed him as a reminder of who he was.

Raphael's thoughts echoed in their mind, Callum recognized the rumble of fear and fury whipping inside of his brother. Their curse—Callum felt it in Raphael's rage. The betrayal, the guilt after killing Bartel would muddle Raphael up, and he couldn't let that happen.

"If anyone is killing anyone, it's going to be me, brother. I can't let you go that road knowing what it'll do to you."

"We need to find Luke; I want to put an end to this before it's too late."

"Leave it to me."

"Threatening my mate and my unborn child, he's no longer yours to end." Raphael's narrowed eyes, rigid and cold, held Bartel's gaze.

"Rightly so. But I know you, brother, this will haunt you, and we can't afford that. So trust me. I will not let anything happen to Priscilla or your child, I promise you." *A little help here,"* Callum slipped into Zachariah's mind.

"I say he deserves whatever he gets."

"We both know what guilt does to us. Knowing our brother, do you want him to feel and bear the guilt of killing the one man he looked up to, after father?"

"What are you going to do?"

"*Take Raphael outside. Davide and I will get Luke's location even if we beat it out of Bartel.*"

"*I must ask, are you going to kill him?*"

"*No, I have other plans for him, but he's going to wish he was dead.*"

"*Make it hurt.*" "Callum has a point, brother. you looked up to Bartel, and he was a father figure to you, so anything you do to him will eat at your conscience and your guilt. You won't be able to help yourself; that's how it is. Let Callum deal with him," Zachariah uttered.

Raphael reluctantly let go of Bartel. His voice, jarringly low, thundered into the room. "I will kill every one of you who concocted this plan, remember these last words before you die. Kill him, hurt him, I don't care, I already buried him seven moons ago." He walked out of the room, followed by Zachariah.

Chapter 29

"You're not going to try to attack me again, are you, if I remove the chains from your wrists?" Rielle felt the chains digging into her wrists and around her ankles. Luke stared at her, his icy silver eyes warning her that he would hit her again if she tried anything. Her face was swollen, and her whole body hurt. She winced, moving on the cold concrete floor, unsure of how much more she could take before giving in to his demands. Whatever the witch did to her, she could fight it, but it was harder to fight when these chains made her feel weak. "Take them off," Luke instructed his men.

"I underestimated her resolve, she's fighting the potion. If you remove them, she'll gain her strength back," the witch protested.

"I believe you will take care of it this time if she does. You're a mage after all, no?" Luke snapped; he was beginning to tire of the witch's failures.

Rielle touched her wrists, feeling a bit of strength in her. Right away, she flicked her left hand. The rebel in front of her flew across the room. Two more rebels ran toward her. Rielle held them to a stop, rooted in place. She mumbled a few words under her breath.

The witch raised her hand, chanting a spell. "No. Let her." Luke stopped her. The rebels screamed in discomfort, kneeling, blood coming out of their mouths and their ears. Instantly both men fell flat on their faces.

Her eyes squinted, Rielle glared in Luke's direction; a burning sensation akin to aggression arose within her. "Pye a te sou genou," she spoke the unfamiliar words with vigor.

Luke sneered, enticed, fighting himself not to give in. "You're tenacious, and it's starting to aggravate me." Immediately he was on her. He gripped her neck and threw her. Rielle huffed in pain, her back hitting the wall behind her. "Leave us."

"I don't think it's a good idea, Luke." The witch took a step toward them.

"I said, leave us!" he shouted. He grabbed Rielle's hair, dragging her to the corner of the room. "Willing or not, you will do what I want," he threatened, cuffing her hands again.

"You are nothing but a soulless brute, yet he still blames himself for what he did to you. You don't deserve his integrity," Rielle spat, suddenly feeling dizzy.

"You think it a coincidence my brothers found you? They knew about you, mortal, and they're not protecting you from me. They're protecting themselves and our people from you." Luke watched her, a sinister look on his face. "The look on your face tells me that they haven't been honest with you."

"I would never hurt anyone." Rielle felt the room spun with her.

"Yet they don't trust that you won't. I read your mind— why do you think my brother bounded you without giving you a choice, knowing that you'd deny him? It's not because he couldn't control himself or that he cares for you. It's because the elders ordered him to. They sent him down here to scout you."

"No."

"You are the daughter of a noble guardian and the last pure enchantress in over centuries. You are a threat to them, and they are afraid of you. Did my brother tell you why I started the war? Why your father got killed?"

Rielle shook her head. "No, Callum wouldn't lie to me." She became scorching hot. Dampness dripped down her body.

"Your father was killed because he defied the elders when they found out your mother was pregnant with you, as they wanted him to kill her."

"You're lying." Rielle felt woozy. Whatever the witch gave her was now working.

"Am I? Didn't Raphael try to kill you once he found out what you could do? And Zachariah, he admitted to you that he was searching for you. It's no coincidence."

"Callum . . ."

"My brother took advantage of you, Rielle, they all did." Luke held her face. "You can read my mind if you want. I know you're a telepath." Immediately he took control of her mind, manipulating her. He planted the death of her father in her head.

"No." The image of Callum standing over a man who looked much like her conveyed in her mind.

"My brother lied to you, Rielle."

The images drilled into her mind like a horror movie scene. She saw Callum plunge the blade into her father's heart, and it seemed real. *"I'm not what you think I am, Rielle. If I had to do it all again, I would."* Callum's words echoed in her mind. Wanting it to stop, Rielle's breathing hardened. "Make it stop." Luke had complete control of her mind, manipulating her thoughts and conveying the same images repeatedly into her brain. "Make it stop!" Rielle screamed, a sharp pain behind it. The lights in the room flickered. The windows splintered into loads of pieces.

Luke watched. He watched the raw emotions in Rielle eyes. Then he smiled, he knew. "You're nothing but a simple mortal to him."

"No, lies." *"I'm a killer Rielle, I've killed, and I'd do it again."* Callum's words reverberated in her brain, and everything turned black.

Chapter 30

*C*allum walked along the covert drive. His chest tightened, he opened his mouth, but no sound could make it past. He felt her anger and her distress; it robbed him of his senses and replaced it with something dreadful. His muscles tensed; pure adulterated fear swept over him. *"Mie cehia,"* he called out to her, but encountered plain dimness.

His chest throbbed—the pain like a dagger taken to his heart. Callum squeezed his eyes shut, willing the pain away; everything around him stopped, his head hammering. Concentrating on the pain, an ominous feel coursed through him, He hardly heard Raphael warning him off.

A tight fist, quick, strong, and potent hit his jaw with force. Callum could taste the cut in his mouth. Forgetting his aching, with two hands he grasped the rebel head, bringing his face down sharply onto his knee cap. Blood flowed from the rebel's broken nose as he staggered backward. Another rebel ran speedily, he drew his fist back and plowed it into Callum's stomach. Feeling the hit to his guts, Callum realized his opponent was enhanced as well.

Irritated, Callum whisked him away, pinning him hard to the wall. With a quick movement, he perforated his blade to his heart.

"We're coming to you," Raphael voiced firmly in his head.

"Not the plan," Callum retorted.

"It is, when your head is not right. What the hell was that?" Zachariah scolded.

"I lost focus for a second."

"A second is all that is needed to get you killed. We're here to get Rielle, and you losing focus isn't part of the plan." Callum heard the wariness in Zachariah's voice.

The old barn was isolated in the wood, next to it was a farm with cows and sheeps. Callum knew it was all a front. Luke was smart, and the metal door was proof enough.

"No man at the door," he sent out, and took a step forward. His feet trod lightly. An alarm rang. His enhanced hearing picked on the feet dragging on the floor toward him. *"Mierdei! Heat sensor."* More than a dozen rebels were already out front, weapons aiming at him.

"Move to your left," Raphael commanded. Rifle shots broke the eerie silence of the wood. One after another, the rebels dropped to the floor.

"Next time wait for me to move before you start shooting people up," Callum rebuked, wiping a drop of blood off his face

"More are coming," Zachariah warned.

Callum glanced at the clans of men running en masse toward him. A wicked smile curved around his mouth. At full tilt, in one fluid movement, he snapped two rebels' necks and stabbed his blade into another one. Shots fired in succession; one grazed his forearms. Callum gulped in pain. He hated those guns.

"Mierdei Raphael aimed at them! Not me."

"You're okay, and it's just a graze."

Four pairs of rough hands tried to seize him. Callum speedily moved to the right. Someone leaped on his back. Brusquely, Callum flipped him over and butted his head. A raging fist hit his left temple. Something dug at his side, sending a firing electrical shock to his body. Callum bent on his knee, frozen all of a sudden. Another blow met his face, and he dropped on the ground.

"Don't shoot. Don't shoot, Luke wants him alive!" a voice screamed out. "Take him inside. Search the perimeters. The others aren't too far."

Zachariah paced around. The night suddenly went quiet. Wherever they were, though far away from mortals, guns were blazing as loud as thunder. Someone, somehow, would wonder what was happening. "We can't risk the human to start asking questions and have them come here. It will be a massacre."

"I know," Raphael joined.

"We have to go in. Callum was motionless, Raphael, whatever they dug in him. If Luke gets to the mountain with these weapons, it won't be a fair fight."

"Trust our brother. He can handle himself."

"Not when Rielle is involved. You saw him earlier. He lost focus, and I felt the fear warped in his mind. Something happened, and my gut is telling me Luke has his claws on Rielle's mind. This isn't a fair fight."

"Guys, we've got company," Davide interrupted.

Raphael gazed toward the shadow of the dark woods. His senses heightened, picking up on the feet and the motion of bodies. "Leave no one alive." His brows furrowed—the words more like a command than a statement.

Chapter 31

*C*allum grimaced, pain throbbed on his side. He breathed slowly, squeezing his eyes shut, his body trying to heal itself. No blood was coming out of him, but his tissues felt like they were on fire. If Luke were to gain entry to the mountain with these weapons, it would be a bloodbath. And whoever in the council was working with Luke, feeding him their technology to use against them, he was going to take pleasure in teaching them a lesson. He glanced around—no windows, only an open steel door.

"Raphael." He reached out but remembered the witch working with Luke might have the place spellbound.

A steady gushing noise was coming from outside of the door, and beneath it was the sound of distant footsteps. The footfalls became steadily louder. Callum writhed to stand.

Whoever stepped into this room was likely not to get out in one piece.

"You're awake." A shiver ran down his spine. Luke came inside the room, accompanied by a few rebels and the witch.

"Where is she?" Callum flung at him. His heavy weight rammed Luke against the concrete wall.

"Stay where you are! This is between my brother and me." Luke forcefully tossed him in the middle of the room and shouted at the rebels walking toward them. Callum landed on his wounded side. Immediately Luke was on him and drew a fist to his face. Gripping his shirt and holding him by his collar, he brought him to his feet. "You are weak!"

Callum tilted his head back and slammed it into Luke's head with every bit of the little strength he had. "Yet you have me in the one thing that restrains our powers. I'd say it's the opposite." Luke sauntered backward, his eyes, menacing, were silver-white. He disappeared from the room. Callum shuffled to his left side, awaiting his attack. A sharp object thrust on his side, Callum growled in pain, and his wound began bleeding openly.

"I'd have thought by now you would know I don't fight fair, brother," Luke hissed. A sudden gush of pain jolted throughout Callum's body. His abdomen ached, his left side strained, and his whole body weakened. He dropped to the ground. "You thought you'd just walk in here and win?" Luke maniacally laughed.

"If you call stabbing me with mortals' weapons to weaken and kill us, winning, then I overestimated you all my life," Callum said.

"You can't stop me, and you can't stop what's about to happen."

"She won't do it," Callum growled, the pain on his side eating at him.

"She won't have a choice; you're leverage, and despite my best effort to turn her against you, for some reason she still sees you as a human being and not the beast that you are."

"Did you know the same council members that plotted with you are plotting to kill her?"

"I'm guessing Raphael isn't too happy learning about the betrayal of those he held in much higher regard—they committed treason against him. Speaking of our dear brother, where is he? Or should I say, where are they? I know he wouldn't let you wander in the woods by yourself." Luke bent his finger, poked it into Callum's wound. "This looks bad; you should heal yourself," he mocked.

Callum scowled. The pain increased in waves. "After all these times, you still can't see how they are playing us. We are nothing but pawns to them."

"You're right, and unlike Raphael, I know. I've always known, but I'm going to let you on in the secret—none of the council members will be alive to see her. Not even the elders. I'm going to murder every one of them." Luke moved away from Callum and walked to the opposite side of the room. "Bring her in," he commanded.

Chains rattled. Callum's breathing hardened. Her face was swollen, her wrists and ankles were bloody. She looked frail and tired, an uppercut underneath her eyes—something broke inside of him. Rigid with fury, Callum clenched his fists, hungry for destruction. Ready to explode, he broke the gold cuff, all but forgetting the pain on his side, he leaped toward Luke and tackled him on the ground. Holding him down, Callum repeatedly whacked his face.

A shot rang, a bullet hit his right shoulder. His dark possession awoke; in a blur, Callum stood before the trigger happy rebel and crushed his head against the wall. Once, twice.

The other rebels stood still, motionless. Callum watched them, his eyes threatening, indicating that he could easily tear apart every one of them. Sensing Luke behind him, he spun around, but it was already too late. Luke stabbed his wounded side, knocking the breath out of him. Callum slumped to his knees.

Rielle quickly ran and kneeled in front of him. "I'm so sorry, I shouldn't have left you alone in the library," he said.

"You're bleeding." She checked his wounds. Her touch alone sent a shiver down his spine.

"Just a graze." Callum forced a smile.

Rielle's watery eyes enlarged, she glared at Luke. "You're bleeding," she repeated. Her breathing slowed. There was deadness to her, a stillness, with ire.

Resentment and fears radiated off her skin. Callum could smell the darkness in her. Hell, he could see it. Luke was manipulating her into giving in to her emotions, and he was using him. "Look at me, Rielle, look at me." His voice was gentle, low, and heart-rending.

Callum cupped the nape of her neck, his fingers sliding in the thick of her wild curls. "No, no, don't," Callum continued. Rielle moved away from him; she wasn't listening. She was fighting something back, and she was losing. Callum worried he wouldn't get through to her.

Standing in the middle of the room, the hallucinations of Callum holding above her father with a blade displayed in Rielle's head. Adrenaline raced through her system, adding to the anger, and the building waves of sheer energy erupted inside of her. Spells floated through her mind; a wicked feel draped around her. A jolt of energy came out of her, clos-ing her palms. "Oxigen, Pa kenbe ex okulus," she whispered under her breath.

Callum's head pounded, every cell in his body screamed for oxygen. In his peripheral, everyone in the room, Luke included, was fighting and gasping for air. As if the room had sucked all the air around them. Feeling his muscles straining, the thoughts in his head turned from fear to a dizzy confusion. Luke and the rebels fell to their knees. Callum was sure they were experiencing everything he was. Whatever she was doing was affecting them all.

Her eyes, darkened, were harsh; he felt the energy pouring out of her. It was like a hurricane inside of her. Wheezing, the conscious part of his brain beckoned her; he had to get through her, and it wouldn't be long now till he blacked out, as the blackness was assailing his mind.

Darkness swathed Rielle, filling her with a deep dread. Red and black streaks danced in front of her. She couldn't remember and wasn't aware of anything but the deep urge to harm Luke and his men. *"Rielle, stop, mie cehia,"* Callum's voice brushed her mind. His anguish and fears immediately snapped her out of her daze.

She looked around the room. Luke was on his knee, coughing up a storm, his men too, and Callum was bent on his side, his one hand supporting him and the other on his wounds. The coldness she felt seconds ago was gone entirely. A desperate hot wave came over. Rielle's heart beat rapidly in panic, and heat rushed through her body, at the thought of her hurting him. Quickly she moved back toward him. "I'm sorry, I'm sorry, I don't know what came over me," she frantically apologized.

By slow, torturous degrees, the coughs eased in intensity and then slowly, slowly passed.

"That was amazing!" Luke's voice boomed in the room, a wry smile on his face. He strolled to them. Briskly he grabbed Rielle's hair and painfully yanked her to his chest. Rielle yelped; her hands automatically went to her head.

"Get your fucking hands off her!" Callum yelled, raising himself.

"You do anything stupid, and I will break her neck. Even with your speed, you won't get to her on time. Aim your guns to her head. If my brother so much as flinches, blow her brain out," Luke threatened.

Callum roared. He felt helpless and was in excruciating pain with a stabbed wound. Luke was right. He wouldn't get to her on time, not when he felt so weak with whatever spell that witch had cloaked this place. A paralyzed hurt spread through his body. He clenched his fists, hesitant to take a step. He couldn't afford to lose her.

"Restrain him," Luke commanded. A glint in his eyes, he stared at the two of them. "How much do you care for my brother?" Luke asked, leaning into Rielle. She ignored him. Her eyes found Callum's. "You care a lot, don't you? Which is why his life is entirely in your hands. Do as I said, and he lives."

"Go to hell!" she spat out.

A rebel was standing three feet away from them, and casually, Luke took hold of his weapon. He aimed it at Callum's left leg and shot. Callum fell to his knees, his eyes wide with horror, his mouth rigid and opened, his nails digging into the palms of his hands.

A scream tore through Rielle. Her eyes widened, and her pulse quickened. Her heart throbbed; pain shot through her. "You bastard!"

"What do you say, Rielle? Another shot—how about his head this time?" Luke continued, his voice threatening, charged with malice.

"No!" tears welled in her eyes. "I'll do it, whatever it is you want me to do. Just stop," she pleaded.

Chapter 32

*R*aphael, Zachariah, and Davide moved into the shadows as they made their way into the old barn. They must have killed a dozen rebels, if not more. Shaken to have found out that the council was feeding Luke's men to create an army and fight his battle, Raphael's ire increased.

"*My wrath will know no mercy*," he inwardly said, conscious that some of these men needed to be in prison, paying for trivial and crucial crimes they had committed instead of being banished from the mountain.

"Ready for round two?" Zachariah's voice snapped him out of his thoughts. A loud alarm rang off.

Several men were running toward them. Raphael walked in front of them. "They're mine." His hard expression indicated and warned both Davide and Zachariah to stay put.

With full force, Raphael leaped in the air, coming down in the middle of the men who now circled him. "Do you know who I am?" he admonished them. "You've disappointed your leader," his voice thundered into the night. With full force and with alacrity, he pivoted around them as he dragged his silver blade into their chests. Writhing breaths followed; the rebels dropped on the ground.

"Should I be worried about you?" Zachariah squinted his eyes. This side of Raphael he knew existed but had never witnessed.

"You guys don't get to have all the fun," Raphael nonchalantly said, walking ahead and signaling them to follow. "The place is spellbound, so our powers are limited in here."

Instantly, guns fired at them, and four men ran toward them. "I'm so over getting shot at." Zachariah threw his knife at a rebel, spinning as he did so, and yanking the gun from the rebel's hands to fire multiple rounds of shots at their opponents. The men dropped to the ground, their weapons hitting the ground. "Though I hate these weapons, they are of use." Zachariah pulled his knife out of the rebel's head and wiped it on his shirt.

⊲⊳

"You two, go!" Luke shouted at the two men standing in front of the door. The alarm had rung off, and soon after, bullets jingled throughout the isolated ranch, feet rushed. "My commandant, we have to get you out of here. It's a mass slaughter outside of those walls, and our men are losing." A rebel rushed into the room. A blast rocked the side of the building; the walls burst in all directions. The witch raced inside the room. Her brow creased, and face tensed.

"Zakian is dead," she pronounced.

"You mean to tell me my best fighter is dead because your spell didn't weaken my brothers?" Luke's face contorted; his curt voice resounded in the room.

"No, your stupid plans got your best fighter killed," the witch snapped. Boldly she held Luke's gaze. "I've done my job, and judging by the look of your beloved brother on the floor, my spells work fine. Your men not being able to defend themselves is no fault of mine."

His face stippled crimson, Luke stomped into the room and advanced toward her. His eyes popped, and his neck strained. The witch's eyes widened, her hitched breath giving away her apprehension. "Your purpose is significantly being weakened in all of this, yet you think I'd want you by my side."

"We had a deal. We bonded, me by your side is part of our bond. If you had listened to me and stuck to our original plan, your brothers would not be on our doorstep, and you'd be home by now, atoned for what they did to you. We just needed her blood, but your obsession with her magics has made you weak and out of focus."

Luke harshly gripped her by the neck and lifted her in the air. "You pathetic human, I can take your life in an instant." His shrill tone warned of his intents. "But I wonder. You think it'll affect me too, since we are one by blood magic." The witch's eyesight went blurry as she desperately flailed her arms, clutching at Luke's firm hands.

In the room, Davide came in fast and silent. He yanked the weapon from the rebel standing next to Callum as he swung his blade. Immediately after, Raphael punched at the smaller rebel's face. The man swore and stumbled back; Raphael shoved his knife at him.

"Trouble in paradise?" Zachariah sarcastically drew in, his knife gutting another rebel with a tattooed face. He smiled in Luke's direction.

Luke released his hold on the witch. She dropped on the floor, coughing, air flood back into her lungs.

"This is no way to treat your witch brother."

"I would think we'd be in accord, seeing how she tortured you." In a blur, Raphael quickly moved to Callum's side. "Take another step, Raphael, and I will blow her brain out," Luke growled, aiming his gun to Rielle's head.

"You're outnumbered, Luke, it's three of us, and there's only you. Your rebels are dead," Zachariah rejoined.

"And you think I need help to kill all three of you?"

"You've lost your mojo brother; I mean, if you need mortal toys and witches' spells to slow us down, I'd say very much that I alone can kick your pompous ass," Zachariah provoked. The fiery glare in Luke's eyes told him his distraction was working.

"Callum," Raphael called out, but the barring spell in the room was too strong.

In and out of consciousness, the cuts on his side infected, blood clotted around the edges of the wounds. The bullet still in his leg, the slug was eating at his flesh like a virus. Though their powers were weakened, Raphael felt Callum's pain as his healing powers and body were battling whatever infested his body.

Davide was standing next to him, and Zachariah was on the opposite side of the room, none of them would get close to Rielle fast enough if Luke were to pull the trigger. Raphael hadn't felt cornered like this in a long time, and it infuriated him.

The only person who could heal Callum was Callum himself. The magic spell in the room needed to break. "He's not breathing," Raphael spoke, his eyes solely on Rielle, hoping the young warrior next to him wouldn't give away his lie. He needed Rielle's attention. Whatever spell the witch had concocted, if he pushed Rielle enough, he was confident she'd be able to break it.

"What?" Zachariah's eyes enlarged; fear rose in his chest. He noticed Raphael's knitted eyebrows, the subtle grief, and worry on his face. A tumultuous thump in his heart. At once, he flew across the room toward Luke. A shot rang, stopping him midair. Zachariah roared in pain and fell to the floor.

"I told you I'd send you to hell myself," the witch voiced out loud and cocked the loaded gun, ready to fire again. "Still think you don't need me?" She glared in Luke's direction.

A grin on his face, Luke walked over to her. "You surprise me."

She read approval on his face. "Kill them! Get it over with," she uttered.

Luke turned his body around, facing Raphael. "I am feeling noble and fair, my lord, so I won't let you go through the pain of burying both of our beloved brothers, at least not at the same time." He irreverently smiled and bowed his head mockingly. "So choose, my lord, and I'll tell my witch to do her best to save the one you choose, and heal him."

"You call it weakness; I call it strength. It personified our mother's essence. You think you're making a point, but here you are, yet again deluding yourself about your contrived views of your reality. There are only two ways you're getting out of this. Dead, or caged," Raphael calmly said, the foreboding tone of his voice lethal.

"Is that so?" Luke cackled maniacally, as he hunched over Zachariah and stuck his index finger into the wound shot on the lower shoulder left collarbone, a hint of evil glistening in his wicked eyes. Zachariah growled in pain.

Raphael went straight for Luke; his fists powerfully met his jaw. Toppled on his back, instantly Luke kicked his legs, but Raphael was already on top of him, his knuckles harshly pounding Luke's face blow after blow. The witch fired her gun, and the bullet speared the wall above Raphael's head.

Zachariah turned around. Pain jolted throughout his body; his arms were losing tension, and he felt weak. Using the little strength that he had, he grabbed the foot of the witch and pulled her to the ground. The gun flew out of her hand, quickly she pulled away and was on her feet. She hummed a few words; both Zachariah and Davide held their heads, screaming in pain.

Drifted away, Rielle had become a ghost of herself. *"Callum is not breathing."* The words had washed over her, and a dreadful emptiness swam within her. Rooted in place, she had watched it all unfold as she became a shell of herself. Waves of hollowness, dejection pounded at her seeing Callum lying on the ground unmoving. A raw pain swamped her heart. The ripples of agony threatened to drown her body, mind, and soul. Something altered in her, dark, unyielding. It encompassed her. The murkiness of it suffocated her. Her eyes darted around the room, anger and the urge for revenge pulsed through her as she focused on the witch.

"Respire mort de l'esprit," Rielle spoke of the words swirling in her mind, waving her hands. Her power pulsed through her.

A gust of wind with a black smog erupted into the room. The woods and the walls exploded. The witch had lost her concentration. Raphael and Luke rolled on their opposite sides just in time. Dimly, Rielle heard both Zachariah and Davide wheezing.

Moments later, a thick haze rose in front of Rielle, and it expanded gradually toward her. The witch had regained her focus, directing a waning spell at her. Quickly Rielle unfolded her hands at her side and lifted her palms. An ominous force took over her core. It was seducing. The magic within her was tempestuous and rampant. It urged her to ravage and flare up everything. It was entrancing. She shoved her palms forward. The thick haze dissipated from the room. The witch collapsed on the floor; her spell fell apart.

"I should have you killed then," the witch spat. Her eyebrows forced together into a pronounced frown. She started to rise but suddenly was slammed to the ground, unable to move.

"Frape acatar desou pa deplase." Rielle closed her palms. The unfamiliar words and language emitting from her mouth held the witch firm to the ground. "You tried, bitch. You're just not as good as you fool yourself to be," Rielle snarled the iris in her eyes, flashed a darker shade of brown. The witch hands went around her own neck, her eyes widened as she clutched for air

A renewed sense of force hit at Raphael. He felt the vitality of his powers all at once, nearly escaping the blow on his left side when he speedily spun around Luke and his knuckles met his jaw, sending him through two broken walls.

"She broke the spell." Raphael casually slipped into his brothers' minds. *"Rielle, you broke the spell."* A sensation of discomfort swept over him once he brushed her mind, and her dark aura sent a chilling sensation down his spine; trepidation hit at him.

"She's not herself. Her aura is wild and entrancing. Should I stop her?" Davide uttered, his gaze on Rielle.

"No, we don't want to risk her losing more control. I'll deal with Luke. Get Callum to wake up. Zachariah, it was stupid of you to jump on Luke like this," Raphael pronounced.

"*I got shot, our brother's mate is about to go shit crazy with her magics seducing her to the dark side, and yet you're scolding me about jumping on Luke at a time when reason wasn't my priority,*" Zachariah rebuked.

Luke roared back into the room and met Raphael's fists this time as he stumbled backward.

Chapter 33

*C*allum woke up suddenly, every part of his body in high mode. Rielle thoughts, her anger, an ill-omened force looped around her. It took over her consciousness. His eyes took in the room, Rielle stood over the witch on the floor. There was fear and terror on the witch's face. Zachariah and Davide were at a loss for words and actions, Callum realized she had tapped into that part of her. He'd seen it before, sensed it back then, but this was different as her feelings mirrored the same thing he felt when he ended a life. His dark possession roared in bliss, his senses urged him to claw his way to stand. Callum moved to get up, the pain on his ribs was unbearable. He was slowly healing; whatever was spreading through his blood, his body and healing power was fighting. That could mean one thing. She had broken the spell.

"Yes, she had, and if you don't do something about this, it will be too late," Zachariah slid in his mind.

"Zach, you're shot! The virus will spread if not contained," Callum met his gaze.

"I feel it, but your mate has indulged in the Arcadien side of her and is seducing her."

"I'll need some time. Davide, keep Luke at bay."

"I'm not saying the witch doesn't deserve this torture. But Callum, this is ethereal."

"She's not herself," Callum defended, moving slowly toward Rielle. *"Mie cehia."* He forced his way through her head. A frightening buzz filled his head.

Abruptly Rielle turned around. The witch dropped her hands and tumbled to the floor. Uncertain, she stared at Callum. Her eyes locked right on his, her rage like a wildfire poured into him. The flames were roaring in her. She was ready to ignite anything and anyone.

"You can't kill her. This isn't you." Callum sang the words, his voice compelling, using his magics trying to charm her.

"No, you're dead. You're not really here," Rielle shook her head.

"I'm right here, mie cehia. I'm hurt, but my body is healing. You broke the spell."

"You're dead. This is another one of your tricks," Rielle turned to the witch and continued to speak the foreign words. The witch held her stomach immediately. Her wailing agony echoed through the room.

Callum couldn't see what was hurting the woman, but he knew she was in pain. Whatever Rielle was doing to her was internal. *"You can control it, mie cehia. Let me help you."* Rielle felt the enchantment of his voice through her head, a part of her fighting with the mesmerized tone.

"Callum, I don't think using your coaxing ability on her is going to end well for any of us here," Zachariah cautioned. The anger in Rielle's face was clear to see.

"Get out of my head, Zachariah. I need to concentrate."

"I would, but Raphael has filled me on the scenario the first time you did it, and you're playing with our lives here."

"Mierdei! Do you have a better idea?" Callum snapped and shut his younger brother out of his head. Cogently he continued to invoke her mind. The commanding tone of his voice immersed in her thoughts. Rielle hissed, turning around to face him. Her jaw clenched, and her muscles tensed. She wrinkled her nose. Callum watched her face contorted into an expression she had never worn before.

Unexpectedly, Rielle raised her right hand and flicked it. Callum flew across the room, his back hitting the wall. He dropped on the ground. "I'm not your pet. You can't just do your magic tricks on me and expect me to abide," she seethed.

"Now you've just angered her more," Zachariah pestered.

Callum winced at the pain on his leg. *"You think!"* A loud thump, Raphael was forcefully thrown next to him. His face was almost unrecognizable. Luke did a number on him.

"You are a disgrace! And those who chose you over me discredited our people, our father's legacy, and our home,"

Luke roared and stopped in his steps, taking in the scene in the corner of the room. "Hmmh . . . I can taste it. So wild, so commanding and so dark." His attention on Rielle, a genuine smile split across his face.

Forgetting about Raphael and unaware of Callum next to him, he was fascinated by Rielle's vibrations, and the darkness in her was gripping. "Kill her! You want to. She's the reason why I found you. She sent those creatures after you. She killed your aunt, finish her!"

"No!" Callum screamed, Adrenaline ran through him. He grabbed Luke's feet and, with enhanced force, threw him against the opposite wall.

Luke laughed maniacally, raising himself. "My darling brother, rose from the dead?"

"It takes more than stabbing wounds and bullets to have me killed," Callum voiced calmly but lethally.

"I know, brother, which is why I wanted you to see this," Luke whispered under his breath.

Callum's enhanced hearing picked up on the words. His eyes widened, panic came over his face. "I will fucking kill you," Callum thundered, his voice murdering ice cold. Luke had tied himself into her mind using the mage dovetail forbidden dark spell.

"Afraid she'll relish the dark side, brother? All that power, all that magic. What's inside of her is to behold, yet you want her to hide it. You want to tame her, and I want her wild with magic like the burgeoning flowers on our mountain. You don't deserve that power. I do. With a little guidance, she'll have the world in her palm, and I will be unstoppable. But first, she needs to lose her humanity. Right now, she is angry, but she's still mortal."

The images of him standing over a dead Gabriel conveyed to Callum's mind. Whatever ruse Luke had planted in her head, all of a sudden she was confused about it.

"I'm a monster, Rielle, and I'm not what you think I am."

"I would do it all again."

"You do, as I said."

The words were echoing in her head, and they resonated with his mind.

She didn't want to believe that he could have killed her father, but the dovetail spell was in full effect. Worries and griefs had galvanized her anger, strong-arming her mind by using his gifts, Callum made it worse. *"Rielle, look at me. Look at me, mie cehia."* When she ignored him, Callum leaped toward her, and they stumbled on the ground. His body covered her; he gently pinned her hands down against the floor. The way her eyes squinted when she glared at him, Callum gulped nervously.

An uncanny wave of sensations poured into him; he was sweating all of a sudden. His ears were ringing. His bones cracked as if they were coming out of his body. Callum growled in pain, feeling the inside of his stomach detached. And it was getting worse, he was losing his balance.

The room spun with him. Callum dropped on the floor next to her. Rielle hovered over him. The burning aversion emerging in her eyes struck his heart.

"From the beginning, you wanted to control me. You've bonded me to you without my consent. You marked me without my consent. Even now, you're trying to force my mind. I'd rather kill you than spend a lifetime with your constant need to control me."

Her eyes carved into his soul; they dug deep every word she threw at him. There was no tenderness or honey in those beautiful brown eyes he loved, just emptiness. Callum knew it wasn't her talking, it was the dark spell, but still, hearing them cut him overwhelmingly. He was losing her. Seduced by her anger, the darkness inside of her was powering and dominating the other side of her magics. He had to get through to her one way or another.

"Then go ahead, mie cehia, kill me. Without you, in a lifetime, I'm dead anyway," Callum acquiesced. Sorrow encompassed him.

With an unmoving gaze, slowly Rielle breathed as if she was fighting something back and losing. Tears welled up around her eyes. She brought her hands to her side. "It's battling with me; I can't help it. I'm so angry," she confessed. The pain left Callum's body, and relief swept over him. "I hurt you," Rielle sobbed.

Callum gently stroked her face. "I have a hunch it won't be our last. But it's worth it as long as it brings you back to me."

"How mundane and human," Luke's voice snapped in the room. Both Rielle and Callum looked in his direction. "This would be sweet if, in the next few seconds, I don't put a bullet in his skull." He stood over Zachariah, pointing his gun to his face. "Now come with me, Rielle! Unless you only care for one brother."

Rielle looked around the room.

Raphael was unconscious, Callum wasn't fully healthy, and Zachariah bleeding. He had a gun to his face. She would never forgive herself if Luke shot Zachariah.

She gripped Callum's hands, picking on his thoughts. He was in no condition to fight, not after what she had done to him. *"No, I won't let you. It'll be okay. It will give you enough time to heal them and yourself."*

"Rielle . . . You can't open the portal. It will be the end of us."

"You have to trust me."

"I'll be right behind you."

"I know." "I'll come with you." Rielle's eyes met Luke's.

"You try anything clever, I shoot him." Rielle did as she was told. Immediately Luke cuffed her hands. "Whatever connection you have with them, soon enough it will be a thing of the past."

"I feel sorry for you," Rielle answered.

A ball of energy hit Luke. It pushed and knocked him off his feet. The witch held her hands up, intoning a spell. A loud growl came out of his mouth instantly, Luke was back on his feet and rushed to the woman on the floor. Violently he grabbed her by her neck and threw her against the wall, hard.

"After everything I've done for you, you chose her!" the witch cried out.

"You were always a means to an end." Luke gripped her neck tighter as the witch fought for air, until she didn't. Her body dropped on the floor. Luke turned around to face Callum and Zachariah in the room. He smirked. In a flash, he disappeared with Rielle.

Chapter 34

Raphael stood next to Davide, a contrived look on his face. Luke had beat him to unconsciousness, and it became personal for him now. Callum managed to get the virus out of Zachariah and himself, and it was at a high cost. Though his brother wasn't going to admit that he was weak and needed at least a day or two to rest and regain his strength, Raphael knew how much energy and fuel it took for those with the healing gift to restore to health. "Can you still feel her? We need to go!"

"Yeah," Callum answered.

Raphael's nerves heightened as Callum was too calm, and it scared him for the first time. "She's tough, she'll run circles around Luke before she opens that portal."

Callum ignored him and grabbed a couple of guns off the floor. He marched to the door.

"I'm not able to get into his mind," Raphael spoke telepathically to Zachariah.

"He shuts me out too. I worry about him."

"We keep an eye on him. Turning is not an option at this point."

The forest foreboding warned them off. The darkness of the night was practically absolute, a few stars scattered the sky. Even the moon faded through the clouds. Streaks of light bolted through the mist; Callum knew she wasn't far. He brushed her mind—she was still in there, and he worried. How long before Luke gets her to tap into that anger inside of her again?

Tying himself into her mind using the mage spell was reason enough for him to kill Luke. At this point, he didn't care about the portal or the elders who betrayed them. *"I'm on my way to you, amoirei mio,"* He sent out to her, unable to stop the fear taking over his body and senses.

"This way." Davide turned to his left. Immediately all three men were on their knees.

The dark spell lingering in the air hit them at once. Callum growled, remembering the specific tormenting spell.

"Don't give in to your impulses." Raphael gritted his teeth, knowing how deliberate and enchanting the familiar hex could be.

Callum knew he lived his life in danger, but no words could describe what he was feeling this instant. Lost in his fury and the torment his brain was in, he was unable to think clearly, and nothing else mattered.

"Callum, freio," Raphael called out. He'd seen it first in Callum's eyes, the tightness of his muscles—he was giving in and getting lost to the spell. "Mierdei!" Raphael uttered as he glanced around. Davide was battling the guilt he felt for liking his brother's mate, and Zachariah was in excruciating pain, heartbroken, with a secret that was eating him alive. Heaving a sigh, with all his power, Raphael raided their minds all at once as he tried to alleviate them of their burdens mentally, commanding them to fight the spell.

A scream rang out, Callum ran fast toward it. Soon afterward, all three men followed.

Chapter 35

*L*uke clenched his fist. A vein popped out of his forehead. He swung his arm. Suddenly Rielle felt his fist on her face. She stumbled backward, and blood trickled from her nose. "Enough play! You'll do as I say, or next it will be my blade," Luke threatened.

Her vision blurred, Rielle tried not to show that she was hurting inside. What else could she do? A lot of people would die if she gave in to that anger boiling inside of her. After what she had done to Callum, she never wanted to tap into whatever curse or thing was inside of her, although that was what Luke wanted. "I'm thirsty," she whispered, crumbling to the ground. Her legs gave way. She was weak, thirsty, and her face was burning.

He dragged her for miles into the forest until they found the portal. "We're here." Luke smiled, standing in front of vast wild hibiscus flowers. Rielle felt the energy hammering this side of the forest. "Home sweet home," he uttered and pulled a wooden piece out of his long coat, then turned to her. "Get up! You try anything clever again, my brothers won't know the difference between your head and your legs if they find your body." Roughly he pulled her back on her feet, uncuffing her wrists.

Rielle tossed her arms. Luke's body flew the opposite side of her. "Arme van fo pa kenbe exhaulus andeye," she spoke. Immediately a strong gusty wind went around Luke, lifting him, the air thrusting him hard on the ground. "Ak san sou ou ekle e loraj." Lighting flashed; thunder roared; Luke barely escaped a tree breaking in two.

He disappeared for a moment. Then next, he punched Rielle's abdomen. She cried out, crouching on the ground. She curled her body into a fetal position. Pain seared through her, eating at her stomach. She gasped, a single tear sliding down her face.

"Get up!" Luke kicked her and pulled her by her hair.

Pressure built inside of her; she had enough of the abuse. Everything shut down. Her mind pushed together; a murkiness took control of it. It engulfed her.

"*I'm sorry.*" Rielle thought of Callum.

The wind howled. "Du feu," Rielle whispered, feeling a surge that came from the ground. The trees around them leaped to life in flames. Luke quickly released her, his eyes sparkled with admiration. The expression on his face was reverent.

The feeling of control ran through Rielle's veins. She drew power from the wind, the earth, and the fire burning around them. Her eyes flashed in his direction. She was fuming. Pulling every ounce of power from the air around them, she pushed it at him. She could hear the blood rushing through her veins as her anger controlled her senses.

"On the other side of this forest, there are others like me, Rielle. And you have a chance to end our tyranny once and for all. Just read the spell and open the portal."

Rielle felt Luke tapped into her mind as she watched him stand slowly. He was connected to her as she felt him pulling her.

"It is your purpose, Rielle. Do it now, or my brother will always bear the burden of our actions." If there were others like Luke, it would be right to kill them all. Apprehensions ran down her spine. She remembered how broken Callum was, and the guilt and responsibility he carried. They did this to him. They had turned him into what he was.

"Callum deserves peace, Rielle. He will never get it until they're all dead." Luke strong-armed her mind reading her thoughts. *"Do it, do it for Callum, open the portal."*

Rielle pulled just enough power from the earth, the wind, the air, and sent it in the direction of the hibiscus. A static of energy flared around them.

"Ouvert a prezan a terre a prezan fuis." She kept repeating the words. Thunder roared. A loud sound came from underneath the ground. She was doing it for Callum—he deserved peace.

Luke's eyes widened. Staggered, he looked at the wooden piece in his hands where the witch had written the magic. "You never needed the spell. You were the spell."

Rielle stepped a few feet closer and repeated the words, sending them with a force that would reach inside of the portal. Like an earthquake, the ground shook; the flowers around the magical veil froze.

A shot rang. The bullet hit Luke's shoulder. He faltered a bit. In a flash, Callum was on him like a caged animal. Raphael, Zachariah, and Davide fenced Rielle in. "Rielle!" Raphael screamed out. She ignored him as she continued chanting the words. "Rielle, Look at me!"

"She thinks she's doing it for Callum. Luke had gotten in her mind," Raphael spoke to Zachariah.

"Can't you persuade her as you did with us?"

"Luke linked himself to her mind; he used the dovetail spell. I can sense it in her mind. It'll make her angrier."

"That son of a bitch manipulated her bond to Callum to get his ways. We must be ready for anything. Whatever we do, we cannot let her open that portal." Zachariah watched her.

"Callum, we have a situation right now."

"I'm in a situation right now, Raphael." Callum threw a blow to Luke's face. Luke stumbled back, a smirk on his face. "You make me proud, little brother." He rushed toward Callum.

"You must talk her off the ledge. She thinks she's doing it for you. I don't want to risk making her angrier."

Callum focused immediately on Rielle. Luke swung his fist, knocking him out of breath. He coughed, trying to recuperate his lungs. In his rage and desire to beat Luke to a pulp, he forgot about the portal, *"mie cehia,"* he brushed her mind.

Raphael was right, and she was on a warpath because of him. *"Rielle, I know you're angry, but I need you to focus on Raphael. Listen to him."*

Another blow this time at his mouth. Luke was now on him. His fists were repeatedly meeting Callum's face. Blow after blow.

"They did this to you. If I don't do this, you will always feel like a monster."

"No mie cehia, they didn't. My demons are mine and mine only. I'm responsible for them."

"We must rid the world of those like Luke; it's the only way."

"Yes, accordingly, when the time comes. There are children in the mountains, women as gentle as you. If you open that portal, then Luke wins."

Callum sensed the apprehension in her mind. He was getting to her. Kicking his legs, he head-butted Luke. Quickly he was on his feet. Luke disappeared. Callum kept an eye on his surroundings. Knowing at any given moment Luke would attack, "You still don't know the meaning of a fair fight. You coward," Callum roared.

"Why would I fight fair when I hold the powers that I hold?" Luke came into sight. Forcefully, he stuck his blade through Callum's heart with a killing blow. Blood splattered from Callum's mouth. He fell on the ground. "I told you, little brother, fighting fair never wins battles." He smiled roguishly.

Chapter 36

*S*orrow sneaked up on Rielle. Quietly it immersed through her heart and her mind. She instantly froze and looked at Raphael. The ground stopped shaking. A torrential rain cascaded from the sky, putting out the flaming trees. "Rielle?" Raphael called out her name. She stopped the chant.

She glanced over Raphael's shoulder, Callum was on the ground. Luke hovered over him. Hurriedly she ran in their direction. In waves, angst consumed her, overwhelmingly stifling her veins. Cradling his head on her thighs, she cried out, her throbbing agony behind it. "No, no." There was something in her scream. It sent shudders through all three of them.

Zachariah watched her, and his eye turned to Luke. He immediately knew what was about to transpire next.

His fury became nothing but a shield for the sudden dread he felt.

A rushing energy flashed past him. It was Raphael, his emotions mirroring every bit of what he was feeling. Moments later, Davide also rushed toward Luke. Zachariah wasn't sure when he'd joined them, as everything was a blur to him, and only one thing was on his mind.

The fight was like a choreographed dance. Three against one, Luke was still the better fighter out of them. Throwing a blow to Raphael's head, Luke was as strong as they remembered. Zachariah knew only one would lose his life, and it wasn't the three of them.

Luke's blade stained with Callum's blood; it lit a fire within Zachariah. He shuffled to the side, anticipating another move from Luke. Another blow, another hit.

Davide charged at Luke. In a fluid movement, Luke dodged sideways, swiveling in Raphael's direction. He knocked Raphael on his back, hovering over him.

His menacing eyes were blazing ice. Luke lunged his blade forward. In a speedy blur, Zachariah leaped on him, seizing the blade from his hands.

"I warned you to kill me when you had the chance." Without hesitation, Zachariah plunged it in the back of Luke's head.

Luke's body thumped next to Raphael.

The air grew thicker around them. Rielle's sobs evened out the quietness of the night, Callum's head still cradled in her lap. Raphael kneeled next to her gently. He placed a hand on her shoulder.

He wanted to alleviate her heartache—a sharp pain in his heart and a numbness pounded his brain. Zachariah was standing a few feet away, his eyes glued on Callum's body. A wave of hollowness engulfed his mind. It scared him.

"We have to take him home," Davide quietly whispered. Rielle looked at him, her eyes glazed with a layer of tears dripping from her eyelids down to her cheek as she blinked. Davide's heart sank.

Rielle's lower lip quivered as words slowly made their way out of her mouth. "No . . . you . . . ," she began. What followed was engulfed in tremors.

"It's the only way." Raphael's morose tone amplified her griefs.

All choked up, Rielle couldn't breathe. Her body tied into knots, she couldn't escape. Surely this couldn't be their fate. She thought. The pain dug deeper inside of her, swallowing her whole, and buried into her soul. Her gaze fell back on Callum's lifeless face. The realization that her life would be without him was too much for her to accept. Time stopped, and it undid her completely. "*Barikad, bare,*" she whispered, the words dancing in her mind. A glowing yellow light swiftly went around them, separating Callum and her from everybody.

Raphael jumped to his feet, stepping away from her. Tears flowed abundantly down her cheeks and dripped from her chin. She wasn't going to let them take him from him.

"You arrogant Neanderthal . . . You can't do this to me . . . it was your idea to tie us together." Lightly she stroke his face then kissed him. "I love you," she somberly whispered. The words unexpectedly sounded out of her mouth.

Chapter 37

*S*torms clouds were now gathering in the sky. The wind shouted like a roar, howling. Both Raphael and Davide paced around the magical barricade light, unable to see Rielle or Callum. "What are we going to do?" Raphael asked.

"Her pain alone is too much to bear, now taking his body away from her would simply be cruel," Zachariah replied. He had detached, dissipating his anger.

"We can't leave him in this realm. He belongs in the mountains."

"Would Priscilla give you away?" Zachariah cruelly said. He knew he was misplacing his anger, and Raphael was trying to do right by their dead brother. But internally he was exploding. "Deisolei," he apologized.

"Io se, freio." Raphael sent him a comforting push in his head.

Chirps rippled around them; they came in bursts, bringing an apprehensive look on their faces. The air suddenly became cold. High above them, a red tyto soumangei owl flew. Perched on a branch, the rare bird believed to appear only once a decade as a spirit.

A thick mist covered the forest. It glistened luminously in the new full moon formed in the sky. Raphael stood still, his eyes following the trail of plants emerging from the ground in the direction where Rielle and Callum were. "*Bas ba gnongolo nolo la vie ka revive,*" his acute hearing heard Rielle speak.

A sudden fear ran down Raphael's spine, and the hair on his head prickled. He took a step toward the magical barricade. Zachariah and Davide did the same.

"No, she can't do this," Zachariah frowned concernedly. He picked up on the words too. "Several spells focused on the *ba* of the deceased—a principal aspect of someone, the body, the shadow, and their life force. Ba is our spirit or soul. Raphael, if she does this, she won't survive it. The magic is too strong, and she doesn't have that ability. Enchantresses can heal, yes, with herbs, but not like this."

"A life force for a life force," Raphael repeated. Fretfulness filled him. If he were to let Rielle do this, Callum would never forgive them, and it would also be the end of them. "We need to stop her."

A ray of yellow-white light shot up into the air. An instant later, a blinding flash with a varicolored force brought up winds of tiny static sparkles.

The magical wall separating them dropped.

Rielle dropped on the floor next to Callum. All three men bolted to her.

Raphael grabbed her hands, feeling her pulse. "Stay with me, Rielle . . . come on, stay with me." The plants retracted to the earth; the roaring wind stopped. The owl turned into remnants. "Mierdei!" he screamed out loud. "She has no pulse." Raphael sat on the ground looking at his brother and his mate. He mentally was lost and genuinely didn't know what to do.

Seconds passed, maybe minutes, but it felt like an eternity. Callum jolted awake, gasping for air, his body alert. He felt his chest where Luke had plunged the blade into his heart. He wasn't supposed to be alive right now. He had died; he knew he had died. He lifted his head. Zachariah, Raphael, and Davide were looking at him, a shocked expression on their faces. a sharp squeeze in his heart, he glanced next to him and saw Rielle.

"She brought you back," Raphael said, astounded that she had, and dreading what was to come next if she didn't wake up.

"No . . . Come on, mia cehia, you have to wake up. You brought me back, so you have to wake up." Callum felt her pulse, immediately using his healing gifts, sending his energy into her and taking over her mind and body. "You have to wake up, do you hear me? You wouldn't let me die, so don't you dare think of failing me." He ripped her shirt apart, forgetting about his brothers and Davide as her bra was out for everyone to see. Surprisingly, right now, he didn't care who saw her chest. He needed to get a pulse out of her. "She's completely shut down. We have to get her to the mountain. I'm not strong enough right now to sustain her, energy wise. I'll need to get her in the healing pool."

"Whatever you need, brother." Raphael opened the door to the portal.

Chapter 38

*B*ringing him back to life had taken her into this unconscious state, split her soul and broke her mind. The
magic had been too strong for her, and ripped her apart. It
was ten days now that she had slept. The healing pool had
done the job of bringing life back into her, but she was unre-
sponsive. "You heard Eloh. She has to heal herself from within
and wake up on her own," Zachariah said, as he walked into
the room where they kept her. Callum wouldn't let Rielle stay
at the medical ward, so Raphael had to intervene and make
him compromise on letting her stay at the manor.

"Well, she's not doing it. It's been ten days, and she's still
not herself. I feel no fight inside of her. She's empty."

"Patience, loverboy, she has the gift just like you and her
father. Give her time."

"Any news on the council and the elders?" Callum questioned.

"Yeah, Raphael took a book out of your page and went wild on everyone. Sael, Kael, and Solamon are locked in prison. But we believe a couple more knew about what was happening though they're claiming they didn't, so we're watching them closely. Everyone is on their best behavior, as Raphael has become the ultimate you but with common sense. You would have been proud."

"What did they say about Rielle?"

"What can they say? The leader of our people told them to shove their rules and their decrees up their asses. So Rielle is a citizen of the mountain like everyone else. Besides, Althazar wants to see her soon."

"Over my fucking dead body." Callum clenched his brows' furrows.

"I get it that you don't want anyone near her, but you're going a little overboard with this one. Althazar is her uncle." Callum growled, Zachariah smiled. "Seven hells, once these fire blooded men around here start looking at her what are you going to do?" Seeing the look on Callum's face, Zachariah held his hands up in surrender. "I was teasing. And the truth is, we both know she won't put up with your shit."

"Get out! Get out, Zach!" Callum roared. He didn't want to think about other men looking at her. Indeed, he wasn't in the mood for Zachariah's taunting. Callum climbed in the large bed with her, cuddling her against his chest.

"You have to wake up. You have to. I need you." *"You can do this, mie cehia. I have so much to show you, share with you. The mountain, my favorite places, our home. I'll even go to Raphael and Priscilla's pointless gatherings with you, but you must wake up,"* he brushed her mind for the umpteenth time. "You're stronger than this. I need you. Mierdei, I need you."

Rielle heard him, his heart connected with hers. She could sense it all. She was awake in her mind, but nothing made sense. His scents were calling out to her, cradling in his arms. She paced inside of her mind, trying to fight the blackness and nothingness that slipped into part of her mind. It was seductive and comforting.

"You can't be here; what are you doing here?" A silhouette flashed.

"I thought I was alone."

"You're never alone." The silhouette took a woman's form, and she looked like her.

Wild curly, coily hair, brown eyes, and an upturned nose. *"Mom? Mom?"* Rielle questioned, *"No, just an image of what she would look like if she were alive."*

"What are you then? Who are you?"

"Her essence. You can't be here," the woman repeated.

"I don't know how I got here. I don't know how to get out."

"You do know."

"No, I don't. Why would I want to stay here in this barren and dark place?"

The woman looked at her and raised her eyebrows.

"*I . . . I . . .*" Rielle stuttered, feeling disconcerted all of a sudden.

"*Go! This place is seductive once you get comfortable. There's no leaving it. Being scared isn't reason enough to be here.*"

"*I'm not scared . . . It's just all too much.*"

The woman looked at her, understanding in her eyes, then nodded, a gentle smile on her face.

"*Yes, it can all be too much, but you're a Petion. Our fear is our strength. You are scared, and you should be. But you must believe that you're strong enough to weather any storm. You have proven it to yourself. You've accomplished what no one else in our lineage could, and others have dreamed of.*"

"*What if I give in to it? The darkness inside of me. I feel it. It's there. What if I hurt him again? What if I can't control myself and harm the people that I love?*"

"*We all fight the darkness inside of us. Some of us are just better battling it and don't let it win. You're a Petion, and you are also a Mallovoi. We balance each other out. Whatever dark- ness is inside of you, it can neither take nor control you if you don't allow it,*" the woman talked to her. Gently she held her face, removing a piece of hair out of Rielle's face. "*He would have been so proud of you. And so would I. Now, it's time to go home. There's nothing for you here.*"

"*But . . .*"

"*Go, Rielle! Now!*"

Rielle couldn't breathe. Her heart kicked into overdrive; it pounded relentlessly in her chest. Callum's fear hit her so raw. It consumed and took hold of her brain. Hands pulled her closer as she fought her breathing and her mind to calm down.

"Easy . . . easy," Callum said softly. His arms tightened around her, his scent calming. The sunlight filtered through the large windows and into the room. She blinked a few times to help her eyes adjust to the brightness. "You're awake," he sighed.

"I think I'm hungry," Rielle faintly said, her stomach growling.

"Of course you are." Callum stared at her, a boyish smile on his face. Those brown eyes were his soul; looking back at them again brought a sense of euphoria he didn't know existed until now. "We unquestionably need some ground rules about using your magic." He leaned into her, and softly, he brushed his lips against hers.

"Thanks for letting me know she's awake, sire," Eloh said, as he walked into the room. Davide strolled in, fol-lowed by Raphael. "Mierdei, freio, let her breathe, she just woke up."

Zachariah sped in the room. "Yea, thanks for letting us know she's conscious."

Callum growled for everyone to hear. Of course, Eloh, that was his gift as a doctor and his brothers connected to him, they would know she was awake.

Rielle chuckled, relieved that she hadn't hurt any of them. They were all here.

"You didn't hurt any of them, though I would have liked you hurt Zachariah a bit. Just a bit," Callum slipped into her

mind. The familiar touch—she shuddered and looked at him. A faint smile curved her face.

"You can. It's not too late," Callum continued.

"Not in a million-years, brother, she likes me. You two have got to put your shields on," Zachariah said out loud.

"Enough, sires, you're disturbing my patient," Eloh smiled, happy to see all three men chatting freely. It had been a while. "Good morning dear, I'm Eloh, these hardheaded boys' doctor. I have been, for over a century now." Rielle raised her eyebrows, puzzled. "Yes, I am a hundred and five years old. How are you feeling?"

"Good, but hungry," she answered.

"Yes, you've been out for days. It's only natural to desire food." He flashed a tiny object in Rielle's face. It blinded her momentarily. Checking her pulse, his hand rested on her neck, and he touched Callum's mark. A quiet snarl slipped out of Callum's mouth. "Now, now, sire, no need to feel guarding. I'm simply making sure your mate is of health," the old man soothingly said. Waves of calming energy spread through the room.

Rielle glared at Callum. Embarrassed, Callum looked away. Both Zachariah and Davide were grinning. Raphael did his best to stay neutral.

"I told you she wasn't going to put up with your shit," Zachariah pestered.

"Keep at it, and Raphael won't find where I bury you," Callum sent the threat. Zachariah's laughter boomed in his head.

"All done. Everything seems fine." Lightly, the older man touched her hands. "Gabriel, your father, would have been very proud of you."

"Can she leave the manor?" Raphael asked.

"Yes, my liege, other than needing some food, she's as healthy as one can be. She has the gifts just like her father, and you, master Callum. That's how she was able to bring you back."

"The healing gift? So it's true?" Raphael asked.

"Yes sire, mixed with her magics once she learns how to use it, she will be the most powerful healer in our midst. You no longer have that role, sire." Eloh tapped Callum's shoulder. "Happiness is with you on the mountain, dear." Eloh left.

The room grew silent; all eyes were on her. Rielle felt nervous all of a sudden.

"You heard the doctor. I'm fine," she whispered.

"That night when I healed you, I felt vigorous. I wasn't only curing you, I was absorbing from your magics too," Callum whispered, amazed, remembering how the energy from him transferred to her and vice versa.

Rielle watched them, perplexed.

"Ease up, brother, you don't want to scare her more about her magic."

"Thank you for reviving my brother, Rielle." Raphael took a step closer to her. His eyes were full of appreciation. "You are one of us now, and you always will be. As of this moment, you are a citizen of the mountain, and if you decide to remain on the mountain, we will be lucky to have you, and so would my brother. But that's a decision you have to make yourself." He shifted his gaze to Callum, cold.

Tension suddenly gripped around the room. Rielle felt Callum's trepidation. "Thank you for everything, guys. Thank you." She held back the tears threatening to come out.

"Of course. We are forever indebted to you, and you're stuck with this one forever, so you're stuck with us," Zachariah pointed at Callum, smiling at her.

"Yeah, I missed our morning coffee routine Rie, and I can't wait to bring you to my favorite teashop around here. Maybe you can advise the chef on adding coffee to the menu." Davide hugged her.

"I'd like that," Rielle smiled at him.

"Alright. Let's give these two some space. Callum, I expect to see you at our council meeting tomorrow morning, or I'll send for you in the deep end of the mountain, military-style. We have much to discuss," Raphael said.

"Good luck, Rielle. If you decide you don't like my brother's far from civilization ways of life in that cabin of his, my house is your house."

"Get out, Zachariah!" Callum roared angrily.

Everyone left; silence fell between them.

"If you want to stay here, then we will, and if you want to come home with me, we will too." Callum stared at her.

"I have the option to choose?" Rielle sarcastically asked.

"Of course you do, mie cehia, you always have option. As long as it doesn't put you in danger," he quickly said. Her face was unreadable. It bothered him that she even said that. He wasn't that bad, was he?

"You are that bad, but you are charming, so it balances it out."

She was in his mind, Callum felt the tease in her voice; it relaxed him a bit.

"Let's go home," Rielle said out loud.

Callum nodded. Lifting her, he carried her out of bed, teleporting them out of the room and out of the manor.

Chapter 39

*I*n the lush of the forest, the cabin sat on the hilltop site of the mountain. A cyan-colored waterfall, an intermediate between green and violet, tumbled down the hill. It flowed over the rocks and the clear magical serenity pool at the bottom. Ferns of forest green, yellow, purple, and red plants waved gently in the depths of the forest, boasting an excellent view with a stunning vision of the surrounding landscape.

Equipped with modern and Tuscan style amenities, the open floor and offset planks of wood contributed texture to the interior wall. They flawlessly blended with the natural surroundings and rounded double gleaming, floor to ceiling window frames captivated the views of the inclosing wilderness while illumining the woods and inside of the cabin.

The smell of the earth, the aroma of the flowers, birds chirping—Rielle felt attuned with herself.

Slowly she made her way to the bedroom. Glass windows transported the outside scenery inside of the room. A plush king-size bed with a pendant lamp in the middle of the ceiling provided an elegant yet grounded touch to the room. "It's beautiful," she whispered.

"I had some help. Come, I have a surprise for you." Callum took her hands in his, lightly dragging her behind him and into the kitchen.

The sizeable cozy kitchen was by far the biggest room in the house. Another waterfall calmly flowed in front of the floor to ceiling windows. Different types of birds flew around, singing.

"Wow," Rielle gasped.

"I know how much you loved our kitchen in Kannan, so I asked Zachariah to help."

"It's beautiful. It's all so beautiful, the mountain, everything. Your home is beautiful."

"Our home," Callum corrected.

Rielle tensed up, removing her hands out of his hands, "Callum, . . ."

"Before you say anything, I want to say that Raphael was right. Staying here with me, or going back to Kannan . . . it has to be your decision. I know you feel overwhelmed, and it's a lot to take in. A new place, new people, coming to terms and adjusting to who you are now and who you were before all of this, but whatever you decide, I need you to know one important thing—you're my home and my place is next to you always. Wherever you go, mie cehia, I will follow." Tears welled around her eyes. Callum pulled her into his arms, her head against his chest. his fingers caressing her back.

Rielle closed her eyes, willing the tears away. She felt secure and safe with him.

But the pain she felt that day regurgitated. She couldn't bear it again if anything were to happen to him. "You have to talk to me, mie cehia. I feel your distress, but you are shielding me out."

"You died," Rielle choked, moving away from him

His features empty as he watched her, Callum didn't say a word. He couldn't, not when the pain and exhaustion she felt this moment was so clear for him to see. He was sad that he had inflicted it on her. It grieved his heart that she went through that because of him.

He watched her intensely, as she too did. No words were spoken as they were having a silent conversation staring into each other's eyes.

Callum propped forward. Her pulse raced. A small ringlet of curly hair tumbled in front of her face, resting in on her cheek. Swiftly, he slid his thumb and brushed it out of the way. Looking into his eyes, she saw the burden. The cerulean in them displayed the angst he was feeling in his soul.

"Mie cehia," Callum whispered in her head. His lips touched her cheek. *"I will forever be making it up to you for putting you through that. And I vow to breathe my last breath in this world or the next after you, and never before you."*

Time stopped. Rielle's heart came to a halt. Her breath caught in her throat. Their fingers intertwined, Callum's supple mouth left the side of her face and down to her neck. He kissed the spot where he had marked her. Her body tingled; a burning sensation flamed inside of her. He pulled away silently, their eyes locked. "I love you. and I always will, even after an eternity."

The blue in his eyes turned yellow green and purple, they were a mixture of each other. Rielle was lost in them. She's never seen his eyes like this before.

A warm fuzzy feeling formed inside of her heart. She leaned more into Callum's chest, capturing his lips into a kiss that conveyed everything she was feeling.

Callum's brain ignited, warmth spread throughout his body. Her kisses, her lips—she was his salvation and his torment. Slow and honeyed, their kiss was comforting in ways that words would never be. Rielle ran her fingers down his spine, pulling him closer until there was no space left between them, and she could feel the beating of his heart.

An eternity later, reluctantly, she pulled her mouth away from him, her eyes met his asking him a question.

Callum smiled, giving her the answer she needed. He wanted her as much as she did, if not more. Gliding his hand down her back, he found the zipper of the robe she was wearing. Slowly he undid it. The dress slithered down her body to lie at her feet. Callum growled. In a flash, he pinned her against the wall, his knee between her legs. "I missed you."

His mouth crushed hers gently as she opened for him. His other hand reached down and pushed past her underwear. He rubbed over her core. Fire lit up her inside instantly.

Callum groaned as she moaned against his mouth. He removed his hand and picked her up as he pressed her against the wall. Rielle ripped the buttons from his shirt, impatiently wanting to feel his skin. Callum grinned. His mouth claimed hers again with grave urgency. Seconds later he positioned her on the bed. His pants magically disappeared; a fully naked Callum stood in front of her. A throbbing need hit her core. "I need you now," Rielle asserted.

Usually, he'd drag and prolong before giving her what she wanted—showing her that he had the upper hand in their bedroom, at least. But he was as impatient as she was and wanted as badly to bury himself into her. Callum hovered over her. Slowly, he entered her.

The purple color flashed around his iris. He drove inside of her, losing himself to her fire and peeking at her essence. Rielle wrapped her legs around him, getting lost in the unruly color for the second time around. Callum pushed himself in and out of her. She met his thrusts until she exploded.

Shaking, she dug her nails into his shoulder as he threw his head back and found his release and rested his forehead against hers as they gained control of their breathing. Callum rolled to his side, and they lay there for minutes.

"I love you." Rielle spun around, she rested her head on his chest, draping a leg around him.

Callum smiled, his heart somersaulted. "You do?"

She kissed him. Callum grabbed the back of her neck, deepening the kiss. "I brought you back from the dead without even thinking of the consequences. If that doesn't scream I love you, I don't know what does," Rielle teased.

He squeezed her tight and kissed her hair. "So you're staying with me? You're not leaving?"

"No, I'm not leaving you. Give ourselves a couple of months up here, and then we can decide if Kannan is home or if this will be our permanent home."

"Deal. Wherever you go, I go," Callum smiled. "I can't wait to show you around. And for you to meet Priscilla—Raphael's mate. I think you will like her."

"Not so fast. I need you to promise me a few things. First, you're not going to go Neanderthal on everyone that approaches me."

"Not everyone. Just the males around here," he casually said. His fingers were playing into her hair.

Rielle quickly sat up looming over him. "Callum?"

"Rielle?" he grinned.

"I am serious."

"So am I." He heaved up and took her lips.

"I can always go live with Zachariah if you become impossible."

"Over his dead body," Callum said, nibbling on her neck

"Or the manor, it's like a palace over there. I'm sure Raphael would have no problem."

"Not if he wants half of our family's home burned down."

Rielle gripped an amount of his hair in her hands and pulled his head away from her. "Promise me." She pulled harder.

"I'll try my best." Callum winced.

"Your best is not good enough. Tell me you won't be a caveman."

Callum grinned mischievously and kissed her earlobes. "I can't tell you that, mie cehia, but I can tell you that I got an icebox. I had Davide fill it up with fruits and vegetables and other stuff if you wanted to cook."

"You got an icebox?" she asked, confused.

"Yes, you humans call it a fridge, no?"

"You didn't have a fridge before? Do people around here have appliances, or do they use magic for everything?"

"No, not everyone has powers or abilities. Those of us who do, are duty-bound and serve one way or another. And no, I didn't need a fridge then, and yes, we have appliances. We're not that different. We're just a bit more advanced here than the mortal realm."

"Coffee? Did he get coffee?"

"Yes, from Kannan, and he demanded one of our experts to figure out a way to grow the damn thing on the mountain. You got him addicted to it." His tone was accusatory.

Rielle laughed out loud. "I merely introduced him to it."

"Amoirei, mie, you fed it to him every morning, so you're an enabler." Her laughter filled up the room. A sense of peacefulness, and something else he couldn't quite put his fingers on, sneaked up in him. Her bed hair flung below her shoulder; the room seemed brighter, livelier, and had more warmth than he could remember. She was irresistible, and she was his.

"What?" Rielle snorted as she stopped laughing.

Callum stared at her with adoration in his eyes, "Nothing, just don't scare me like that again."

Rielle saw the fire in his eyes. Immediately she understood what he meant. Being comatose for ten days must have been hard for him too. So focused on what she felt, she had forgotten that it was the two of them in the same boat. "Just don't give me a reason to scare you like that again."

"We'll need some ground rules about using your magic. Mie cehia, I can't have you going out every time you use more magic than you should. There are plenty of books that can help you learn about your gifts in our general library, and I'll get us some for here too," he said, matter-of-factly.

"And we'll need some ground rules about you putting yourself in danger. Because, baby, I can't have you coming home wounded or not at all." She used his tone. Callum smiled inwardly. She was a firecracker, and he loved that about her though he would never admit it to her.

"You just did," Rielle's voice caressed his mind.

"I also hate it, should you know." He smiled. "You have to eat. There is plenty of good food on the mountain. We can go out to eat, or I can teleport and go get you something to eat."

"No, I'll just make something here with whatever's in the icebox," she mocked.

Callum wrapped his hands around her back as he pulled her closer. His mouth crushed hers, kissing her passionately.

Much later, Rielle sat on the dockside of the cabin. The sun a tangerine blush, a sparkling gold-plated, dipped below the horizon. She understood why Callum made his home here, away from the noise and the town. Though Zachariah was right, and she realized indeed that Callum was a loner, this place was just breathtaking.

"I'm not a loner, and please don't start siding with Zach," he slipped into her mind.

Rielle chuckled, teasing him. *"Hey, I was having a moment to myself. You're intruding."* She grew fond of the intimacy of being in each other's mind and talking telepathically to one another.

"My offer still stands, join me?" She could feel his lips brushing hers.

"Stop that! Enjoy your outdoor shower." They had made love in every corner of the cabin, yet he still wanted more. He was insatiable, and she was almost right there with him. Removing a full amount of wild curls out her face, she heaved a sigh. It was going to be an adventure, and she had no idea what to expect. Though Raphael told her she was one of them, and her father's blood ran through her veins, she wondered if others would accept her too.

Callum told her about the rules of humans and Arcadien consorting with one another back then.

She was mortal, and she was Arcadien at the same time. That was different. And whether human or Arcadien, people didn't like change and were skeptical about things out of the ordinary.

"The Elders and the council can shove their rules up theirs. You're Gabriel's daughter, a Mallovoi. Your uncle is an Elder and head of the council. Your brother-in-law rules our people, and your mate is the guardian of Arcadin. But most importantly, you, mie cehia, are a pure half enchantress and Arcadien noble. So they won't dare cross us. And if they did, I'll kill them all." He leaned over her and kissed her forehead.

"Not every solution needs to involve somebody dying, you know."

"Strike first, ask questions later. That's the adage."

Rielle rolled her eyes at him. "They have a therapist on this mountain too?"

"Don't even say what you're about to say." Callum kneeled in front of her, laughing at her thoughts.

Rielle giggled. "I have to let Syrah know that I'm ok. She's the only family I have left."

"We can visit her. You have to tell me when."

"Isn't it against the law to cross the portal without permission?" she asked.

"It won't be without permission. Tell me when you want to see Syrah, and we will."

Rielle reached up, her arms around his neck. She kissed him. "I want to do this mate thing with you for as long as I can."

"No, mie cehia, we're doing this mate thing until our last breath and after that." His eyes were soft, Rielle saw the yearnings and fire behind them. His forehead touched hers. His warmth absorbed her heart like she had never experienced before. It energized her and filled her with a desire and hope that overpowered and encouraged her. Gently but passionately, he pressed his lips into hers.

Epilogue

Rielle looked at herself in the mirror, ready for the small gathering of their friends and family turned into a full-on black-tie affair. Priscilla had insisted on having a reception for them because they didn't have one after Callum bonded them months ago. She had quickly become friends with Raphael's mate, and Priscilla was the sweetest; hence, it was hard to say no to her. Rielle glanced in the mirror one last time. The alluring, lightweight Chantilly lace gown made her look ultra-feminine.

A daring deep V-neckline was balanced by detachable bows at the shoulders. The bodice of the dress, adorned with a hint of metallic thread, accentuated her small waistline with a ribbon belt and a back bow and a deep open back that showed off beaded spaghetti straps. The applique accented skirt resembled a chapel train.

"Rie, everyone is waiting. If you don't go out there, we both know that man of yours will come in here roaring," Syrah walked in the room. "Wow, you look gorgeous! That man of yours will absolutely be roaring," Syrah exclaimed, teasing.

Rielle smiled at Syrah, the two of them facing the mirrors. "You look beautiful too, Sy. My god, that dress will be the talk of the night." A pale champagne sequin rounded neckline sleeveless bodice maxi dress with a sexy cowl back drapes and a mermaid hem clung to her friend, flaunting her curves.

"She is just about exposed and needs to put some better clothes on." Davide strolled in the room. Both women turned in his direction.

"Don't be mean, Davide. She is not. And she looks beautiful." Rielle hit the young warrior shoulder.

"I didn't say she didn't look beautiful. I said she needed to put some clothes on." Davide glared at Syrah. His brows furrowed, he seemed frustrated all of a sudden.

"And your opinion matters why?" Syrah hit back at him. Tension cut in the room, Rielle looked between the two of them. Their constant match was starting to get out of hand. The two didn't get along, but it had escalated the last couple of days. "Look, you two, enough of the snide comments and the mean remarks. You two are my best friends, and I love you both dearly. Can you at least pretend to get along for my sake? At least for tonight?"

"Now you've upset her," Davide accused, and scowled at Syrah.

"Oh, I did? I'm not the one who barged in here and took upon himself to be a dick," Syrah fiercely spat.

Rielle had never seen her friend riled up like this. Yes, Sy had her moments, but this was completely off base. "Guys! Please, for the love of god! A couple of hours, that's all I'm asking of you." She was starting to get frustrated with the two of them herself.

"Mie cehia. Are you ok?" Callum slid into her mind. He must have also felt her frustration.

"Syrah and Davide are driving me mad with their senseless feud."

"Want some backup?"

"No. I got it all under control."

"Well, get out of here, woman! I'm starting to be impatient."

"A couple of hours, that's for how long I need you guys to pretend to like each other." When they were about to argue with her, Rielle raised her hand, stopping them. "I'm not ask-ing, I'm telling." Both Davide and Syrah glowered at each other, then nodded at her. "Thank you! Now let's get this thing over with." She walked past them, leaving them behind her.

The last seven months were a whirlwind, learning how to control her magic, assimilating, and getting to know the Arcadien people. Callum was still a pain in the ass, and his overbearing ways knew no boundaries once she opened her café in the city. His Neanderthal ways became worse after she stubbornly made the mistake of using a spell that sent her body into another dimensional realm for a day. He couldn't help himself.

Her uncle Althazar had become a father figure, and like Priscilla, he was also adamant about this reception. He and Callum butted head constantly regarding her, and the two didn't see eye to eye on anything, except when it came to reprimanding her about not being safe.

Zachariah had become the brother she never had, and Davide was her best friend. She was grateful for them and couldn't imagine living on the mountain without them to make her laugh or burst Callum's bubble.

The last few months had also shown her that despite being graceful and polite, Raphael was as overbearing as Callum. Surely it was an Arcadien male trait, though Priscilla was the apple of his eye, and he loved her tremendously. Everyone was excited about the baby.

Rielle walked down the stairs. At the bottom, Callum waited for her. He held her gaze, holding his breath until she stood in front of him. He was handsome. His hair in a slit back low braid emphasized his beautiful face. His fitted black suit with a white shirt underneath displayed his muscles, drawing attention to his form.

"Hello, handsome. You're wearing a bow tie."

"You look so beautiful, mie cehia." His eyes sparkled; a sly smile flashed across Callum's face. Briefly, he unconsciously bit his lips. "Let's call it a night so I can take this dress off you," he hissed in her ears, drawing her in. Hearing his husky voice, frissons ran down Rielle's back.

"Priscilla alone would send wild dogs after us," Rielle chuckled.

"She'll get over it, and we don't need this reception. Most of these people I don't care about." Callum kissed her earlobes.

Rielle was in his head, and she knew what he was thinking. Though Callum wanted people to fear him as the guardian of the people, he also took it to heart when people saw him as nothing but the killing machine that they deemed him to be. This reception was the perfect occasion to prove that he was more than their guardian, that he wasn't a mon-ster, that he was more than his abilities and skills. "Not a chance warrior, I didn't get a wedding, so this is as close to a wedding as I'll get. Unless you want me to start planning a whole wedding where I invite everyone on the mountain," she smiled mischievously.

"I have to warn you, people will . . ."

"It's you and me. Lumiie forricei, you're the only one who matters." She caressed his face.

A smile curved across Callum's mouth, hearing the native words from her lips.

"Now I am urged to rip this dress off of you, hearing you speak Acad."

Rielle laughed and took his hands, intertwining their fingers. "Come on, you and me."

The room buzzed with excited chatter. Live music vibrated in the hall. Once they entered, applause spread across the room. Everyone got up for a standing ovation as they made their way to their table, smiling and holding hands. Usually, he would get strange and apprehensive stares; Callum was shocked by the surprise welcome and the round of applause.

After a few moments, Raphael rose from his chair, and everyone else sat down. He raised his wineglass, signaling everyone to silence. "To my brother and his life mate. Rielle, you've not only turned my bother somewhat sane. But you have made him the happiest man in this realm, and for that, I will always be grateful to you. He never attends any of our gatherings, but I'm sure things are going to be different now because I will deliberately hold you responsible for his absence." The room exploded in laughter.

"You're enjoying this, aren't you?"

Raphael smirked and ignored Callum's voice in his head. "To the Guardian of Arcadin," he toasted.

"To the Guardian of Arcadin," everyone reiterated. The clinking of the glasses reverberated across the room. And soon after, people went to their conversation, enjoying themselves.

The jazzy tune resumed, and people flocked to the dance floor. "May I have this dance?" Someone tapped Rielle's shoulders.

"Sure," she grinned, giving her hands.

"Keep your hands to yourself!" Callum warned.

Zachariah smiled, pulling Rielle onto the dance floor. "You look beautiful, Rie." He turned her around.

"Thank you, Zach. Stop provoking him, or one of these days I'll have to send out a search team for you,"

"And here I thought you mellowed him, but it turns out you turned him into a complete animal."

Rielle laughed, hitting his shoulder. "Hey, he's a gentle beast."

Zachariah feigned to throw up. "But seriously, thanks for giving him back to us. We almost lost him to darkness, and also for good. but each time you brought him back to us."

"It was purely for a selfish reason," Rielle joked.
"Regardless of the reasons, thank you." Zachariah kissed her temple.

"What part of keeping your hands to yourself don't you understand? That goes for your lips too," Callum was in his head. Zachariah laughed out loud and dipped Rielle on purpose.

"Dip her one more time, Zach, and our brother won't know where I buried your fingers."

Zachariah laughed out loud and dipped Rielle one more time. "That mate of yours is threatening me. If I come up missing, I hope you'll tell everyone he's responsible."

"Zach, surely you must know I'll always be his accom-plice and alibi," Rielle giggled.

"And here I thought you had my back. You both deserve each other," Zachariah feigned, being shocked. *"How about you get off your heiane and come dance with her? I can assure you, many are waiting for me to clear the way so they can take turns dancing with her."*

"Over my dead body," Callum snapped.

In seconds, he was next to them. "Go away, Zach, I'd like to dance with my woman."

Zachariah kissed Rielle's temples, a smirk on his face pro-voking Callum, and walked away. "Hi," Callum smiled at her.

"Hi." The slow music whirled around them. Rielle rested her head on his chest, their body becoming one on the dance floor. The saxophone came in, then the piano. A slow melodi-ous voice echoed in the room. Callum's hands on her back, making little patterns, sending shivers to her spine. *"Io Lovia."* He kissed her hair.

"I love you too." Rielle looked up into his eyes and reached up. She kissed him.

End

About Author

Inspired to create entire worlds she could explore, Sherdley S began telling stories at the age of ten. She uses her art of writing as a driving force to empower the authenticity there is in creating one's world. She currently lives in Miami, Sunshine State, with her sidekick, a clever Lhasa Apso named Juno. Outdoorsy when she's not writing, she's either kayaking or getting lost in nature. You can learn more about Sherdley on her website and subscribe to her newsletter she makes it a point to answer to all fans.

Website: www.sherdleys.com
Instagram: @sherdleys

Made in the USA
Columbia, SC
13 August 2020

15184209R00212